Where Merlin Rests

Book Two of Myfanwy's People

By

Joseph H.J. Líaigh

DEDICATION

To my family: my wife, Mandy, and my sons, Timothy, James and John, who have graciously and generously put up with my writing; and to Isabella, for encouragement and generous criticism.

Published in Australia by Leach Publications.
PO Box 2123, Parkdale, Vic. 3195, Australia.
Email: leachpublications@gmail.com

First published in Australia 2016
Copyright © Leach Publications 2016
Cover design: Giuseppina Danna
Editor: Isabella Kružas

ISBN: 978-0-9943481-3-5

Liaigh, Joseph H.J.
Where Merlin Rests: The Second Book of the
Myfanwy's People Series

This is a work of fiction. Any resemblance to actual people, living or dead, is entirely coincidental.

Acknowledgments:

This book would not have been written without the encouragement and support of my family. I would also like to thank Isabella Kružas, the chief editor for the Myfanwy's People series, for her encouragement and advice.

My thanks also go to the staff and students of St. Joseph's Primary School in Chelsea, Victoria, who acted as my test readers. Their enthusiasm, encouragement and comments were all greatly appreciated.

Prologue

The beast slouched from the forest and moved towards the figure on the hill. The bright sunlight hurt its eyes, although it had no effect on the thick skin and bone-like growths that covered its body. It stopped and stared hopefully at the figure standing in front of it. This person was dressed all in white and appeared luminous: light seemed to come from their face, their hands and even their clothes.

"I know what you most desire and I can help you," the figure said. "I can change you from the monstrous thing that you are now and make you human. I can give you the form you were meant to have, the one you long for, so that you can walk unmarked among other men." The beast listened eagerly. "But there is a cost. First, in your native form, I require that that you put fear into the heart of my enemy and then, when his courage has been crushed, I shall require that you kill him. Are you prepared to pay this price?"

The beast hung its head and closed its eyes against the fierce light of the sun. A deep, guttural sound came from its throat. It might have been a growl of rage or even a cry of despair. Then the beast was silent for a long moment. Slowly, it nodded its head and the figure on the hill smiled a thin, cruel smile.

Chapter One
A Spate of Kidnappings

There was a swell rolling in from the Southern Ocean and I'd started the day surfing. I rode down and across the face of each wave as it curved and crashed behind me, crouching slightly until the curl of the wave caught up with me. I'd been surfing since I was little and while I surfed I found myself lost in the moment: with only myself, my board and the ocean. I loved to feel the power of the ocean and I joyed in my ability to ride with it. On that day, however, it was winter and I knew that it wouldn't last long. I'd been out for less than an hour and, even though I was in my thickest wet suit, I was already starting to feel very cold.

I was surfing off my home beach at Angle Creek, on the southern coast of Australia. So there were no selkies, beings who were both seal and human, trying to call me into the deep. When the wave broke it was just white foam, there were no water horses galloping and rearing towards the beach. These were things I had encountered when I had tried to surf the beaches of Annwn: an island off the coast of Wales. Don't try looking it up on a map, it won't be there, and you'll never find it if you go looking for it in a boat. It is not a normal kind of place. It is a strange place, outside of our space and time, where many mythical creatures still exist. It's also the home of Myfanwy, and her people: a strange land and a strange people. They have the ability to use quantum uncertainty to make highly improbable things happen. In short, they can do magic.

Although it was winter in Australia, I was here because it was the summer school holidays in England. The last Australian summer, my Mum had taken a job as a fashion photographer in London while my Dad worked on an oil exploration rig in the South China Sea. It was at my new English school that I'd met Myfanwy. I found out about her magical ability and she found out that I was immune to magic, things that neither she nor I expected. Despite being wary of each other at first, Myfanwy and I had become very close and I was now happy to call her my girlfriend. Still, I had missed my Dad and Mum and I had made a point of coming home during the holidays to spend some time with him. Myfanwy and her family had joined us for the last few weeks of the holidays. Soon we'd be flying back to England for our final year of school.

I decided it was time to finish and rode my last wave's shore break up onto the beach. Myfanwy was the only other person on the winter beach. She was wrapped warmly in a large woolen jumper and reading a book of the French poetry she liked. She looked up as I ran over to her.

"Have you finished?"she asked. When I nodded she simply disappeared for a moment. When she reappeared, she handed me a cup of steaming, hot chocolate. On a winter beach, when you've just been surfing and the wind is coming straight off the Southern Ocean, there are advantages to having a girlfriend who can do magic.

"Thank you," I said as the warmth of the hot liquid seeped through me.

"You're very welcome," she replied smiling. "Can we go somewhere warm now?" I liked it when she smiled. Her face was so often solemn from the strain of keeping her magic talent hidden that her smile was like a great flash of joy. I nodded in reply and was about to pick up my board and head off home when I noticed an odd figure walking towards us. He was large and excessively pale. He wore knee length shorts, a thick water proof jacket, sandals and a white, broad brimmed hat. I knew him straight away, even before I could see his face, though I was very surprised to see him here, on a surf beach in southern Australia. He was way out of his normal context.

"Hello Dr. Jones," I said as he walked up to us. "What brings you to Australia? Has Director Smith recovered yet?" Dr. Jones was the Chief Scientist of DIAP, the Division for the Investigation of Anomalous Phenomena: an agency of the British government which tried, with decidedly mixed success, to bring Myfanwy's people under the control of British law.

"Hello Tom," he said. "The Director is recovering slowly. Thank you for your concern. He has the help of a particular psychiatrist that Professor Rhys recommended. He seems to have a talent in such cases and the director has made good progress." Director Smith of DIAP had had his mind and memory altered in a disastrous confrontation with Cadell, a psychotic magic user, and Apophis, his equally deranged son. Since Professor Rhys was Myfanwy's uncle, I assumed that the psychiatrist was also one of Myfanwy's people and was using magic to try and repair the damage. Dr. Jones turned and shook hands with Myfanwy.

"Miss Ferchwyn I presume," he said. "I am pleased to meet you formally and under better circumstances." Previously they had only met briefly during the battle between DIAP and Apophis; a battle that had gone horribly wrong. "I am here because there are some curious events happening in England and it seems that they may be of concern to you. Can we go somewhere a bit warmer to discuss the affair?" Myfanwy nodded vigorously and I picked up my board and indicated the path back to my house.

Sometime later, after I'd had a shower and my Mum had made everyone a cup of tea, Dr. Jones told us the reason for his visit.

"There's been a spate of strange kidnappings and murders in England," he said. "All of the victims have been university professors who specialized in the period of history that followed the withdrawal of the Roman Legions from Britain, both historians and experts in literature and folklore. The victims are normally tranquilized in broad daylight and then taken to some deserted warehouse or factory and interrogated – tortured actually. Some of them have died. The police have been active and they have interrupted several of these interrogations and have caught the kidnappers. These invariably turn out to be only hired muscle, local thugs, who know nothing about who hired them. The chief interrogator has always evaded capture, even when the police had the building completely surrounded. Even more curious is that all the victims were asked about only one subject. They were all asked about the location of Merlin's tomb…" At this Myfanwy sat up and started to pay close attention. She was descended from Merlin's family.

"Dr. Jones, while I agree that this is really odd, what does it have to do with us?" I asked.

"Well," Dr. Jones said. "The interrogator has always escaped but often not by much. On one raid he left his iPhone behind. The stored information somehow erased itself completely and irretrievably but not before DIAP had managed to copy two folders. In one there was a list of the professors who had been kidnapped. In the other was Miss Ferchwyn's name, along with an address: 16 Golflinks Rd. Angle Creek, Australia." At this my blood ran cold and Myfanwy looked at him in shock.

"I take it that is where your family is staying over these holidays," Dr Jones said, looking to Myfanwy for confirmation. Myfanwy nodded mutely. Dr. Jones looked directly at me. "Tom," he said. "I know you have kept secrets from us in the past but these men are dangerous. I urge you to tell us anything you know."

I shook my head. "I'm sorry," I said, "but I really have no idea what any of this is about."

"Why do they want to know about Merlin's tomb?" Myfanwy asked.

Dr. Jones sighed. "I was hoping that you could tell us that, Miss Ferchwyn."

Myfanwy shook her head vigorously. "No one knows where Merlin is buried," she said. "No one!"

Dr Jones hesitated and then asked softly, "Not even members of your…ah…community?"

"No one knows," she said forcefully. "Don't you think that if we knew we would go and free him?

Dr Jones looked at her closely. "Free him," he repeated softly. "Which means that Merlin isn't actually dead." Again Myfanwy shook her head. Dr Jones stood up quickly and started to hurry to the door.

"Thank you for the tea Mrs. O'Malley. This conversation has really been very helpful. I must be going now. I have a flight to catch back to England." He paused at the door and turned to look at Myfanwy. "Be careful Miss Ferchwyn," he said. "These men are dangerous criminals and they may well be after you and your family." He then turned and left.

"What a strange man!" Mum said. "I swear Myfanwy, sometimes it's your people who seem normal." Mum had only known about Myfanwy's magic for a short while and she was still getting used to it. Fortunately, Mum was a photographer and Helen, Myfanwy's Mum, was a painter. They had worked together and had become close friends. I think this had helped Mum to adjust. We hadn't told Dad, although keeping the magic from him was a bit of a challenge and we would have to tell him eventually.

"Come on Tom!" Myfanwy said. "We have to go warn my family!" Then she grabbed my hand and we were suddenly in the large house that Myfanwy's family had rented for the English summer holidays. I really don't like it when she does that, especially without warning. It is really upsetting to suddenly just find yourself in another place.

Myfanwy called all her family together and repeated what Dr Jones had just told us. Helen looked worried and she pulled Gwyneth, Myfanwy's younger sister, close to her. Nain, who played the role of house keeper but was far more than she seemed, looked thoughtful. Only Carwyn, Myfanwy's brother, looked unconcerned.

"I don't think we should worry about it," he said. He held out his hand and a ball of fire appeared in the air. "Magic people we are. Remember? Ordinary criminals wouldn't know what hit them."

"Stop that Carwyn!" Nain said crossly. "You are being foolish. We must take this seriously."

"Carwyn, Nain's right," I said. "You're really more vulnerable than you think. You can't defend yourself against a threat you know nothing about and these people seem to know more about you than you do about them." Nain nodded approvingly.

"What do they want with Myfanwy?" she asked.

"They want to know the location of Merlin's tomb," Myfanwy said. This really surprised Nain and it was clear that she had no idea why a criminal group would want this information. There was a bit of further discussion but, since we didn't know anything other than that a threat existed, it really didn't get anywhere.

I walked back to my house slowly, looking at every passing car to see if it contained a gang of kidnappers. Angle Creek is a small tourist town and it's almost deserted in winter. Out local police constable was very good at catching speeding motorists but I didn't think he'd be much of a match for professional criminals. The more I thought about it the more worried I became.

However, nothing happened over the next week and we would soon be returning to England where Myfanwy would have many more people to protect her. The fear and worry began to fade. We did make sure that Myfanwy never went out alone, even though this began to irritate her after a while. Then Friday came, a warm sunny day with no wind and a flat sea. Myfanwy and I decided to take the two kids into town for an ice cream.

The main shopping strip of Angle Creek was an eclectic mixture of grocery and hardware stores for the locals and specialty shops for the summer tourists. Most of these were shut for the winter but for some reason the ice cream shop, with its thirty six flavours, stayed open. As we were coming out of the shop Myfanwy suddenly dropped her ice cream and slumped against me. There was a needle sticking out of her arm and across the car park a man was reloading what looked like a gun.

A large man dressed in motorcycle leathers walked up and said, "Don't try and be a hero kid. I'm going to take the girl. No one needs to get hurt, this can all be civilized, but if you try and stop me I'm going to have to hurt you – badly. Just give me the girl." I didn't think so. Still holding Myfanwy tight, I shoved my ice cream in his face and kicked him as hard as I could in the stomach. I know a bit about martial arts, so I can kick pretty hard. The man went down, gasping for air and trying to wipe the ice cream out of his eyes. Just then Carwyn and Gwyneth came out of the shop. Myfanwy was unconscious so I dumped her in Carwyn's arms.

"Carwyn!" I said. "Take her away. Anywhere but here!" I'll say this for Carwyn. He took in the situation with a glance and didn't hesitate. He grabbed Gwyneth's hand and the three of them were just gone. It was then that I felt the needle thud into my back. I tried to turn around but my legs had turned to rubber and everything seemed to go dark. I was vaguely aware that the guy in motorcycle leathers was swearing at me and that a dark shape moved very quickly across what remained of my vision. Then I seemed to be falling into darkness and I don't remember anything more.

Chapter Two
Return to London

I woke from panicky dreams of falling to find myself lying on a bed in a strange room. Mum was sitting in a chair next to the bed reading a book. I struggled to remember how I came to be here.

"Myfanwy!" I said anxiously as the incident at the ice cream shop became clear. "How is she?" Mum smiled and put her hand gently on my chest to stop from trying to get up.

"Myfanwy's fine," she said. "She's still asleep. She took the same dose as you but she's a lot smaller. I'm glad to see you awake. How do you feel?" I gave up on the struggle to sit up.

"Terrible," I replied, "and my head is all fuzzy. Where am I?"

"You are in Carwyn's room at the rental house," Mum answered. "We felt it would be easier to protect you both in the same house. The doctor is still watching over Myfanwy in her room and the police are checking the needles to see what tranquilizer was used. The tranquilizer gun was stolen from a vet, so they seem to think it might be one normally used on horses." She held up her hand to keep me calm. "Doctor Jamison still thinks you'll both be fine with a bit of rest." At that point Gwyneth stuck her head into the room and gave the kind of squeal that only a nine year old girl can give.

"Carwyn, come quick! He's awake," she yelled. She then ran into the room and mum had to stop her from jumping on the bed. Carwyn followed but with his usual casual coolness.

"We've been out with Nain making a spell to protect the house," Gwyneth said. "It's a really complicated one so that anyone who comes near the house intending to harm us will forget all about us and the house and just sort of wander away."

"I wanted them to be displaced to about twenty feet above the deepest part of the river," Carwyn said, "but as usual I was told that that was too extravagant." He gave a theatrically deep sigh. I smiled. I had sympathy for Carwyn, he was caught between two worlds. In Annwn he missed surfing the net, Facebook and connecting with his friends. At his expensive boarding school in Ireland he was frustrated by not being able to use his considerable magical ability.

After that the room started to get crowded. Dr. Jamison heard that I was awake and came in to check on me, followed by Nain and Helen. Dr Jamison said that I should rest for about half an hour but that after that I should be able to get up and go home. He, of course, knew nothing about magical protections. When he left, the crowd followed him down the hall and I was left alone. I started to get out of the bed and found that I was almost too weak to stand. Still, with the help of the bed, the door and wall I made it out of the room and down the hall to Myfanwy's room. I needed to see for myself that she was alright. She was lying on her bed sleeping, her breath slow and steady and her hair a mass of dark curls on her pillow. I sank gratefully into the armchair near the door. The short walk down the hall had exhausted me and I closed my eyes to rest. I vaguely heard voices down the hall,

"O come on people," one of them said. "Where do you think he might have gone!" I didn't care. I drifted off to sleep. I awoke to find Myfanwy awake and watching me.

She smiled. "Hello you," she said.

I smiled back and said, "You know, Myfanwy Ferchyn, going out with you is never dull: often dangerous and painful, but never dull." I walked over to the bed and held her hand.

"That's very touching," Nain said behind me, "but now that you have seen that she is alright, you, Thomas O'Malley, can leave my god daughter's bedroom. Your presence is not appropriate." I don't know how old Nain actually is, the magic people live a long time and time sometimes runs differently for them, but she has very firm views about such matters. It's also complicated because once magic people form a romantic bond, the bond itself has a kind of magic. It can't be broken, ever, without disastrous consequences. This means that even a casual romance could be a lifetime commitment and that magic people tend to be very careful in such matters. Nain is also very protective of her godchildren.

That night Mum and I went back to our unguarded house since we figured that the kidnappers had no interest in us. It seemed we were right because no one disturbed us.

I was eating breakfast the next morning when Mum and Helen came in laughing. They had been down in town shopping and I looked at them curiously.

"What's so funny," I asked.

"Nain may need to adjust her protection spell," Helen explained. "There are TV news crews, newspaper reporters and photographers all wandering around Angle

Creek, wondering what they are doing there. Obviously, according to the workings of the spell, the paparazzi and reporters are out to do us harm so they come up to the house and then just forget why they're there." The spell's assessment seemed pretty accurate to me, so I didn't see any need to adjust it. It would have been even funnier if Carwyn had got his way.

Later that morning I was interviewed by the police. There was an Inspector Browning, a detective sergeant from Melbourne and a man introduced as Inspector Barnabas from the Criminal Intelligence Unit at Scotland Yard. I, however, knew him as Sergeant Fisher of the 5th Lancashire Lancers, on detached duty to DIAP. He was military Special Forces and one of the bravest men I knew. Dr. Jones had clearly left him behind to keep an eye on things.

After I had told my story I asked, "Did you catch the guys who did this?"

"Yes," Inspector Browning answered. "Inspector Barnabas was apparently coming to warn Miss Ferchwyn about some intelligence they had of a threat to her when he observed the incident and ...ah, apprehended the two culprits. One will get out of hospital next week and we hope the other will be well enough to be interviewed in a couple of days." The Inspector paused and looked at his notes. "There is one thing I don't quite understand," he said. "After you gave the unconscious Miss Ferchwyn to her brother, how did he get her out of harm's way?"

I shrugged. "I don't really know," I said. "I was pretty out of it with the drug about that time. I guess he must have just dragged her behind a car or something." The Inspector nodded, still looking doubtful.

"Yes," he said. "I guess that's how it must have happened. That's pretty much what the boy said. Perhaps people just remember strange things with the effect of post-traumatic shock." The phoney Inspector Barnabas just smiled. He knew who he was dealing with.

Two days later we packed up and left for England. The flight was terrible, as it always is: cramped seats, bad food, toilet queues, old movies and long periods of intense tedium. Carwyn wanted to speed things up by making the plane go faster but I pointed out that a passenger jet flying over the Middle East at three times the speed of sound could very well be mistaken for a large, incoming missile and this could have unfortunate consequences. After some discussion he was persuaded to simply endure the flight, which he did by expanding the space around him and turning his seat into a bed. It took all of Nain's talent to ensure that nobody noticed.

When we got back to England, there was a uniformed chauffeur from a stretch limousine company waiting for Myfanwy and her family. This was a bit of a surprise because Professor Rhys, Myfanwy's uncle, had arranged to meet them. Apparently he'd been delayed. As I helped Myfanwy out with her luggage, I noticed that there was another man sitting in the front passenger seat. "Why are there two of them?" I wondered. About this time Gwyneth pulled anxiously on my sleeve.

"His mind is all dark and mucky," she said, pointing to the chauffeur. "I think he is a bad man." I nodded. I had just seen a bulge in his jacket; he had a handgun shoved into the waistband of his trousers. I looked at Myfanwy and imitated the hand gesture she uses when she wants to stop time. This is a useful talent that she is very good at, although I remain unaffected since I am immune to all magic. Myfanwy looked at me questioningly, so I repeated the gesture. Then she did what I asked and stopped time, without really knowing why. Everything just stopped, frozen in place.

"Thomas, whatever you need to do you will have to do it very quickly," she said. "I can't stop an international airport for long. There are big planes coming in to land and they have an enormous amount of energy." I was already pulling the gun out of the chauffeur's waistband.

"Don't worry," I said. "This won't take long. When you let time go again, yell 'He's got a gun'." I put the gun in his hand, wrapping his fingers around the handle. As I stepped back, time started to flow again.

"He's got a gun! He's got a gun!" Myfanwy yelled. It is remarkable what effect those words can have at a modern airport. People dived for whatever cover they could find and armed police and security came running. The chauffer looked a bit stunned to find his gun in his hand and felt around his back to make sure that it was missing. There were now a number of things he could have done. If he were a DIAP agent he could have placed his gun on the ground and waited for things to be sorted out. If he was a smart crook he could have placed his gun on the ground and have been arrested on firearms charges. A less smart crook could have got in the limousine and tried to make a run for it. A really dumb crook would try to use his gun. This crook was really dumb. He fired two quick shots at Myfanwy, presumably to keep her quiet. Simply shooting at magic people isn't that effective, the bullets just stopped in mid air and fell to the ground. By this time the security forces had arrived.

"Put your weapon down! Put your weapon down!" they yelled. When an armed policeman tells you to put your weapon down, you should do it. You shouldn't turn around to face him still holding it. A single rifle round caught him in the chest and he went down.

By that time, the other guy in the limousine had scrambled across to the driver's seat and was trying to drive off. Carwyn gestured casually and the car engine stalled. He made another gesture and the guy started to panic as he found that there were now no door handles on the inside of the car. He seemed almost relieved when the police opened the door and arrested him.

It was at this time that Professor Rhys drove up in his classic 1960's Rolls Royce and quickly set about extracting us from the situation. First all of the luggage, including Mum's and mine, disappeared into the boot of his car – a boot which simply expanded to hold however much luggage was required.

"All in," he said, opening a rear door. "I think it best that we go and that no one remembers we were here. Mrs. O'Malley, I think it would be good if you and Tom could come with us," he said to Mum. "Less complicated all round." So we all climbed into the back of the car which expanded to something like a sitting room: everyone had plenty of space. Professor Rhys then set about smiling and waving at all the people and police: altering their memories and deleting us from any retelling of the incident. We then drove off towards London at Professor Rhys' normal breakneck speed.

"Remember the security cameras," I said.

"Thanks Tom," he replied, "But I have already taken care of that. Now, can someone tell me what just happened?" Nain started to explain how the chauffeur had been waiting for them because Professor Rhys had been delayed. She looked puzzled for a moment, then she said,

"Then, all of a sudden, the chauffeur had a gun in his hand and tried to shoot Myfanwy. There is something very strange here. Something I do not understand." It suddenly occurred to me that when Myfanwy slowed or stopped time, she did that for the magic people as much as for anyone else and they might not be aware that she had that particular ability. The sly smile Myfanwy gave me confirmed my hunch.

"I told Tom that he was a bad man," Gwyneth said. "Perhaps Tom did it."

"Sorry, Gwen," I said smiling. "I can't do any magic. I can only stop other people from doing magic."

"Well, whatever happened, it was clearly another kidnap attempt," Professor Rhys said. "I was delayed but I certainly didn't send any limousine. Alwyn ap Bryn has had a series of computer attacks on his business interests all day and he asked me for help. It seems clear now that these were orchestrated with the express purpose of delaying me. Whoever these people are, they know a lot about our community. I don't like that at all." Alwyn ap Bryn was another of the Nobles of Annwn, a kind of ruling council. Like Professor Rhys, he also spent most of his time in our world.

"Professor, has Iolo caught Cadell yet?" I asked.

"No Tom," he replied. "You make a very good point. If Cadell has joined forces with a criminal organization, or even if he is simply using the resources of such a group, it could be very bad news indeed." Cadell was a powerful but twisted magic user who had escaped, wounded, from a battle with the Special

Operations Unit of the Swiss Pontifical Guard: a battle that took the life of Apophis, his son.

As we drove, it was decided that, since the kidnappers had shown no interest in us, Mum and I would probably be safe in our London home. It still had some magical protection left over from our battle with Apophis. The others would go to Aelred Abbey, the castle they owned in Norfolk, where they would be safe even if a whole army attacked. They also decided that Myfanwy should return to St Agatha's school, since it would be easier to protect us if we were both in the same place. I didn't actually feel in need of protection but this would mean more time with Myfanwy, so I didn't argue. Myfanwy, on the other hand, had always hated her new school, the school she had been sent to to keep us apart, so she didn't argue either.

We got to our London house in a ridiculously short time. As we were saying our goodbyes and thank yous, our luggage was magically deposited in the hallway. Then, just as the car was about to drive off, time stopped. Myfanwy got out of the car, came over and hugged me tight. In the middle of a London street, with traffic and people frozen still around us, we were perfectly alone.

"So long surfer boy," she said. "I'll see you at school." Then she kissed me hard on the lips, turned, and got back in the car. Time started to flow again. I couldn't help grinning like an idiot as I watched the car disappear into the traffic.

I didn't notice it at the time, but in the small park opposite our house there was a young man sitting on one of the park benches. He had lank, dark hair and he was staring intently at our house with faded green eyes.

Chapter Three
Myfanwy at St. Agatha's

Returning to school, to St. Agatha's, was a strange experience. I couldn't help but feel dislocated. A few days before, I had been sitting on my board and waiting for a wave off the beach at Angle Creek, looking at the sandstone cliffs and the forested hills behind them, then I was sitting in a bus on my way to a school on the outer fringes of London, looking at row after row of drab streets and small houses. At Angle Creek I was at home and in harmony with the place. In London I was, and always would be, an outsider.

The school, however, was familiar: for better or worse. The opening assembly was the headmaster at his pompous best. He gave his speech, a speech which was essentially the speech he had given many times last year and which I knew I would hear many times during the coming year. It was all about being the best we could be and living up to our parent's expectations.

After the assembly I returned to Mrs. Brown's homeroom class and sat at my old desk next to the window. Now, however, the late summer sun streamed into the classroom and the garden outside was a vivid green: very different from the rain and bare branches of my first arrival. I watched as the rest of the class arrived. Horace and his mates swaggered in. They didn't do much that was out of order, just pushed when there was no real need to push. It was just enough to let everyone know that if you got in their way there'd be trouble. Phil came in talking excitedly to an Indian boy, whose name I could never remember, about some soccer match. He was followed by Gabriella and a bunch of girls who just looked bored. When Wilson came in he rushed over to my desk and put a thick book down with a thud. It was a book on astrophysics.

"Hi Tom, welcome back. I hope you had a good holiday," he said in a rush. "I spent mine reading this book. You have got to read it! It gives you a whole new appreciation of the dark matter problem." There aren't too many people who are as passionate about astrophysics as Wilson is. In fact, he became my friend partly because I could protect him from Horace and his crew and partly because I was the only other person in the class who understood what he was talking about.

"Thanks Wilson," I said smiling. "I did have a good break and I'll get this back to you as soon as I've finished it."

"Great!" he said going over to his desk, "but I'll need it back before Christmas. The National Physics Association is running its student essay competition again and I want to do a piece on the expansion of the universe." This was the same competition that he'd won last year. If they kept letting him enter, no one else would ever win.

The 'in' girls came in last: heavily made up and with the blondest hair modern chemistry could provide. They had probably waited in the corridor until they could make a grand entrance. The effect was a bit spoiled when Rachael, a wannabe goth with unkempt black hair, slouched through the middle of them with a look of utter contempt on her face. Myfanwy was not at the assembly and she had not come in to sit in her old desk in front of me. I kept looking anxiously towards the door.

Mrs. Brown came to the front of the class to make her welcome back speech. She was wearing a nicely tailored dress that somehow still didn't seem to fit her properly. It sort of slumped around her shoulders and bagged up around her armpits. Her speech was all about how we should work hard, how this year was so important and how she was confident we would all do well. Unfortunately, the expression on her face suggested that this year was going to be deadly dull and we were all doomed to failure. It was halfway through this speech that the Headmaster knocked on the door and walked in. Myfanwy was with him, dressed in her St. Agatha's uniform.

"If I may interrupt," said the Headmaster. "I am pleased to announce that Miss Myfanwy Ferchwyn has decided to rejoin us here at St. Agatha's after a short stay at another educational institution. I am sure you will all join me in welcoming her back."

Myfanwy gave an embarrassed smile and walked back to her old desk. The welcome back was decidedly muted. Beyond a small circle of friends, Myfanwy was not very popular at school. The care she needed to take to hide her magic powers placed a great strain on her and this caused to her to be very reserved. She'd also been raised in another time and place and had little sense of modern fashion or manners. This often made her seem aloof and distant to those who didn't take the time to know her well. Horace and his mates, as well as some of the 'in' girls, openly scowled at her return.

At lunch we gathered together again: the table of outcasts, misfits and rebels. As well as myself, an

Australian who didn't know his place, there was Wilson who was both black and the very model of an *uber*nerd, Rachael who had the utmost contempt for just about everything about St. Agatha's, Phil who tended to get a bit lost when no one was talking about soccer, and, of course, Myfanwy. Although no one at the school, other than myself, had any idea of the extent of Myfanwy's power, they knew enough to know that she was special and this made them fear and isolate her. The people seated around our table were her only real friends in all the school.

This lunch time the talk was all about the massive earthquake that had occurred in Sicily. Whole towns had been destroyed and centuries old churches had been reduced to rubble. The number of people dead was not known yet but it was clear that there were a lot of them. Many nations were sending in rescue teams to help the Italians who were frantically searching through the ruins. In Australia we have bushfires, floods and drought but earthquakes that bring down mountains are beyond our experience. The shear horror of it was on everyone's mind, although Phil was mostly concerned with the effect it might have on the European championships. Myfanwy was very quiet and looked worried.

When I asked her if anything was wrong she shook her head and whispered, "Later. It might be nothing. Sometimes things can just happen."

Towards the end of lunch, Horace came over, put both hands down on the table and leaned threateningly over Myfanwy.

"You shouldn't have come back witch girl," he said. "Last year you had me fooled but I'm not afraid of you anymore so you can't protect your little nerd friend.

I know you only played on my mother images to make me think you had powers. Your supposed powers are just a maternal projection." Horace had obviously spent some of the break in therapy. It didn't seem to have improved his character.

Myfanwy looked at him calmly. "You know my name is Myfanwy," she said. "I don't like it when you call me that other name."

"What?" Horace asked sneeringly, still leaning over Myfanwy. "The witch girl doesn't like being called witch girl? Well, that's just too bad…witch girl." Horace had no idea who he was talking to or of the power that he faced. How could he?

Myfanwy pointed her finger at Horace and said softly, "I think you should be quiet now." Horace tried to make a sarcastic reply but found that he couldn't make a sound. He tried again and still nothing came out. He stood up, grabbing at his throat in panic. He tried to scream but still no sound came. He looked at Myfanwy with horror, still trying to scream.

"Myf, stop it!" I said. "Let him go!" Time froze in the dining hall: Horace standing as a horror stricken statue, the faces of the kids around us frozen in expressions of surprise. Myfanwy turned to me and pointed ferociously at Horace.

"He is a pig!" she said angrily, placing equal emphasis on each word.

"I know," I said as gently as I could, "but this isn't good. You've used your power in public and you have humiliated and badly scared Horace. He is going to hate you."

"He hates me anyway," she said sulkily, "and you sound just like Nain."

I gave a wry smile. "At least I don't dress like her. Look, you really do have to fix this and you have to be more careful. I know it's hard but you can't afford to lose your temper." She nodded reluctantly and time started to flow again. Myfanwy spread her arms wide and yelled, "Forget!" Then she stood up and said "boo!" into Horace's face. There was surprised laughter around the dining room. After that, all that anyone, including Horace, remembered of the incident was Horace taunting Myfanwy with the 'witch girl' jibe and Myfanwy standing up and saying 'boo!' in response. It was a good response and left Horace looking a little silly. Naturally, being Horace, he did try to regain some of the initiative.

"A projection!" he said. "That's all you are: just a mother projection! I'm not afraid of you." He then stormed back to his own table. I'm not sure Horace really understood what he was saying but Rachael did.

She leaned across to me and whispered, "If his fear that Myfanwy is a witch is a projection from his relationship with his mother, what does that say about his mother? What sort of family does he come from?"

After we had all gone back to class, one thing that struck me about the incident was the look on Horace's face as he sat down at his own table and looked across at us. The memory of his humiliation may have been wiped from his conscious mind but I think that perhaps some remnant still lingered in his subconscious, because the look he gave Myfanwy was one of real hatred.

That evening, I walked Myfanwy home. Unusually, we walked in silence, each feeling the tension of the lunch time incident. We only walked a few short streets from the school to an old wooden gate. It seemed to be a perfectly normal gate except that it didn't lead anywhere, behind it there was only the wall of an old church. It was, in fact, a kind of portal and by stepping through it Myfanwy would be at Aelred Abbey, her family's castle in Norfolk. Before she stepped through she turned and kissed me lightly on the cheek.

"Thank you Tom," she said. "I really needed you there today. Without you I might have done something very foolish."

"Don't worry," I said. "I'll always be there for you. Remember?" I had said that to her once before. That time it had turned out that she was the one who was there for me.

"I remember," she said with a sad little smile, "but today I'm really ashamed of myself. I shouldn't need you to tell me my duty." With that she turned and walked through the gate and down the path through the birch wood that led to Aelred Abbey. When the gate shut behind her there was once again only the wall of the old church. I turned and walked back down the street to the bus exchange at the foot of the hill. As I walked I thought that Myfanwy had, in fact, done something very foolish and had then used her power to apply a sort of band-aid patch up. The way Myfanwy's people used their power to manipulate normal people's perception had always annoyed me and it annoyed me now, even if it was Myfanwy doing it.

The next morning the news from Sicily was mostly bad. There had been a few notable rescues but the confirmed death count just kept climbing. Naturally, the British news focused on the number of Britons who had been killed, were injured or were just desperately trying to get home. There was also a curious story from Yellowstone Park in America where a geyser had exploded violently, badly scalding a bus load of tourists.

Chapter Four
Threats and Danger

At school, the lessons progressed pretty much as they always had and so did the student's lives. At lunchtime I learned that Gabriella had given up on trying to get Phil to pay more attention to her and less to soccer and had broken up with him. If anything, this only made Phil even more fanatical about the game that he loved. Ida Bruin, one of the blondest of the in girls, had also dumped Jack Smithfield, one of Horace's henchmen. Apparently she thought she would have better prospects with a basketballer from another school. This may have been a good judgement call on her part but it left the aforementioned Jack in a particularly foul mood. Even Rachael was finding that nuclear physics wasn't as wild and radical as she had thought and was beginning to pay a lot less attention to Wilson. I'm not entirely sure that Wilson noticed. The next day both Myfanwy and I were called to the headmaster's office, where two uniformed police officers were waiting for us. The headmaster greeted us without getting up from behind his large, antique desk.

"Thomas and Myfanwy," he said, "These two officers are from the Metropolitan Police and they are here to take you to be interviewed about a regrettable incident that I understand occurred while you were in Australia. It's all voluntary, of course, and you are free to go back to your class if you wish. However, your mother has agreed Thomas, as has your uncle Myfanwy, and it may well help your own security. I believe the police will see you home afterwards." I sensed the hand of DIAP in all this but we were taken in a perfectly genuine police car to a perfectly genuine police station. There they showed us a whole series of photographs and mug shots and asked us if we recognized any of the men or had seen any of them recently. Neither Myfanwy nor I remembered ever seeing any of them. They then ushered us into an interview room, offered us tea or coffee, and left us alone.

A short while later, Dr Jones and Sergeant Fisher walked in, confirming my original suspicions.

Dr. Jones did not waste time on pleasantries, "I assume you were involved in that fracas at the airport," he said. We both nodded in confirmation. "I thought so, didn't make much sense otherwise. Look Miss Ferchwyn, this confirms that you are still at risk. It would seem that someone knows a lot about your movements and has found the weak point in the magic community's security. Your magic can't protect you against things you know nothing about. If they can get a sneak attack in before you are aware of it, then they have you. Miss Ferchwyn, you and your people both need our protection."

"Hang on," I said before Myfanwy could reply. "This doesn't really make sense. Why do they want to kidnap Myfanwy and, if they know about Myfanwy's ability, how were they planning to hold her? I assure you that if she wanted to, Myfanwy could simply walk out of the most secure prison in this building and the whole of the Metropolitan Police Force could not stop her." Dr. Jones looked sharply at Myfanwy who gave him her sweetest smile.

Turning back to me he said, "We don't entirely understand what's going on but there are a few things to consider. One is that the group who attempted to kidnap Miss Ferchwyn are the same group who have kidnapped and murdered a lot of experts on Late Roman Britain. The method used in all the attacks was identical. This suggests that they want some information: perhaps about Merlin?"

"But I don't know anything about Merlin that isn't common knowledge," protested Myfanwy. "Being distantly related to someone doesn't give you special access to some collection of arcane information."

"Perhaps they don't know that," Dr. Jones suggested. "One answer to the problem of holding a kidnapped magic user is to keep them permanently drugged." Dr Jones looked a little embarrassed at this point and I wondered how much research he had done in this area. "This would, of course, render them useless as an information source. There is, however, another possibility." He turned to Myfanwy. "We understand from your uncle that there is still a rogue magic user on the loose." Myfanwy nodded. "It is possible that this magic user is the mysterious interrogator. In which case, he might use his own power to hold Miss Ferchwyn and to question her. Would this be possible?"

Myfanwy nodded slowly. "Even though he is wounded, I couldn't fight Cadell. He is too skilled and powerful." she said. "But he would already know far more about Merlin than I do."

"So, we are left with a conundrum," Dr. Jones said. "Until we work this out we have arranged to upgrade your security. Sergeant Fisher will take a position at your school. He will be there ostensibly as a teacher but his real task will be your security. Don't hesitate to go to him. Somehow, you two hold the key to this mystery."

The police drove us both back to my house and I walked Myfanwy around to another of the portal gates to Aelred Abbey. This one was, conveniently, just around the corner from my London house. At the gate I hugged Myfanwy tightly to me.

"Be careful, Myfanwy," I said. "I'm worried. If Cadell is behind this, he won't want to talk to you. He'll want to kill you."

"I know," Myfanwy said with her head resting on my chest. "But I have strong friends to protect me." Then she reached up and kissed me softly before turning and walking through the gate. As the gate closed, I was left staring at an empty wall.

It was getting dark when I got back to the square where my house was and the park in the centre of the square was full of deep shadows. It was out of the corner of my eye that I noticed something moving in the park, something large and misshapen which lurched through the shadows. However, as soon as I turned to look directly at it, it was gone. I stood still and waited as the dark deepened but still all remained quiet. Eventually, I went home. That night the news showed pictures of a spectacular volcanic eruption at Mount Ruapehu in New Zealand. Fortunately it occurred in a national park and there was no one around to get hurt.

It was hard to concentrate on schoolwork the next day because I was worried about Myfanwy. Cadell was a brilliant and powerful magic user but he was also a murderous psychopath who had a long standing grudge against Myfanwy's family. He had already sacrificed his son to this grudge and he would not hesitate to kill Myfanwy. Mr. Chester, our geography teacher, took the interest in the recent earthquake and volcanic activity as an opportunity to start a discussion about the physical underpinnings of geomorphology. He talked about the great hazard posed by volcanic eruptions and the violence of some known past eruptions. He also showed how even Britain, which was currently far from any volcanic centre, has been formed by past volcanic activity. Knowing I was in the class, he pointed out that the same was also true of Australia. It was interesting but my mind was elsewhere.

At lunch there was a pretty brown haired girl crying at one of the tables and being comforted by Gabriella and her friends. Apparently she had been dumped by some boy. Gabriella and her friends glared at every boy who came into the dining room, clearly blaming the entire male gender for what had happened to their friend. As I sat down I commented on the rapid turnover in relationships around the school.

"That's really not unusual, you know," Rachael said. "It's quite normal."

Myfanwy sighed and said, "Here we go again." I took it that she had already had this discussion.

Rachael ignored her and said, "Teenage relationships don't last very long because they are all about exploring different possibilities; about trying to find out which persona best suits you. Who you would be if you were in relationship with x or y and so on. It's you and Myfanwy who are unusual." Rachael had no idea how true that was. She also didn't know that when Myfanwy's people form romantic relationships, the magic gets involved and the relationship becomes permanent. Bad things happen if it is broken.

"Tom," Rachael continued, "don't you ever wonder who you would be, what type of person you would be, if you had never met Myfanwy and had gone into a relationship with Susan?"

I shook my head and said, "I would just be me in relationship with Susan. I wouldn't be a different person. Look, they say the same sort of thing about travel: that travel changes you. Yet in Australia I live in a small coastal town and go surfing. Here, I live near the centre of London, the nearest surf is miles away but in both places I'm the same person. I'm just me living somewhere else. I don't change just because the world around me does."

"He really doesn't, you know." Myfanwy chipped in. "He can be in the most peculiar situations and he's still just him ...for better or worse," I don't know what Rachael made of that comment because just then Phil came up to the table with what he considered urgent news. Predictably, it was about soccer.

"Tom," he said. "I have two tickets to Saturday's game and my dad can't come. Tottenham is playing Real Madrid in the Champions League. It's going to be a great game and it'll be a really good way for you to learn about football. Want to come with me?" He looked at me almost pleadingly. "Come on, if you're living in this country you need to know about the football played here. Give it a go!" How could I refuse? We arranged to meet at 6.00 o'clock at Liverpool Station to go out to the game. One thing was clear, Phil was always Phil. Yet, despite my answer to Rachael, she had planted a nasty little worm of an idea in my head. I was young, perhaps too young to commit to something for the rest of my life. Why should I be forced to make a permanent choice just because that was the way it was for Myfanwy's people?

Before I could sort these thoughts out, the bell rang and we had to go back to class. As I was leaving the dining room, I noticed Horace busily writing something in a small notebook. The idea of Horace writing something he hadn't been forced to was strange enough but when he saw me looking he smiled and waved. Henchmen one and two joined in. I didn't like the idea of Horace and his crew being friendly. I didn't like it at all. There was something unnatural about it.

That afternoon we had a Physical education class and Sergeant Fisher, under the name of Mr. Black, turned up as the instructor. Instead of the usual boring exercises and medicine ball drills, he decided to give us a class in self defence. It was mostly a demonstration, using me as his test partner. I think he was using the class to try and sort out my ability: to find out how much I knew and how good I was. It was interesting. I was probably more technically correct and had a wider range of techniques but he was much stronger and far more direct in his approach. He called me aside after the class.

"That was good Tom," he said. "You have excellent technique and you would be a real problem for most people. However, you need to work on your power and focus and you need to keep it simple. Remember, it's a fight, not a dance." He then pulled a small medallion and chain from his pocket. "Since I'm meant to be responsible for your security, I'd like you to wear this. It could be important." It looked like an ordinary piece of jewelry, not something I'd ordinarily wear, but, to humour DIAP, I slipped the chain around my neck.

"Thanks," I said.

That evening was the first time that I noticed the homeless guy who seemed to have taken up residence in our park. He was dressed in jeans and a tee shirt under an old army great coat. Even from a distance I could see that he was young and yet his shoulders were bowed as if in despair. In spite of this, there was still a great sense of energy about him, as if he were engaged in a mighty struggle. As soon as he saw me looking at him, he shuffled off to a large clump of bushes where I guess he had made his camp. That night the news carried more footage of the spectacular eruption at Mount Ruapehu, only tonight it was paired with the eruption of a previously dormant volcano on the northern tip of Sumatra. This one had disrupted air travel and caused thousands of villagers to be evacuated.

The next night Phil and I met up and traveled out to the Tottenham Stadium. I found the first half of the soccer game interesting: not for the game itself, which I couldn't follow at all, but for the passion of the crowd. The playing field was much smaller than that used for an Australian Rules match. This meant that, even though we were near the top of the stand, we were much closer to the action than we would have been at an Australian game. I think this increased the intensity of the crowd interaction. There was also the national sentiment issue. Judging by the comments around us, this was a real factor, even though there were Spanish players playing for Tottenham and English players on the Rial Madrid team. As for the game itself, for the whole of the first half the ball passed backwards and forwards between the two teams with neither team being able to score, The tension building up in the crowd was palpable.

It was just before half time that one of the Spanish players was red carded for something that seemed pretty harmless to me. The whole crowd was up on their feet and yelling: everyone except Phil who seemed to be asleep in his seat. It was as I turned to see what was wrong with him that I noticed the small dart sticking out of my own forearm. Everything started to go dark. The last thing I was aware of was a voice I didn't recognize saying,

"Hey, we'd better get these two young fellas home. It looks like they may have imbibed a bit too much."

Chapter Five
Cadell Returns

I slowly woke out of the depths of a very confused dream to find myself sitting up and secured to my chair with windings of cling wrap. My head felt like it had been stomped on by an elephant. I looked around and saw Phil in a chair next to me. He was bound in a way similar to me but still asleep. We seemed to be in some sort of old factory. There was a lot rusty metal and disused machinery and I could hear water dripping somewhere in the background. The light inside was dim but sun light was showing through gaps in the wall.

"Eh, it looks like the big one's awake." A voice said from behind me. Three men came into my field of view and I could hear another one behind my chair. They were big men, roughly dressed. They looked at me intently but didn't say anything directly to me. Instead they discussed the situation among themselves.

"Yeah, this one's awake. You'd better call him."

"Do I 'ave to? He gives me the creeps."

"Yeah, he gave Fred the creeps too. Look what 'appened to him"

"Right, good point. I'll make the call."

They then went out of my field of view and I was bound too tightly to turn my head very far. The one behind me came up and whispered in my ear.

"Now you're for it. You are not going to like this at all." Listening as hard as I could, I was expecting to hear a conversation on a mobile phone. Instead I heard one of the men knock on a door somewhere off in the factory.

"Sir, you wanted to be called when the prisoners woke. Well, one of em's awake: the big one." The speaker was clearly using his most formal and deferential voice. In fact, he was almost groveling and I wondered what could cause that much fear in such men. I still couldn't see much but I heard the door swing open and something creak towards me. Eventually a figure emerged from the gloom on my right, with the four men standing behind him. It was Cadell, his body broken and bound to a wheelchair, his face filled with malicious glee.

"Well, well," he said. "I do believe that it's Master O'Malley, come to be my guest again. You do seem to be a very hard person to kill. I can assure you, Master O'Malley, that I will not be so ill mannered as to throw you out this time. No indeed, I think that this time you should have a long stay." He wheeled his chair up so close to my face that I could smell his breath. "It's not that I enjoy your company, not at all. Rather, you are valuable to me as a tool. I have a task that requires your peculiar talent."

I looked him straight in the eye and answered as calmly and distinctly as I could. "I will never help you do anything."

"Are you sure?" he asked. "Are you really sure? Because if you're really sure, I could just kill you now. Not my preferred option, no, but a very good second best and one that has its own particular satisfaction. You see, I have found a way around your unnatural ability. Quite properly, these men fear me. After watching one of their colleagues die in agony just because I wanted him to, you can understand why. Now, because they fear me, they will do as I say. So, if I want to hurt you, they have very large fists, and if I want to kill you, they have guns. I don't really need you, you know. Things are so well advanced now that they can't really be stopped. You are just insurance and I can do without an insurance policy." Phil chose that moment to regain consciousness. At first he just looked confused, then his eyes widened in fear as he took in his situation.

"Hey! What's going on? Where am I? Why am I tied up like this?" He started to struggle so hard against the cling wrap that he nearly tipped over his chair. "Help! I can't breathe properly." Cadell leaned even closer to my face, so close that we were almost touching.

"Tell your little friend to be quiet or I will silence him myself – permanently" he said.

Phil turned as he heard the voice. "Tom?" he said. "Tom, what's going on? Who are these people?" Cadell pointed his finger at Phil, probably to hurt him or even kill him, but I concentrated on willing him to lose his magic. This was what Cadell called my 'unnatural' ability, the ability to make magic users lose their magical power.

Cadell felt his power vanish and he turned to look at me with pure hatred and hissed, "As I said, I have found a way around you." He waved to one of the men and pointed at Phil. "Hit him. Hit him hard." The man walked over and without any hesitation punched Phil in the stomach. I heard the breath leave his body and then Phil really did have trouble breathing. He was left in pain and gasping for air.

"You see Master O'Malley," Cadell said. "These methods may be crude but I can cause you and your little friend here real pain. Now, I need to kill someone but it's hard for me to get to them. I'm not even going to ask you to do the killing. I'm a reasonable man. All I want you to do is to open the door, as it were."

"You are a bitter, twisted, insane excuse for a creep," I said. "I don't care what pain you cause. I will not help you kill anyone." Cadell shrugged and signaled to the thug again.

"No! No!" Phil yelled. "I'm not a part of this, I just went to the football. I don't understand. Tom, what is this all about?"

"It's Myfanwy, Phil." I said. "He hates Myfanwy's family and he's afraid of them. He wants to use me to get at her." Cadell jerked back as if I had hit him.

"Fool!" he yelled. "Do you think I am afraid? I do not fear the children of Owyn Ap Rhys. I killed the father, why do you think I would fear his half breed pups?" He gestured again to the thug. "Hit him again." Phil only had time to yell "No!" before the man punched him so hard in the face that his chair was knocked over. When they picked his chair up, he was unconscious and there was blood flowing from his broken nose.

"I'm sorry Phil," I said to his unconscious form. "I'm so, so sorry." It really wasn't fair. All he had wanted to do was take a friend to a football game. Cadell turned to the man who had hit Phil.

"You ape," he said. "You hit him too hard. He is useless to us now." He swung his wheel chair around to look at me. "You must decide now. Will you help me, or do I have the pleasure of seeing you die?" He pulled a face full of mock sorrow. "Think of how upset poor Myfanwy would be." I didn't spend any time thinking about it. If I had thought too much about it the fear that was pushing at my heart might have come to the surface. I was sweating and if my hands had been free, they would have been shaking. There was this dull feeling in my stomach. I realized that it was dread. I was dreading what seemed to be inevitable. To my shame, I realized that I wanted to cry. Still, I was determined that none of this would be allowed to show, let alone determine my actions. I didn't want to die but co-operation with Cadell was just impossible.

"Go jump!" I said.

Cadell smiled with what seemed to be genuine pleasure and said, "There is a prize for the first man who shoots him." All four pulled guns from their jackets. Just then there were three very loud bangs in quick succession and a flash of blinding light filled the space. As the afterimage faded from my eyes, I saw that dark figures in flak jackets and helmets already had the four thugs on the floor and handcuffed and Cadell had gone. I had lost concentration and he had used his ability to teleport away.

One of the uniformed figures came and said something to me but I couldn't hear him because my ears were still ringing from the bangs. He had 'police' written across the front of his helmet and he pulled out a battle knife and cut through the cling wrap to set me free. Next to me two men were tending to Phil. Someone opened up a door and let the light in. I slumped in my chair. It was over.

Later on I was sitting in the back of an ambulance, after I had been checked out by medics, given a detailed statement to the police and spoken to my mother over the phone, when one of the uniformed figures approached me and took off his helmet. It was Sergeant Fisher of DIAP.

"Hi," I said. "I thought you were probably involved. How did you find us?" He smiled and pointed to the medallion that he had given me.

"That," he said, "is a GPS tracker. As soon as we realized that you were missing we were able to track you. Unfortunately it was only after you didn't return from the game and by that time you were already in Yorkshire. We're lucky you weren't in France – or Russia. I'm sorry we were a bit late but it took us some time to do all the official co-ordination with the Yorkshire police and get a team together. Then we had to do the proper surveillance. If we'd just blundered in there, we could have gotten you both killed. We were ready to go just before they pulled their guns."

"I'd have to say that you did cut it uncomfortably close. Still, I was very glad to see you. Unfortunately, I have bad news. The rogue magic user, Cadell, was here but I'm afraid I let him get away. I'm sorry but those Flash-Bangs of yours made me lose concentration."

Sergeant Fisher shrugged. "Don't sweat it," he said. "Those things are designed to make you lose concentration. The police, however, are very puzzled about how a guy in a wheelchair could escape their security cordon. I'll leave that to Dr. Jones. Dealing with those sorts of complications is way above my pay grade. Any idea of why they snatched you?"

I thought for a while before I answered. "I think it was probably to get at Myfanwy," I answered in a doubtful voice.

Sergeant Fisher nodded. "Makes sense," he said. "If a direct attack proves too difficult, you try an easier, more indirect approach." I nodded but there were still many doubts in my mind. It didn't quite fit. I worried over this for a short while until I heard Phil's voice coming from an ambulance next to mine and I had to smile.

"Can't anyone tell me the result of the game?" There was an inaudible answer. "The result of the Spurs, Rial Madrid game of course!" This time I could hear the paramedic say that Tottenham had won 1:0 after Rial Madrid's key defender had been red carded off.

"Yes!" Phil yelled. "That's great. This is just fantastic." As I said before, Phil is always Phil. Eventually he was taken off to the hospital for observation, they were worried about concussion and setting the broken nose, but I was deemed well enough to go home with my mother.

It took most of the day before we could get back to London. I tried to act cool and nonchalant around Mum when she came to collect me, as if being kidnapped and threatened with death was no big deal, but in the car I started shaking and couldn't stop. I knew it was a reaction to stress, I had gone through it before. Mum didn't say anything but I think she noticed. It was dark by the time we got home. Mum was still fussing and worrying around me, urging me to get to bed and rest, so I didn't really get a good look at the park opposite us. I just caught a glimpse, a glimpse of something that looked a bit like a very large man, only massively twisted and deformed. Mum then rushed me inside and I wasn't unhappy. I had an instinctive reaction that I really didn't want to see what that thing actually was.

I didn't go the school the next day. I spent most of it resting and watching the 24hrs news channel where the story of our kidnapping was repeated over and over again. The consensus seemed to be that our kidnapping was the work of organized crime and an attempt to set up some sort of extortion ring. They typically led the story with something like this:

"The kidnapping of two schoolboys from a soccer match is believed to be linked to an attempt to pressure leading financial figures into supporting organized crime. The two boys are known to be friends of the niece of Professor Cadfan Rhys. Professor Rhys, a professor at the prestigious City of Westminster University, is a well known figure in financial circles."

In the afternoon a very nice lady came around for a preliminary counseling session. We had a pleasant chat about how I really didn't like being kidnapped and how people threatening to kill you can ruin your whole day. In the end I think she went away satisfied. After school, Myfanwy came to visit. As soon as I opened the door I found myself crushed in a bear-like hug. She's only short and very lightly built but she's surprisingly strong.

"You could have been killed!" She said into my chest. A memory of four men all racing to find their guns flashed into my mind.

"Yes," I said. "I could have been – but I wasn't." I pulled back and looked at her face, her dark curls were an untidy cascade and her brilliant green eyes were full of tears." I wasn't. I wasn't even hurt. I'm fine." I lightly brushed a tear away from her face.

"If only you had never met me you'd be safe," she said in a miserable voice. Professor Rhys appeared behind her and gave a small, embarrassed cough. Then Mum came up behind me and invited Myfanwy and her uncle in for tea.

It was during tea that the professor posed a very interesting problem. "What I don't understand is how they knew that you and Phil would be at that soccer game. It wasn't part of any routine, in fact it was a complete one off. So, how did they know?"

It wasn't a question that had occurred to me before but as soon as he posed it I knew the answer. I decided then that I would go back to school early tomorrow.

As they were leaving, I hugged Myfanwy close and whispered in her ear. "If the choice was between living or knowing you, I would still want to know you." It's the kind of thing you say when no one is pointing a gun at you.

Chapter Six.
A Fight and its Aftermath

I got up early the next morning and, despite my mother's protestations that I needed another day's rest, set off for school. I seemed calm but actually I was in a blind rage. I waited at the school gate until Horace and his three henchmen came walking up from the bus exchange. They were laughing and obviously feeling very satisfied with themselves. This changed as I came up to them, grabbed Horace by the front of his blazer and pushed him back onto the school gatepost. The henchmen tried to grab me but I was so angry I just didn't pay any attention.

"It was you," I said. "You told them where to find us! We got kidnapped, tied up and almost killed because of you. Phil is still in hospital because of you." At this time two of the henchmen got serious in their attempts to separate us. I was having none of that. I let them pull me away then did a backhand strike to one and a spinning heel kick to the other. They both went down. Being as angry as I was, I probably hit them a bit too hard. The third henchman ran off to get a teacher and Horace also decided to make a break for it. I grabbed him in an arm lock and pushed him back up against the gate post.

Pressed up against the gate post, Horace had difficulty talking but he managed to say, "You don't know, you're only guessing. You can't prove I had anything to do with it." We were now surrounded by a growing crowd of yelling kids. I pulled him round to face me.

"I don't need proof to beat you to a pulp," I said. Then the world was engulfed in a total silence except for Myfanwy saying,

"Tom stop! You must stop this now." I looked around to find that time had been stopped, the yelling kids caught in mid yell, the two henchmen frozen still while trying to get to their feet. Myfanwy was on the edge of the crowd with a horrified look on her face.

"Myf, he did it!" I said. "He was taking notes in the dining hall. He told them where to find us."

"Even if that's true," she replied. "This will do no good. It will only get you into trouble. You can't just go around beating people up." She pushed her way through the frozen crowd and stood close to me, looking directly at me with her emerald eyes. "What is the difference between you using your martial arts ability and me using my magic talent? The need for control doesn't just apply to magic."

I knew she was right. "Okay," I said. "I won't hurt him." Now that the white heat of my anger had passed, my mind started to work again. "But could you wait a bit before you let time go?" Myfanwy looked puzzled but time stayed frozen. I searched the frozen Horace and quickly found what I was looking for. In the inside pocket of his blazer was the notebook I had seen him writing in. "Okay, I'm ready now," I said. Time started to flow again and the world was full of the sound of yelling kids. Horace was looking at me with real fear and my stomach clenched in disgust to think that I was the cause of that look. I had a sudden insight into the mind of Cadell. He enjoyed the feeling of power that that look carried. I hated it.

"I'm sorry," Horace said in a whiney voice. "Look, I really didn't know what they were going to do."

Just then 'Mr. Black' pushed his way through the crowd. "Break it up, break it up," he said. "Anyone who is still here in five minutes gets a detention." That had the effect of rapidly dispersing the crowd. "Not you four," he said to me, Horace and his henchmen. "You are coming with me to the headmaster's office."

In the headmaster's office the henchmen were able to show off impressive bruises to bolster their claim that I had attacked them. Mr. Black stood at the back of the room, observing quietly.

The headmaster started to use his most pompous voice. "I must say that I am shocked and disappointed Mr. O'Malley. I have always regarded you as a model student: a credit to your country. Is it true that you launched a vicious and unprovoked attack on these, your fellow students?"

"I did attack them, Sir," I said. "But it was not unprovoked. These students have been passing on information about my movements to the criminal gang that kidnapped Phillip Trenton and me. It is because of them that I was nearly killed and Phil is in hospital." Horace and his mates started to protest but the headmaster silenced them.

"That's a very serious charge Mr. O'Malley," the headmaster said. "Do you have any proof?" Here Horace gave a smug little smile.

"I do," I said. "In the inside pocket of his blazer, Horace Trimble has a notebook that he has used to write down my movements and plans so as to pass them onto the criminal gang." Horace looked shocked and 'Mr. Black' moved forward with surprising speed.

"Hand over the book," he said.

"I don't have any book!" Horace protested but Mr. Black, aka Sergeant Fisher, could not be put off or fooled by a schoolboy, his voice just became firmer and more insistent.

"Hand over the book – now!" There is often a special energy and directness about Special Forces soldiers which can be very intimidating. Horace handed over the book. Mr. Black looked briefly at the last few entries.

"It would seem that Mr. O'Malley is correct, Headmaster. This note book contains a written record of his movements, including details of where and when he would meet Mr. Trenton to go to the football match. I think we need to call the police."

The police came and there was a series of tedious interviews. It was after I had told the story of the fight that 'Mr. Black' took me aside and quietly said to me, "A spinning heel kick? Really? You know that if you miss, and trust me you will miss; you end up looking stupid and being vulnerable. Remember what I said, it's a fight not a dance – keep it simple."

The wash up of the police interviews was that Horace and Co. were taken off to the police station for further questioning and I was suspended from school for the rest of the week for fighting. I was lucky I wasn't charged with assault and battery. I think they all thought I was suffering from post traumatic shock.

That afternoon I didn't go directly home but went to visit Westminster Cathedral near the centre of London. I needed to work things out and I knew that the quiet stillness of that place would help. I sat towards the back where the domes of unfinished brickwork, still awaiting their glittering mosaics, resembled a cavern with its columns and its darkness. There, in the presence of God, I could face the shame of the fear that I had caused in Horace, the fear and anger that I felt at what had happened to me and my new awareness of my own mortality. At the core of it all was a single question: what sort of person am I? When I left I didn't know the answer but at least I had asked the question.

Mum wasn't very happy with me, to say the least. When she got home from work, I got a long lecture on the need to control my temper and about how disappointing my behaviour was. I even got a shorter but punchier version from Dad, via satellite phone from his oil rig in the South China Sea. They didn't tell me anything I didn't already know, and my promise to try and be more careful was heartfelt.

That night the social network was very active. Rachael and Gabriella told me not to feel bad and that I was perfectly justified in what I did – something I now disagreed with. Phil let me know that he was out of hospital and sent me a video link with a single word annotation: "Cool!" The video, which must have been taken on a student's phone, showed me doing a spinning heel kick to knock down Frank Bullfinch, Horace's henchman. Several other students also sent me that link and I hoped it wasn't going to get out of control. Wilson sent me notes on the day's schoolwork and promised to keep me up to date. This was really good because his notes were a lot better than mine. Myfanwy, of course, didn't contact me. She would be up at Aelred Abbey where no electronic communication was possible.

I had a lot of time on my hands over the next few days and I started to pay more attention to the homeless guy living in the park. He was always dressed the same way, always sitting in the same seat and always, apparently, staring at our house. On Wednesday, I decided to go for a walk in the park, primarily to get a closer look at him. I could see him stiffen as I approached. He had fine features, pale skin and long, dark hair that really needed a wash. His eyes were green: not the brilliant green of Myfanwy's people but a faded, almost olive colour.

As I walked past I said, "Good morning." My greeting was polite and cheerful but he simply nodded in reply and turned away. I didn't know if he was just being rude, if he was wary of strangers or even if he was a refugee from somewhere who didn't understand English. Perhaps I was becoming paranoid but I decided to keep watching him because now anyone watching me made me nervous.

The next day was cold with gusts of wind carrying a light rain. At lunch time I made myself some toast and heated up a can of soup. I went to the front sitting room and looked out into the park while I sipped a cup of the soup. The homeless guy was there again, still in the same seat, shivering in the cold. A thought occurred to me and I poured the rest of the hot soup into a mug and took it over to offer it to him.

"Here," I said. "This'll help keep you warm." At first he looked at me suspiciously but he accepted the mug, wrapping his hands around it for the warmth. He drank the soup slowly, almost reverently and when he had finished he handed the mug back to me in silence.

Then, as I turned to go, he spoke in a deep, rough voice that sounded like river gravel.

"Pax vobiscum," he said. I looked at him in surprise. That was Latin! Moreover, it was formal, church Latin. I had done four years of Latin in Australia before giving up languages to concentrate on the Maths and Sciences, so I knew that it meant 'Peace be with you'. It was one of the formal greetings with which a priest would address his congregation during the liturgy. Fortunately, I also knew the correct response.

"Et cum spiritu tuo," (and with your spirit) I said. As I walked back to the house I wondered why a destitute, homeless guy in the middle of London would be conversing in Latin. It didn't make sense.

That night Professor Rhys came to visit. He suggested that my mother and I come to spend the weekend at Aelred Abbey so that we could discuss a serious and developing situation in detail. I was eager to go, not just because Myfanwy would be there but because it was a great place to visit. It was an old castle and the site of a ruined monastery on the Norfolk coast. Also, I was going stir crazy stuck in the house.

Mother, however, was a little more reluctant. She had heard that the place was haunted, and this made her rather nervous. After much pleading, however, she agreed and Professor Rhys made arrangements to pick us up early on Friday afternoon. Aelred Abbey is in fact haunted, not by the spirits of the dead, but by the echoes of its past which flow easily into its present.

The next day the news carried the story of a massive earthquake in southern Japan. It had sent a giant tsunami across the East China Sea and devastated the eastern coast of China, including the city of Shanghai. It had also funneled up the valley of the Yantze River as far as Nanjin. Hundreds of thousands were feared dead.

Chapter Seven
Earthquakes and Merlin

On Friday we packed two small weekend bags and waited for the Professor to arrive. I had thought that we would go to Aelred Abbey in his classic Rolls Royce. However, to my surprise, he turned up on foot.

"I thought that since you would only have bags for a weekend, we might as well walk," he said. "There is a gate close by." This puzzled my mother a great deal.

"I thought that you said Aelred Abbey was on the Norfolk coast. How can we walk there?" She asked.

The professor smiled. "Tom knows well enough," he said as he set off down the street. "Follow me." We walked around the corner from the square and along the street up to an old gate that seemed to have no purpose: it simply led to a wall. I knew what was coming but Mum was sure we were all mad when Professor Rhys opened the gate and held it for her to walk through.

I whispered to her, "Just go with the flow Mum. Believe me, in Myfanwy's family anything can happen." She raised her eyebrows and hesitantly stepped through the gate. I followed her. Mum was standing on narrow path that led down, through a birch wood, to a stretch of salt marsh. Her face was frozen in shock and surprise and I wondered if I had looked like that when I first stepped through the gate. Behind us, Professor Rhys was closing the same old gate that had been on the London street, only now behind it were the green fields of rural

Norfolk. The professor led us down the path to the causeway and to the familiar view of Aelred Abbey.

There are places that you tend to forget as soon as you're not in them; perhaps most places are like this, certainly most city suburbs are. Then there are places which, once you've visited them, become etched in your soul and become an indelible part of your view of the world. Aelred Abbey is such a place and a place like no other. It sits on a small island of high land between the sea and the salt marsh and it is really two buildings joined together. On one side there is the heavy, square defensiveness of the tower keep: a building once garrisoned for coastal defense but now converted into a comfortable home. On the other side is the ruin of the monastery itself: older than the tower and built on the site of a still older monastery. The grace of its ruined arches and colonnades are a marked contrast to the dour solidity of the keep.

Here time flows differently and the past has an unsettling tendency to intrude into the present. This is the refuge that Myfanwy's family uses when they have to live and operate in our world. It is certainly no ordinary place. Here the mythical and the magical hold sway over the mundane.

It was only a short walk across the causeway to the Abbey. There we were greeted at the huge door of the keep by Nain. She bustled us into the kitchen at the rear of the tower where she already had hot tea and cakes waiting. Our bags disappeared and I knew that later on we would find them ready in our rooms. It was good to be back. After our tea and much general talk, it was agreed that the serious discussion would be left for tomorrow, we were shown to our rooms to refresh ourselves and to settle in.

A little while later I checked my watch, I had something to do. I left the keep and crossed over the causeway. In the birch forest I sat down to wait. It wasn't long before the gate swung open and Myfanwy, dressed in her school uniform, walked into the forest from a rather dreary outer London street. She looked at me and smiled and that smile shone brightly and caused my heart to thump in my chest.

"Hello surfer boy," she said. "What brings you out here?"

"My Lady Myfanwy," I said bowing. "I have come to escort you to your castle."

"Great," she said. "Then you can carry this. It's really heavy." She handed me her school bag which I threw over my shoulder. Then I took her hand and we walked back across the causeway. Myfanwy was chatting about things that had happened at school but I wasn't really listening. Just being with her in the brightness of her smile was enough. Nain was there to meet us at the door: her expression unreadable.

"There's hot chocolate ready in the library," was all she said. That night we had dinner in the cozy confines of the kitchen.

This caused Professor Rhys some irritation but Nain said, "Don't worry Cadfan, we'll have your grand meal sometime: just not tonight. Tonight we can relax together around the table." Leek Soup was followed by Shepherd's Pie and a good deal of discussion about the state of the financial market and the differences between fashion and landscape photography and which was more rewarding: none of which concerned me at all. We finished up with Bread and Butter Pudding and big mugs of hot tea. The mood was spoiled a bit when a desperate monk came running through the kitchen wall followed by a large Viking with a plaited blond beard and a vicious looking axe. Mum sat pale and frozen at the table. Professor Rhys' only response was to give an explanation.

"The Vikings raided the monastery here in the year 800 and again in 821. After that they deemed that there was nothing left worth stealing and they left the place alone. In each of the raids, however, many monks were killed or taken into slavery. These events echo strongly in the history of this place and will occasionally intrude into polite conversation or quiet moments. It is best to ignore them."

Mum nodded, the colour slowly returning to her face. "I'll do my best."

Next morning I was woken by a scream from Mum's room. I rushed in to find her starring horrified at four wounded royalist soldiers from the civil war groaning on the floor.

"Remember Mum, they're just echoes of the past," I said, "a kind of real, 3D movie." As soon as I said this I saw her expression change as she started to think like a photographer. She turned to get her camera but by then the room was empty.

The day had dawned clear, with a warm sun and a fresh breeze coming off the sea. Nonetheless, we were indoors as Professor Rhys gathered us in the Library to discuss his concerns. We sat in a rough semi-circle around the empty fire place while the professor stood on the cold hearth and addressed us – for all the world like he was giving a lecture. He started by listing all the recent earthquakes and unusual volcanic activity.

"To that list," he said. "I must add two earthquakes that occurred almost simultaneously: one just to the east of Yellowstone National Park in the United States and the other near Lake Taupo in New Zealand. The problem with all this activity is not just that it is unusual, nor even that human lives have been lost. Such things do just happen. It is part of the cost of living in a wild universe. However, these events are not just unusual – they are way off key. Myfanwy and Nain will know what I mean and will have sensed this themselves." He turned to look directly at Mum and me. "However, for the sake of our guests, I will need to explain something about magic."

"Magic works because the world is not fixed and deterministic, as some believe, but rather, it is a tangled mix of probability: from the randomness of Quantum Physics to the inherent uncertainty of chaos theory. Those of us with magical ability can sense the probable outcome of events and also all the other improbable outcomes: even very improbable outcomes. Knowing these improbable outcomes, we have the ability to choose the one we want. There are limits to this and the more improbable something is the higher the energy barrier there is to make it happen." Mum was fascinated by all this but I had heard it before and I think the Professor could sense my restlessness.

"Okay, Thomas," he said. "I will come directly to the crux of the matter."

"I really wish you would Cadfan," Nain interjected. "You do go on and wander off the track sometimes." The Professor ignored her and continued.

"All of this means that we can sense when magic is being used. When events do not match what we sense as the probable range of outcomes, we can see when magical selection and energy has been used. Just as a person listening to music will expect a certain range of possible resolutions to a chord and will notice if something discordant happens, so we can sense the flow of reality. These catastrophic events are not just part of the random activity of the Earth. To follow my music metaphor, they are discordant. They show all the signs of magical activity: someone is causing then to happen. The questions we must answer are who, why and how can we stop them?"

"But Professor," I objected. "You yourself said that there are limits to magic and I know how tired some things can make Myfanwy. The energy involved here is huge. You're talking about the energy of many, many hydrogen bombs. How could a magic user do this?"

The professor nodded as he replied. "The energies are indeed huge, Thomas, far beyond the ability of any human magic user. However, it may be that they do not have to produce those energies themselves, nor do they have to control them; all they have to do is trigger them. The energies are already there, coiled in the Earth. To trigger them before their time would be difficult. It would require great, subtle skill and knowledge but the energy barrier might not be impossible."

"In that case, I think I can answer two of your questions," I said. "Cadell is still at large and he is a subtle and skilful magic user. He is the most obvious answer to 'who?'. This also answers 'why?'. He is a psychopath bent on destruction for its own sake. Since the world won't accept him as their natural overlord, he wants only to destroy it, even if he destroys himself doing so. The only question left is then; how do we stop him?"

"I tend to agree with your conclusions Thomas," the Professor said. "However, this leads to another mystery: the key role that you seem to play in all this. Cadell had you kidnapped and we know now that he was not interested in Myfanwy: so he was not planning revenge. He kidnapped you as his insurance policy. Well, if you were insurance against something going wrong with his plans, then that means that something *can* go wrong with his plans, even now. I don't really know but my guess is that if you can stop things going wrong then you can also cause them to go wrong and we need you to do that. You, Thomas, are the key to all this."

"Maybe," I said doubtfully. "But I don't think I'm really the one who can stop him. Cadell wanted to use me to help him kill someone. I thought it was Myfanwy but that didn't really fit. I think it's the person he wants to kill who can stop him."

"But weren't there other kidnappings as well?" my mother asked. "I'm sure that strange, English public servant type said something about other kidnappings while we were still in Australia."

"Of course!" Myfanwy said. "It's Merlin. He's trying to find where Merlin sleeps. Yet even if he found him, he would need Tom to break any protective spells so that he could kill him. But why Merlin?"

Nain drew a deep breath and relied solemnly, "Because Myrddin Emrys, whom the Romans called Merlinus Ambrosius and who you know as Merlin, was a terramage, perhaps the greatest that ever lived. He understood the lore of the earth and could feel its moods. If anyone can calm the violence within the Earth, it's him. That's why Cadell wants to find him. He wants to kill him while he is still in his enchantment. Clearly, Cadell thinks there is a risk that Myrddin Emrys could stop what he is doing. He's a risk to his plans. The trouble for us is that Myrddin Emrys sleeps forever, trapped in a hidden cave. A cave that is so well hidden that after fifteen hundred years of searching, it has never been found."

"If he was so great a mage, how is it that he got himself trapped like that?" Mum asked.

"Because," Nain replied, "even though he was wise and powerful, he was also human and as he grew older, loneliness clouded his judgment. A young maiden, Nimwe, came to him and pretended to love him in order to learn his lore. The old fool couldn't see that she was just using him, or perhaps he just didn't care. Anyway, he opened his heart to her and when she had learned from him all that she could, she used his own lore against him and bound him in an enchanted cave. He was lost forever."

"What happened after that?" I asked.

"Well," the Professor said. "The absence of Merlin precipitated war between the Dux Arturos, who you know as King Arthur, and the witch queen Morgana. This war was so bloody that Nimwe was shocked at the result of her actions and she became one of the six mages who sealed Annwn off from the rest of the world and separated our people from the rest of humanity."

"Well," I said. "I think it's pretty clear that we have to find Merlin before Cadell does and get him to stop whatever it is Cadell is doing."

"Not you Thomas," the Professor said firmly. "Your job is to stay safe and keep low until we need you. Cadell must not get near you again. You are far too important to risk in the search." That was a sentiment that my mother and Nain heartily agreed with. I argued the point but they were adamant: my only job was to stay safe while the Council of Nobles searched for Merlin. When they had found him, I was to be escorted in to help break the enchantment that held him. It was like I was some sort of tool to be called on only as needed. Eventually Nain called an end to the discussion by insisting that it was time for lunch.

Chapter Eight
Questions, Advice and Plans

There seemed to be little point in continuing the discussion after lunch, so Myfanwy and I took the opportunity to go for a walk along the beach and up onto the coastal path. After we had walked a while, there was an oak tree off the path and we sat down in its shade, looking out to sea. Myfanwy was so quiet that I knew she was about to ask me something important.

"Thomas," she said eventually. "Does all that stuff that Rachael keeps going on about, about relationships breaking up and new possibilities, worry you?" I didn't answer for a long time. I was trying to figure out how to respond. The trouble was that Myfanwy's question confused me. I really didn't know the answer. In the end I answered as honestly as I could, trying to voice the confusion that I felt.

"I don't know," I said. "Perhaps a little. When I'm with you and just think about now, then everything is fine. It's just that when I think of the future, maybe years and years, it can be a bit scary. Also, our relationship has not, by any stretch of the imagination, been normal. I can't help but wonder about what it might have been like if I didn't have this peculiar talent, if we hadn't got caught up in trying to stop Apophis. What would our relationship have been like then? The trouble is that Rachael's talk just feeds all these little doubts and fears and I can't make them go away."

"Do you feel trapped Thomas?" she asked in a very small and quiet voice. "Because if you do, it may not be too late. The bond between us hasn't been finally sealed. If you just walk away now, I think it might be okay. Our bond will just fade and die. I don't want you to feel that you are stuck with me against your will. If you feel trapped, I want you to walk away now: to go back to London, to Australia, to anywhere. Especially if you feel that you have been tricked into something you weren't really prepared for, I really want you to go."

I looked at her in surprise. Where had all that come from? She was staring fixedly out to sea and there were tears in her eyes. I put my arm around her and tried to pull her towards me but she resisted: holding her body stiff.

"Myf," I whispered softly. "I will always be your friend, remember? Don't let Rachael do what the Council of Nobles couldn't. I may be confused and I might be a bit afraid but I could never just walk away from you." She relaxed then and put her head on my shoulder.

In the same small, quiet voice she said, "You might be afraid of how long the future could be but I am only afraid that it will be without you." This really upset me. Myfanwy is so sensible, so strong and positive that she's not afraid of anything much at all. She also never gets sentimental and mushy. Rachael's talk must really have upset her.

"No need to be," I said. "After all, without you and all this crazy magic stuff, my life would just be really dull. I'd probably even end up going to the soccer with Phil." She smiled at this and the feeling between us became more comfortable. We sat quietly for a long time.

"Come on," she said at last, getting up and brushing off old leaves and bits of twig. "We need to get going or we'll be late for dinner."

That night, Professor Rhys got his way and we had a grand, formal dinner to welcome my Mum to the house. This sent Mum into a bit of a panic and she insisted that I "dress" for dinner. Given what I had packed, this presented me with a real problem. I did, however, have some mildly formal clothes that I had included for going to church. So I put these on and headed downstairs. On the landing I found myself facing a door in the western wall, the wall facing the ruins of the monastery. This door had not been there when I had gone up to my room. Naturally, I opened it and went through.

As I expected, I found myself in a long, austere room with stone walls and a tile floor. Halfway along there was an old Benedictine monk sitting on a wooden bench. He was bald and his face was deeply lined with age. He was also my friend and spiritual advisor, Brother Theophane: a remarkable monk of the fifteenth century. He was a member of the Aelred Abbey community when it was still a proper monastery and during his life he had been famous for giving advice to those who needed it. On his deathbed he was granted, as a favour from God, that those who came to Aelred Abbey needing his advice would always be able to get it – no matter when they lived. Since teaming up with Myfanwy, I have had need of his advice before.

He smiled as he saw me and called out, "Welcome, Thomas, welcome." He patted the bench next to him.

"Come, rest thy limbs and speak to me of what troubles thy heart." I sat down and once again found that I could speak to him very easily. I spoke to him about all my doubts and fears, about what Rachael had said, about my fear of hurting Myfanwy, my fear of a long term commitment in an uncertain future, about feeling too young and unprepared for the decisions I was being asked to make. As I spoke, he listened in silence and I found all my fears and confusion falling into a deep pool of stillness. When I had finished he looked at me and gave a very gentle smile.

"Is she comely?" he asked. "This maiden on whom thou hast set thy heart, is she fair to look upon?" I nodded.

"Very," I said.

"Then how sure art thou that the attraction is from thy heart and not thy loins?" I started to protest indignantly but he continued. "Nay Thomas, calm thyself. I do not impugn thy honour. I merely pose questions for thee to consider, that in answering these, thou mayst find yet deeper answers. See thee that love comes not, as many think, as an emotion of moonbeams and flowers, but rather as a decision. Here now I have heard how thou art attracted to this maiden: to her smile, to her laugh. Now thou must decide to love her or no. As to being young: I have seen men thy age shoulder the burden of raising a family. I have seen men thy age lead others into battle. Aye, and die there too. None of them were prepared and all of them, save the most foolish, were afraid. I myself came to this monastery as a boy and I trembled at what lay before me even as I grieved for what lay behind. Yet I decided to live this life as faithfully as I may and I have had great joy in thus living. One more question I would ask of thee, not for thee to answer now but for thee to ponder at thy leisure: is to love this maiden the way that thou art called to love thy God?" Just then a bell started to ring in the monastery. Brother Theophane got up.

"Ah Thomas, once again I am called away to vespers," he said. "But do not worry, we will talk of these things again." Just before he left the room, he turned and said, "Thomas, thou hath a true heart, I would trust it as a guide." I left by the opposite door and went down the stairs to the dining room - behind me there was only a stone wall.

Dinner that night was very formal, with a proper sequence of courses all appearing as the dishes of the previous course disappeared. To tell the truth, it was a bit creepy. It was like we were being served by a crowd of invisible servants. Still, the food was good and the room looked terrific, with the candles in their silver candelabras reflected in the polished wood of the table and casting a soft glow on the tapestries that hung on the wall. The only problem was that the five of us looked a little ridiculous sitting at a table that could comfortably seat thirty. Over dinner I tried repeatedly to argue that I should have a role in the hunt for Merlin only to be firmly rebuffed on every occasion. The message was clear: the fun and games are over, this is serious and it is time for the adults to take charge. In the end I dropped it because it wasn't getting anywhere and was spoiling the mood of the dinner conversation.

After the dessert we 'retired' to the library where there was coffee and port for the adults and hot chocolate for Myfanwy and me. The conversation was cut short when a troupe of medieval actors suddenly appeared, performing a funny but rather raunchy play about a rich widow. There were also some men at arms sitting on wooden benches who seemed to find the play hilarious. It was really very mild compared to a modern sitcom but Nain was horrified and insisted that Myfanwy and I go to our bedrooms. I lay on my bed but I didn't sleep well that night. I lay awake for a long time; thinking of what Rachael had said one moment and of what Brother Theophane had said the next. When I did sleep, my dreams were haunted by the image of Myfanwy starring out to sea with tears in her eyes.

I had to get up early the next morning to go to mass. After Nain had cooked us all a breakfast of sausage, bacon, fried eggs and cockles, I got ready for mass and met the other four in the main entrance hall. Both of our families were Catholic but with vastly different histories. My Irish ancestors had hung on to their faith through years of vicious persecution and oppression while for Myfanwy's family the reformation had simply happened somewhere else. They still kept to the old, pre-reformation traditions and were more concerned with the struggle against the ancient, pagan religion which was still strong on the island of Annwn.

We walked over to the gate and found ourselves stepping through, not a gate onto the lane to the village but through a gateway in a large yew hedge and into an extensive garden which was laid out formally with paths and rose beds. Across the garden from us was a large building dominated by a massive square tower. Under the tower were the high vaulted roof and stained glass windows of what was obviously a church.

"Where are we?" I asked.

"At Belmont Abbey near Hereford," Professor Rhys answered. "Our family follows the ways of the old church and we are more comfortable in a monastic setting. Also, it avoids embarrassing questions about community involvement." We walked across the garden and joined a small crowd of people who were coming to the church through the main entrance, where a large statue of St. Michael brandished a gleaming sword. Inside, the altar was near the centre and surrounded by the four, high, vaulted arches that supported the tower. Everywhere I looked there seemed to be images or statues of angels: hundreds of them. The monks sat in their choir stalls behind the altar and chanted the parts of the mass, while we sat on chairs in the main part of the church. As everyone was leaving after mass, I lost sight of Myfanwy. I found her again in a side chapel, kneeling down and praying to a Welsh saint I had never heard of. I waited silently not wanting to disturb her. As she got up she smiled at me and took my hand as we left the church.

"It's okay," she said. "I think I know what to do now."

After we returned from mass, it being a warm sunny day, Myfanwy and I decided to walk to the village to get an ice cream. I was still feeling hostile at being sidelined in the search for Merlin and the battle against Cadell and was glad to get out of the house for a while.

As we walked down the lane, Myfanwy said quite casually. "You know, Uncle Cadfan is making a mistake. Our people have been trying to find Merlin for nearly fifteen hundred years without any luck. Cadell might be trying hard too but I don't think he knows any more than we do." I looked at her closely to see where this might be going but her face was carefully neutral. "You are the only new element and I think Cadell wanted to use you to find Merlin's cave as well as to open it."

"How?" I asked. "I really want to be involved but I have no magic and I certainly have no special knowledge of Merlin and his cave."

"No, but you can't be fooled by magic," she replied. "If something was hidden by magic it wouldn't be hidden from you. If you were to be paired with a magic user who could sense when magic had altered an area then there could be a real chance of finding Merlin. That's why I think Uncle Cadfan and the others are making a mistake in excluding you."

By this time we had reached the village. We went over to the small grocery store and bought some ice creams from the owner who served us reluctantly and with very bad grace. The people of the village considered Aelred Abbey to be haunted and were very suspicious of Myfanwy's family. As we were walking back down the lane, eating our ice creams, I asked Myfanwy, "Well, if your uncle is making a mistake, what do you think we should do about it?"

She seemed to take a deep interest in her ice cream for a while and then replied very casually, "I think we should conduct our own search. I'll do the magic part and you'll do the immune from magic bit. You could use the internet to find possible locations and we could visit a different one each weekend." I shook my head.

"No way," I said. "That would mean being away for long periods of time and there's no way we could do that without being closely questioned and watched." Myfanwy just smiled: a very sneaky, conspiratorial smile.

"You know," she said. "We call ourselves girlfriend and boyfriend but we've never even been on a proper date. You've never taken me out anywhere. There are a whole lot of galleries and museums in London that I could spend a whole day in – if you would take me."

I shook my head even more vigorously. "Absolutely no way," I said. "I am not going around sneaking about and lying to people."

"I'm not asking you to, surfer boy. I'm just asking you not to mention where we went *after* we visited the gallery or museum or whatever…" I still shook my head. I didn't like it.

"Okay!" she said in an exasperated voice. "We will not lie. We will not deceive in any way. We just won't be very specific about where we are going and why we are going there and if we manage to find Merlin and stop Cadell, we might just save thousands of lives. Does that satisfy you?"

That morning she had her mass of black curls tied back off her face and she looked at me intently, her green eyes full of challenge. I looked at her and I surrendered. "I give up," I said. "Although, I think I am in danger of being led astray."

She shrugged, as if that was unimportant. "There's something else," she said. "I don't think that just finding Merlin will be enough. We need to understand what Cadell is up to and for that we need the services of a lore master: someone who can make sense of these events."

"I'm guessing," I said, "that these lore masters are not common or easy to find."

"No they're not," she replied. "The only one I trust, and I think the most knowledgeable there is, is

Friar Daffyd. We need to go and talk to him." By this time we had passed through the gate and were walking back across the causeway to Aelred Abbey.

"Um…" I said with a great show of hesitation. "You do realize that he doesn't ever go far from his hermitage on Annwn and that I am still banished by the Council of Nobles."

"I know," she said cheerfully. "We're just going to have to find a way to sneak you in." I sighed a very heartfelt sigh. I would follow Myfanwy anywhere but following Myfanwy had a tendency to leave me broken, bruised and in trouble.

Chapter Nine
The Marlborough Mound

In a similar way to the change between Angle Creek and London, going back to school after time spent at Aelred Abbey was always a bit disorienting. You moved from one world, where time could turn back on itself and magic was normal, to another, mundane world, where time was always linear and magic was impossible: from a world of wonder to a world of traffic jams. I had spent Sunday night searching the net for hints to the possible site for Merlin's entombment. Most of them seemed pretty unlikely and I seriously doubted that we would find Merlin this way. Still, I made a list of the five most mentioned sites to show Myfanwy.

As I sat on the bus, stuck in traffic, on the way to school, I couldn't help but think about the contrast between Myfanwy's world, where it was quite reasonable to try and wake a wizard who went to sleep fifteen hundred years ago, and the noisy ordinariness of modern London. The thought came to me that I really didn't belong in Myfanwy's world, that I was a normal person and I belonged here in the traffic and the noise. I found that thought depressing because so much of the modern world was mean and ugly. However, I also quickly realized that my world, the place where I belonged, was not here. It was the south east coast of Australia, where forested mountains reach down to tall cliffs and sandy beaches. There is nothing small or ugly about it and while its wonders may be different from those of

Annwn, they are still real. Perhaps this was part of the reason for the bond between Myfanwy and me: we were both outsiders and we both came from worlds full of awe and wonder.

At school we were really starting get into the swing of our final year and the exams loomed like an ever present threat on the horizon. In English, Mrs. Brown was introducing us to the modern poets and we were told to concentrate on the work of W.B. Yeats and T.S. Eliot. I sensed a wasteland ahead.

I had a free study period before lunchtime and so was the first to the dining room. As I approached I could see the two serving ladies standing there white faced and frozen in fear. As I walked into the room I could see why. The school dining room had originally been the ball room of an old mansion and now ladies in long, gowns were dancing around the room with gentlemen sporting elaborate facial hair and dressed in either white tie and tails or military dress uniforms. Against the wall a small, string orchestra was happily playing away in silence. I got my plate and went up to the first of the serving ladies.

"Not too many of the beans, thanks," I said. She turned to me slowly, her eyes wide with fear. She showed no sign of understanding what I had just said.

"Not too many beans," I repeated. "They have a nasty effect on me." Robot-like she nodded and began to automatically fill my plate. When the second lady served me some goop that was intended to be mashed potato, I said,

"You know, I think it's great the way these old buildings make you think of the past." They each looked at me in horror. The dancers were fading as I went to my table and they had vanished by the time the rest of the students arrived for lunch.

It wasn't long before Myfanwy came in from her literature class and brought her lunch over to my table.

"Did you get the list?" she asked. I nodded and said,

"Yes, but we have another problem. How long have you been at this school?"

Myfanwy looked puzzled. "Almost six years. Why?" she asked.

"Well," I answered. "You may have noticed the serving ladies were a bit distracted as you got your lunch. They had good reason. You remember telling me how the longer your people stayed in one place the less linear time became, and the more likely it was to fold back on itself and have echoes of the past turn up in the present?" She nodded doubtfully, not knowing why I was talking about this. "Today I was the first in here for lunch and when I arrived there were ladies and gentlemen dancing all around the ballroom. From their costumes, I'd guess they were from the early nineteenth century. It looked like quite a ball." Myfanwy put her hand over her mouth in shock.

"Oh no!" she said. "Tom, there nothing I can do to stop that."

"Perhaps not," I said, "but you might want to ease the anxiety of the two serving ladies. They were scarred out of their wits and they're now probably worried that they're going mad."

"Of course, you're right," she said and turned to look intently at the serving ladies who suddenly seemed to be much happier.

She turned back smiling and said, "Now they think it's wonderful that the historic atmosphere of the place means that you can almost see the past. However, it may happen again. It's pretty random, so it may not happen for a year or it may happen next week. It depends on how significant, how emotionally charged, the events in the old house were. It could become a real problem." I shrugged. There was nothing to be done about that at the moment.

"Here's the list of possible sites," I said, pushing a piece of paper across the table. "Most likely at the top, least likely at the bottom – not that I think any of them are particularly good prospects." Myfanwy looked at the list and screwed up her face in contempt.

"You're right," she said. "But I still think we need to start somewhere. We should visit the least likely first, eliminate them and work up the list. By the way, do you own a bike?" I nodded just as Wilson and Rachael joined us for lunch. The rest of the conversation was about how hard T.S. Eliot's poetry was.

The next day Horace and his mates returned to school and Phil and I were called to a big conference in the school conference room – a room I hadn't known existed until then. The meeting was a bit awkward to say the least. The Headmaster sat at the head of a very large and highly polished table. Phil and I sat on one side while Horace and his three henchmen sat on the other. Next to them sat a large man in a dark suit who we soon learned was Detective Inspector Nielson of the Metropolitan Police. The Headmaster started the meeting by giving a little speech.

"I know there is a good deal of animosity between you and I am not going to ask you to pretend to be friends. However, I have called this meeting so that the whole situation might be out in the open and I can get each of you to promise to be at least cordial in your dealings in this school. Now, Thomas and Phillip, I understand your anger that some of your school mates gave information to a criminal gang that led to your kidnapping and attempted murder. However, they have assured me, and both I and the police believe them, that that is not what they thought they were doing. They thought they were giving information to a journalist who was going to write a story on Australians in our education system." The headmaster and police might have believed that but I didn't for a moment and I could see that Horace knew I didn't.

"I'm not saying that their spying on you was honourable, indeed it wasn't, but it wasn't murderous in intent. I ask you to recognize that. Also Thomas, you must know that resorting to physical violence is unacceptable – no matter what the provocation. Do you accept that?" I nodded briefly. "Good. Now I have rearranged the class assignments so that that you will be separated as far as possible. I am not going to ask you to shake hands; I think that would be a bridge too far at this stage, but I am going to ask you to give me an assurance that you will avoid open antagonism and stay out of each other's way. Can you do that?" The four on the other side of the table nodded readily. Phil and I gave our assent much more reluctantly. All in all it wasn't a bad performance by the Headmaster and he seemed pleased with himself. Detective Inspector Nielson, however, had something to say before the meeting could be finished.

"I want you all to know," he said, "that something good has come out of all this. Because of the information given to us by the boys here, we have been able to break open a particularly nasty criminal gang that has been operating in London for some time. We rounded up their foot soldiers and were able to put a lot of pressure on the gang leadership. Finally, we got phone taps that indicated all the leaders were going to a prearranged meeting with this mysterious character they called the wizard. We actually think they were planning to kill him. It didn't work. As soon as the meeting started a gun fight broke out. Our SWAT teams moved in quickly when they heard the first shot but by the time they got in all six gang leaders were dead. They had all shot each other for some reason. All except this 'wizard' character, as usual he had got away."

"So he's still out there?" Phil asked. I could see his fists clench tightly in fear.

"Yes," the inspector answered. "But don't worry, stripped of his gang connection I don't think he can cause any more trouble. I would really like to reassure you on that point. In fact, he's probably already fled overseas." Anyone can make a mistake and Detective Inspector Nielson had just made a big one. "From the interviews and phone taps we have conducted, the plan seemed to be about some novel way of gaining entry to a bank vault, probably by using threats to get information from Professor Rhys. We'll never know for sure. The only ones who knew all the details are dead. However, it's all over now." Second big mistake in the one morning, the inspector was not having a good day.

As we were leaving the room, the inspector stopped Phil and me. "There's just one small thing," he said. "Are you sure that the head guy who questioned you was in a wheel chair?" We both nodded emphatically. "Strange, none of our phone intercepts mentioned the wizard being a cripple. Hmm…Political correctness among the crims…who've thought?"

It was the next Saturday that I sat looking out a train window as the suburbs of London slowly changed into a patchwork of green fields and trees.

"Where are we going again?" I asked.

"Great Bedwyn," Myfanwy replied. "Then we are going to ride out bikes through the Savernake Forest to Marlbourough to look at the mound in the college grounds. There is a local legend that Merlin is buried under the mound. In fact, the town sometimes refers to itself as the place where Merlin's bones lie. I agree that it the least likely of the places on your list but we have to start somewhere."

I sighed. Early that morning Myfanwy had turned up at my door with a bike and a small picnic basket and announced that we were going to catch a train and go for a ride in the country. Mum approved, no doubt thinking this was a normal and harmless activity, and one that got me out of the house and into the open air — so away we went. I had barely had time for breakfast when we were catching the tube to Paddington and then off into the country. I was still feeling grumpy about being woken up so early as we passed the scattered commuter villages.

"Why are we starting with the least likely sites?" I asked. "That doesn't seem efficient."

Myfanwy gave me an exasperated look. "Because the Council of Nobles will be checking the more likely sites first," she replied. "That will leave us free to explore the less likely places. Then, when we have eliminated these, the Council will have moved on from the other sites." I opened my mouth to object but she answered me before I could say anything. "No, they won't find him. They haven't found him for fifteen hundred years and they won't find him now." I pulled out my phone and googled the Marlbourough Mound.

"Actually," I said. "According to this, a recent core sample from the mound was dated to over four thousand years: way too old to be Merlin's hidey hole."

Myfanwy shrugged. "That's just the date when the mound was built: doesn't mean Merlin wasn't put there later on." She said. It was too early to argue, so I turned and watched the countryside pass by the window.

Eventually the train came to Great Bedwyn and Myfanwy and I collected our bikes. Great Bedwyn was a small village of very ordinary looking red brick houses with the railway and a canal along one side.

"This is Great Bedwyn?" I asked. "What's so great about it?"

"I don't know," Myfanwy answered, pulling out a paper map. "I think it's probably because it's bigger than Little Bedwyn." Now it was my turn to be exasperated.

"Look," I said, showing her the route planner on my mobile phone. "We want to go from Great Bedwyn by bike to Marlborough College. There, let's go." She looked at the route marked out on the phone and muttered something under her breath as she put her map away. We rode off away from the canal and were soon in rolling countryside with a patchwork of fields and forest. Skirting to the south of Bedwyn Common we came to the straight, central avenue that runs through Savernake Forest. The forest was quite strange for me because, even though the trees were old, they had obviously been planted and the whole layout was artificial. To me it looked like a cross between a forest and a park. In Australia, forest is often synonymous with wilderness. However, Savernake Forest was a very pleasant place to ride a bike.

It was a warm, sunny day and riding along that forest road with Myfanwy was, simply, fun. I thought that perhaps my Mum was right: that this was a normal and fairly harmless thing to do. It was the kind of thing that any boy and girl might do, even when they weren't trying to save the world. I suddenly felt a great longing for this kind of normalcy: to be able to be with Myfanwy just for the sake of being with Myfanwy. The ride was only a few kilometers and didn't really take long enough. We rode past some big monument and then down a hill and out of the forest. My phone showed us how to skirt the centre of Marlbourough and come directly to the college.

The burial mound itself was easy to spot. It was a small, tree covered hill in the middle of the school buildings. Myfanwy and I were able to ride our bikes up through a car park to the foot of the mound. A game of cricket was being played on a field nearby. It was a bit strange, just cycling into someone else's school, and as we got off our bikes I said, "I don't think we should be here. This is private property and we're trespassing." Myfanwy waved her hand dismissively.

"I'm witch girl, remember?" she said. "Don't worry, no one will notice us." She looked closely at the mound. "Locally this is known as Merlin's tomb but I don't get any sense of magic being used here. Still, we need to check it out. What I want you to do is walk all around the mound and describe in detail everything you see. We'll see if you can see something that I can't."

We walked around the perimeter of the mound with me describing every bush and every tree. Nothing looked out of the ordinary. There was a small stone building but it just looked like a garden shed. We then walked in a spiral up the mound with me keeping up a running commentary – nothing. I did notice some activity towards the top.

"Boy and girl in school uniform – getting very friendly. We need to reveal ourselves. If they don't notice us soon, it might get very embarrassing."

Myfanwy looked at them and said, "No, I have a better idea." She pointed at some bushes down in the garden.

A few seconds later the girl yelled, "It's a bee! Get it away! Oh no, there's another one." The boy started to wave his arms around, trying to hit the bees, which is actually a very good way to get stung.

"Rotten insects!" he said as the girl started to run down the hill. He followed her shortly after. I turned to look at Myfanwy.

"Myfanwy Ferchwyn," I said. "You have a vicious streak in you."

She laughed, "I don't know what you mean," she said. "I was just saving a maiden's virtue." We sat down near the top of the mound, in the shade of a large oak tree.

"Well, that was a bust," I said. "I think it's pretty clear what happened here. This is a really old and obviously artificial hill. So sometime, probably in the middle ages, people decided it must be associated with the oldest stories they knew: the King Arthur stories.

Since it was sort of mysterious it was naturally associated with Merlin: the most mysterious and magical character in those stories. Bingo, the hill becomes Merlin's tomb."

"Never mind, the day's not a total waste,' Myfanwy said. "This is a nice spot for our picnic." Indeed it was. The picnic basket from Myfanwy's bike appeared and from it she pulled out a plate of pasties, some glasses and a bottle ginger beer.

I smiled and said, "I feel like I've walked into a Famous Five book." Myfanwy looked at me puzzled. "You know," I insisted, "all those 'lashings of ginger beer' they used to have. You did read Enid Blyton when you were a kid didn't you?"

Myfanwy shook her head. "No," she said. "I was raised on Annwn remember. The only modern books we had were those my mother brought across with her in the early nineteenth century. They were mostly by Jane Austin and the Bronte sisters." I had forgotten how differently time flowed on Annwn and how strange Myfanwy's people really were. It was an unsettling reminder.

The pasties, however, were really good: homemade by Nain and filled with a spicy mixture of cockles, potato and leek. Myfanwy's magic meant that they were as hot as if they had just come from the oven and the ginger beer was as cold as if it had just come from a fridge. It was a really good lunch and afterwards we sat quietly together looking out across the countryside.

"You know," Myfanwy said. "This is actually a really good spot for doing what those two were doing when we came up." She turned her face towards me.

Unaccountably, all of a sudden I was afraid and I wanted to tell her not to push, that I wasn't ready.

Instead, I gave her a quick kiss and said, "Come on, we need to move if we're going to catch the afternoon train home."

Chapter Ten
A Chase and a Language Lesson

Myfanwy was unusually quiet as we rode out of the school and skirted around the town. We rode pretty hard through the streets and out of the town precincts. However, once we got onto the forest trail Myfanwy stopped. I turned to look at her and it was clear that she was angry about something: her cheeks were flushed and her eyes flashed with a dangerous fire.

"Thomas," she said. "Why are you in such a bad mood? This was meant to be a nice ride and a picnic in the country but you have been moaning and complaining all day. What is wrong with you?" I shrugged.

"I guess I just wasn't prepared for getting up that early," I said. Myfanwy shook her head vigorously and pointed her finger at me accusingly.

"No, that's not it," she said. "You are deliberately keeping your distance from me. No, more than that, you are pushing me away and I want to know why." I was quiet for a long time, trying to organize my thoughts.

Eventually I said, "I don't want to push you away Myf; that's the last thing I'd want. It's just that this thing between us is real; it's not a game. It's going to determine all our lives. This is all serious stuff and I guess I'm just a bit overwhelmed." Myfanwy gave me a long, searching look.

"Is it all that stuff Rachael was talking about?" she asked. "Because if it is, I don't know what to do. You say you'll always be my friend and then you go and treat me like some sort of paid assistant." I stared intently at the ground, trying to figure out what to say. I didn't want Myfanwy to be upset with me but how could I explain my feelings when I couldn't really make sense of them myself?

"I'm sorry. It's not really about all that Rachael stuff," I said eventually. "It's more that I'm being asked to grow up and leave childhood behind before I thought I'd have to. You and I both know that things are developing between us. Well, I just want them to develop as a result of deliberate choice and not casually or by accident. Does that make sense?"

Myfanwy's expression softened ever so slightly. "Not really," she said. "Still…I won't push. I'll let you work this out in your own time. Perhaps it's because I'm out of my depth in this world but I really don't understand why you have these doubts."

I smiled. "In a way that's good," I said. "Because I don't really understand either and it would be embarrassing if you understood and I didn't."

"Get used to that," she said. "I'm a bit surprised that I don't understand what is going on in that simple head of yours but I'm not at all surprised that you don't." She made to ride off again but I put my hand on her shoulder to stop her. I had seen something in the forest. I had seen a tall figure with long black hair, dressed in an old army great coat. It was common enough attire but I couldn't believe it was a coincidence. I had a creepy feeling that we were being followed. Whoever it was, I quickly lost view of him in the tangle of trees.

"What is it?" Myfanwy asked, concerned.

"It may be nothing," I answered. "But I think we should get to the train as quickly as possible. I'll explain later." We started to ride down the road towards Great Bedwyn but we had only gone a few hundred meters when we were forced to stop as a small herd of panicked deer rushed across our path and moved rapidly into the forest on our left. Myfanwy looked worried.

"Tom, they're not just startled, they're terrified," she said. "What could panic them like that?" Just then we heard something large moving where the forest pressed close to the road on our right. We turned to see something grey, humped and misshapen lurching towards us. It was almost like a rough, broken granite boulder given life and a monstrous pair of arms. It had a lump of a head which turned towards us.

"Ride! Myf ride!" I yelled. Myfanwy needed no encouragement and had already started to race down the road. I followed close afterwards. I had no desire to look into its eyes. As we rode we could hear the thing crashing through the forest, keeping pace with us. Towards the middle of the forest there was a large open area which the road went straight through. Here we paused both to catch our breath and to see what the thing would do. It also paused and then set off to the right, still moving through the forest.

"Tom, I can't teleport!" Myfanwy said in a panicky voice. "Someone is blocking me." It had to be Cadell, somehow he must've found us. I quickly looked around but all I could see was meadow and forest.

"It doesn't matter," I said. "That thing's not coming into the open; it's going round. If we ride fast now we can get ahead of it." Ride fast we did and we didn't let up until we stopped, exhausted, on the outskirts of Great Bedwyn,

"Are you still being blocked?" I asked. Myfanwy shook her head, still struggling to get her breath after the hard ride.

"No," she said. "I'm free. Did you see anyone?" I shook my head and frowned.

"What was that thing?" I asked.

"I have no idea," she said. "I have never seen or heard of anything like that before."

"It's obviously some sort of magical or mythical creature," I said. "It must come from Annwn. Are you sure you don't know what it is? It looked a bit like I imagined a troll would look like."

Myfanwy shook her head decisively. "No, I've not seen anything like that in Annwn and it looked nothing like an actual troll." We rode into Great Bedwyn and waited for the train in silence, occasionally looking towards the forest. There was no sign of the thing.

We remained silent for a long time, even on the train. Eventually Myfanwy said, "Cadell must have generated a list similar to yours and he has decided to use these sites as bait to try and trap us. I don't know what that thing was or where he got it from but it was clearly meant to harm us."

"Or scare us off," I said. "There is another possibility: we may be being followed." I told her about seeing something like the thing in the park opposite my house and about the homeless guy in the coat.

"That's strange," she said. "How could something that big hide in such a small park without anyone seeing it?"

"I don't know," I replied. "How do you do all that stuff at school without anyone noticing?"

"Point taken," she said. She frowned as she stared out the window. "This is beyond my knowledge. I wish I could talk to Nain about it but I can't. If they knew what we were doing, they would try and stop us."

That night Myfanwy stayed with us for dinner. We ordered pizza and watched a bit of TV. Myfanwy, who lives at Aelred Abbey, does not normally get to see much television and it holds a strong fascination for her. She was horrified by the news and intrigued by the Dr. Who episode. She found the whole idea of travelling in time very interesting. Later, as I walked her back to the gate that would take her to Aelred Abbey, we had a close look at the park opposite my house but there was nothing to be seen. The homeless guy was not there.

He did, however, turn up on Monday. During the week I tried to talk to him several times. I tried greetings in a number of different languages; French, German, Russian and even English. He showed no sign of understanding any of them. It was only when I spoke to him in Latin that he showed any response. To prepare for the experiment I had supplemented my meager knowledge of Latin with a set of phrases from a web translator program. I started with a standard medieval greeting.

"Dominus vobiscum" (The Lord be with you.) He responded with the standard reply.

"Et cum spiritu tuo" (And with your spirit). I then tried something else.

"Meum nomen Thomas est. Quod vestrum est?" (My name is Thomas. What is yours?) Somewhat to my surprise, he seemed willing to continue the conversation.

"Michael me vocavit," he said. I wasn't really sure what this meant but I took it that his name was Michael. I pressed on with my set of phrases.

"Quomodo Michael?" (How are you Michael?) He replied with a long string of Latin that I later struggled to remember.

"Ego bene sum sed nocte venit et habeo domum redire." I didn't follow all of this. I knew that the first part meant 'I am well', that nocte meant night and domum was house, but I couldn't put the whole sentence together. I looked at him puzzled. He grew agitated and started to use much simpler language.

"Tenebris adventum est. Ad domum!" Again, I didn't follow all of this but I knew that last part was telling me to go to my house. As far as I could figure out he was telling me to go home and not be in the park at night. I nodded to indicate that I understood.

"Gratias et vale Michael" (Thank you and farewell Michael) I said and turned and went home. Once inside, I wrote down as much of the Latin as I could remember and then typed it into a web translator. Two things stood out. One was that he was clearly warning me about the coming night (nocte venit) and that it would soon be dark (Tenebris adventum est). Clearly, he thought something bad would happen if I was in the park at night. The other interesting thing was that when I asked him his name he didn't simply say 'Meum nomen Michael est' or 'My name is Michael'. No, what he said was 'Michael me vocavit' which means 'He calls me Michael'. Who, I wondered, had given him the name Michael and why didn't he own it as his own? One thing was clear: this was no normal homeless guy.

I didn't sleep well that night. I couldn't stop thinking about this conversation. I needed to know who this guy was and what side he was on. He was clearly involved. It was ridiculous to think that by simple coincidence, a homeless guy who only speaks Latin would turn up in the park opposite my house at the same time as Cadell was trying to involve me in some sort of plot.

I caught up with Myfanwy while she was walking to school the next day.

"Myf," I said. "I need to ask Nain something. Would it be possible to speak to her after school?" Myfanwy put on that exasperated expression she uses when she thinks I've said something stupid. As usual, it was because I hadn't appreciated the power of magic.

"Tom, of course you can come over and ask her. The gates mean that I effectively live just around the corner from your house." I pointed out that I had no way of knowing that Nain would be at Aelred Abbey but she persisted. "You still don't take advantage of the gates. You could walk home with me every night instead of taking the bus. Walk home with me tonight." I had never thought about that but she was right. I could make use of the magic gates. I walked into school with a big smile on my face: I had a girlfriend who lived in a castle on the coast of Norfolk just around the corner from my house in London.

Lunch that day was a gloomy affair. Rachael had told Wilson that she was not his girlfriend and Phil had found out that Gabriella was going out with one of his soccer mates. He had found this out when his mate didn't turn up to kick the ball around. I'm not sure which loss he was more upset about but upset he was.

No one spoke much and it was a relief to escape to mathematics after lunch.

That afternoon I walked with Myfanwy up to the gate and she took me through to Aelred Abbey and Nain greeted us as if it was the most natural thing in the world for me to be there. It was later, as I sat sipping hot chocolate in the kitchen, that I asked my question.

"Nain, how well do you know Captain Pierre and his unit?" Captain Pierre Gauthier was the commander of the Swiss Guard's special operations unit: an ancient unit dedicated to combating rouge magic users and other magical or mythical problems. They operated out of a secret base, St. Martin's Monastery, high in the Italian Alps.

"I know them better than they would want me to and they know me better than I like," she said.

"When we first met them, he greeted you in Latin," I recalled, "but you told him to stop it because his Latin was terrible. Does his unit normally speak Latin?"

Nain shook her head. "No," she said. "They would know a few phrases of course, but most of them are native German speakers, although many speak French. Of course, they all speak Italian and English to some degree."

"So they wouldn't converse in Latin?" I asked.

Nain looked at me curiously. "Tom, no one converses in Latin these days, not even in the Vatican," she said. "Why do you ask?"

I shrugged. "No real reason," I lied. "Just that I did Latin at school and I wondered." Nain went back to her cooking but across the table Myfanwy was staring at me intently: her green eyes trying to bore into my skull.

"What was that all about?" she asked later as we were walking across the causeway to the gate. I told her about my conversation with the homeless guy.

"I didn't think the Pontifical Guard would be watching my house," I said, "but I needed to be sure. I needed to eliminate the possibility."

Myfanwy looked worried. "That is really weird; perhaps you should've told Nain the whole story. He might be dangerous." she said.

I shook my head. "He hasn't done anything to harm or threaten me," I said. "In fact, all he's ever done is warn me to stay out of the park at night."

"Still, I don't like it: that thing in the wood and now this. We need to keep you safe. I think we should be more careful about our Merlin hunting until we can figure out what's going on. We need to plan more."

"Sometimes," I said. "You sound just like your uncle." By this time we were at the gate: behind it I could see the soft, Norfolk countryside, dark against the setting sun. Myfanwy kissed me goodbye and I stepped through into the London street around the corner from my house. As I walked home, the evening shadows in the park were deepening. The park looked empty but I hurried to my house.

Chapter 11
A Fruitless Search

Myfanwy's new found caution meant that nothing much happened in our search for Merlin for a few weeks. I will admit that those weeks were really enjoyable. It was great to be able to forget about mysterious threats to the world and just live a normal life for a while. However, news kept coming of earthquakes and strange volcanic eruptions around the Earth. In the meantime, Mrs. Brown was busy introducing us to the modern poets, starting with the Irish poet W.B. Yeats. The poetry was difficult and simply beyond many in the class. In the last week before the half-term break we studied a poem called 'The Second Coming'. The last stanza stuck in my mind. I somehow knew that it was important.

> The darkness drops again but now I know
> That twenty centuries of stony sleep
> Were vexed to nightmare by a rocking cradle,
> And what rough beast, its hour come round at last,
> Slouches towards Bethlehem to be born?

I couldn't get the last lines out of my head. I didn't know why but I felt that these lines told me something I needed to know. I just didn't understand what. It was getting dark earlier now and each evening the shadows in the park were deeper as I got home. Occasionally I would see homeless Michael shuffle off to wherever he slept but he avoided me during the day and I took care not to be in the park at night.

On the Friday before the Half Term break, the morning news was full of the story of a massive volcanic eruption in Siberia. It was in an uninhabited area, so there were few direct casualties, but it generated a stratospheric ash cloud over a wide area and all polar route air travel was cancelled. One unfortunate Japanese airliner flew into the cloud before the warning was put out. It was badly damaged but managed to limp into Vladivostok. At the same time the final death toll from the Chinese tsunami was published. The official figure was a horrifying 1.2 million but many believed that the real number was much higher. As I looked at that figure I knew that it didn't really matter how risky it was, I couldn't just pretend that it had nothing to do with me. I couldn't just sit around while Cadell was free to do whatever it was he was doing.

I met Myfanwy before school and showed her the newspaper reports.

"We have to do something!" I said, almost pleading. "We need to keep searching for Merlin." It was the only thing I could think of to do.

Myfanwy sighed and nodded in agreement. "But we need to plan," she insisted. "Last time we were far too casual. This time we really need to plan our search." Given the amount of input I had had into the last venture, I thought the "we" was a bit rich but I let it slide. We both had a free study period after lunch, so we agreed to meet in the library.

When we met, the only sound was the drumming of the rain on the glass. We sat together at one of the library computers near the window. I don't know if

Myfanwy had arranged it or if it just happened by accident, but we were the only ones in the Library. I did the same internet search I had done before on the location of Merlin's burial and came up with the same locations: all places where there was some local story about Merlin. I knew the list well and I knew it was not promising. Over the last month I had researched the background of every place on it. I paused for a moment and checked the search results again but I already knew. We went through all the places together but the result was no different.

"The harsh truth is that we have no clue where Merlin is buried. All of these places are mainly promoted by their local tourist boards and none of them are really credible," I said. I banged the computer desk in frustration. "We know Cadell is doing something to the Earth and we are sitting around doing nothing! And the worst of it is: I can't even think of anything sensible for us to do. We really need to find Merlin."

Myfanwy sighed, "This is what always happens when you go looking for Merlin. He just disappears into a mass of improbable legend and contradiction. The good news is that Cadell probably can't find him either."

I smiled grimly. "The bad news is that Cadell doesn't really need to find him. He just wants to kill him on the off chance that Merlin could stop him. If Merlin stays sleepy bys then Cadell just goes ahead and does whatever it is he's planning to do." We were both silent for a while, watching the rain run down the window pane in twisting little rivers.

Eventually I looked at Myfanwy and asked, "What now?"

Myfanwy remained thoughtfully watching the rain. "We are way out of our depth here," she said eventually. "I was wrong to think that we could do this alone. We just don't have the knowledge. We need to confide in Nain." I looked at her in surprise. Nain, with all her excellent qualities, was a member of the Council of Nobles and if we failed to convince her, we could find ourselves watched so closely that we would be out of the game.

"Are you sure?" I asked.

"Yes," she said nodding. "Whatever happens, we aren't doing any good this way. We need to convince her that we represent the best chance of finding Merlin. We really need her help." I sat back and ran my fingers through my hair nervously: convincing Nain was not going to be easy and there was a real risk that she would put a stop to all our activities. Still, I knew Myfanwy was right about our current efforts.

"Okay." I said. "You're right. I'll come with you tonight." Just then the bell rang for a change of period. Myfanwy had to go off to Literature and I had Geography, where Mr. Chester would be talking about volcanoes again. I shut down the computer and we left as other students started to drift into the library.

Later that afternoon, I was sitting at the kitchen table in Aelred Abbey with a cup of hot chocolate. Even though the rain hadn't let up and was now being driven by a wind off the North Sea, so that it lashed at the kitchen windows, the kitchen itself was warm with a fire burning brightly in the old stove. Together, Myfanwy and I explained everything that we had done to Nain. We explained about our theory of combining our talents to find Merlin's tomb, about our visit the Marlborough

Mound, about the strange creature that threatened us, about the strange homeless guy in my park and about his warning not to be in the park after dark. Most of all, we explained that our search for Merlin had come to a dead end and we didn't know what to do. Through all of this Nain sat silently with no readable expression on her face.

She sat still for a while after we had finished then said, "I told Cadfan that it wasn't realistic to expect the two of you to sit quietly and do nothing but he thought it didn't matter since you couldn't get yourselves into much trouble chasing something as elusive as Merlin's resting place. As usual, however, you seem to have pocked a nest and stirred some very strange hornets. Tell me about the places you have researched."

"Well," I said, "Apart from the Marlborough Mound, there was Carmarthen and Bardsea Island in Wales, Drumelzier in Scotland and the Paimpont Forest in Brittany. I think the most likely place would be Carmarthen, at least it's in Wales. It also dates from about the right time." Nain, however, shook her head.

"Oh, it has strong connections to Merlin right enough," she said. "It's the place where he was born. The problem is that at the time of his disappearance, the hill fort was still occupied by the local ruler and the Roman town at the foot of the hill was a busy trading centre. His incarceration would have been complicated and delicate magic. It would've needed quiet and isolation."

"Then that leads us to the forest at Paimpont in Brittany," I said. "It's beautiful, remote, and there would've been a lot of connection between Brittany and Britain at the time, so it is possible. There are also many stories here: that he is imprisoned in a tree, that he is buried in a stone tomb, that the Lady of the Lake cares for him."

Again Nain shook her head. "The people of Brittany were driven out of Britain by the Saxons. These stories are their attempt to hold on to the memory of things they had lost. Exiled people tend to do that." I nodded, thinking of all the stories of Ireland my grandmother had told me: stories that she had heard from her mother in turn. "We have looked at this place in the past," Nain continued. "The problem is that the tree is far too young, the stone tomb is far too old and the Lady of the Lake died years ago on Annwn. These stories are all medieval or later. They are connected with the French romance, not to the original history."

"So, if we now discount Brittany," I said. "The next place on our list would be Drumelzier in Scotland. It has a lot going for it. It's isolated and the time could be about right."

"Again no," Nain said. "The character involved in that story is called Merlin Caledonensis. That name means he comes from Scotland, not Wales. He is the Scottish Merlin. I don't know what his connection is to our Merlin is but he's clearly not the same person. He is not Merlin Ambrosius, not Myrddin Emrys"

"Just as well," I said, "Because he's dead. In fact according to the web site, he died three times. He was stabbed, fell off a cliff and drowned. Then they buried him under a tree. If we were depending on this guy, we'd be in real trouble. That leaves Bardsey Island." Nain sat back in her chair and stared glumly out at the rain driving against the window.

"Again no," she said. "It is for certain a place of great power and significance but it is the same as

Carmarthen. There was already a thriving monastic community there at the time and Nimue would never have been able to work uninterrupted. The story of him being buried there probably came about by simple association: he was an important, mystical figure and Bardsey Island was where important, mystical figures were buried."

I nodded. "We've already decided that it's probably not worth the effort to visit all these places. If there was anything in any of these places, a million tourists crawling all over them would probably have found it. That's why we've come to you. We need a way around this impasse."

Nain sighed. "I don't know that I can help you. In desperation, the Council of Nobles has visited each of these places again and again. They have found nothing. Nimue kept her secrets well hidden. It's frustrating to admit but in this case we know nothing more than the local tourist boards."

"But Tom could help," Myfanwy insisted. "He can see all that's hidden by magic. Not even Merlin or Nimue could hide things from him. You could at least use him to eliminate any possibility that Merlin is in any of these places."

Nain looked at me intently and it was only after a long while that she answered. "This trail is so dead that I don't think it would be worth the effort," she said at last. "But there may be another way. If we can't find Merlin, perhaps we can find what Merlin left behind. In order to seal Merlin in his long sleep, Nimue borrowed, or stole, an artefact of great power. That artefact survives, buried deep somewhere in Annwn. It may be that it can lead us to Merlin, and even if it doesn't, perhaps we can use it ourselves to stop Cadell. Unfortunately, it is hidden so deep that few would know where to start looking or even what the thing is. Indeed, I know of only one. The only person I know of who may know the location is Friar Daffyd on Annwn but this is not information that can be sent by messenger. You will need to go there and ask him.

It is also bound to be well protected so that no one can reach it, except, of course, someone who is utterly impervious to magic. Even for such a person, I think this trip may well be dangerous. Tom, are you willing to go back to Annwn against the decree of the Council?"

I nodded my agreement, it was just good to be doing something, anything. Annwn was also a place of beauty and magic and I really wanted to go back anyway. However, I had been banished by a council of powerful magic users. I didn't want them any more annoyed at me than they already were.

"Me too," Myfanwy said. "If Tom is going off somewhere, then so am I." Nain looked annoyed at this for a moment but then she just shrugged.

"So it goes," she said. "Tom, tell your mother that I'm taking you on a trip tomorrow but that I'll have you back in time for dinner. Be ready around nine o'clock. Wear clothes appropriate for a long hike and it might be a good idea to bring along that walking stick Declan gave you. Think of it as a trip to celebrate the half-term break."

Myfanwy walked with me to the gate. This was just as well, because otherwise the wind driven rain would have drenched me walking across the causeway. As it was we remained perfectly dry. The rain drops just never seemed to hit us. As I have noted before, there are advantages to having a magic girlfriend. Unfortunately, Myfanwy's rain protection ended as soon as I stepped through the gate and I got drenched as I ran down the street to my home. I was too cold and wet to notice if there was anything amiss in the park.

Chapter 12
A Trip in a Caravan

The next day was overcast and threatening showers. I dressed in outdoors gear and took the stick that Declan had given me last year. Declan was one of the Irish Tuatha De Dannan from Tyr na nOg and, if anything, even more magical than Myfanwy's people. He had carved it in intricate patterns and it had the ability to change into whatever stick-like thing you needed at the time, from a fighting spear to a pole for probing the snow after an avalanche. It was a very useful stick.

Mum was a bit wary of me going off somewhere without having all the details; especially after the incident last year where I had run off to France without telling her. That escapade had saved the world but I think that in her heart of hearts she considered that to be an inadequate excuse. She was, however, reassured that Nain would be in charge, considering her a responsible adult. This understanding was challenged somewhat when Nain turned up in her gypsy caravan, pulled by a small, white pony. Her caravan was emerald green with red trim and there were small, white flowers painted along the base. It would be hard to imagine something more out of place in modern London. At first Mum looked a bit stunned but then she shrugged. She had learned to expect the unusual around Myfanwy's people.

As soon as it stopped Myfanwy jumped out of the back and came over to get me. She was dressed in jeans, hiking boots and a red, waterproof jacket. Her hair was tied back behind her head and I was struck again by how beautiful she looked.

"Don't worry Mrs O'Malley," Nain called. "I'll have him back in time for dinner. We're just going on a little day trip. Tom, why don't you climb in the back with Myfanwy?"

I had to bend down to get in through the small door at the rear of the caravan and the inside was quite cramped. Dried herbs hung from the curved roof of polished wooden slats. Along one side there was a miniature, wood-fired stove, a cupboard and a small table. Along the other there was a bunk bed. There was a thick, brightly coloured mat on the floor. I had been in here before but then I had been bruised and hurt from one of Apophasis' attempts to kill me and I wasn't really taking much note of my surroundings. Now I was struck by the simple homeliness of the caravan, with its smell of herbs and the warmth of its interior. It was briefly dark as I closed the door but then a candle on the table magically lit itself and the cabin was filled with candle light.

Myfanwy sat on the bunk and I sat beside her. As soon as we started to move, with the hanging herbs swinging to the gentle rocking of the caravan, Nain came back and sat at the table, leaving no one to drive the caravan. I was way past being surprised by this and I smiled as I imagined the small, white pony picking its way with magical sureness through the busy London traffic.

"Now, you must both listen to me carefully," Nain said. "You must not leave this cabin, you must not even look outside, until I tell you. Our success depends on secrecy and that secrecy is fragile. Even a glance outside, by either of you, could bring it undone. Do you understand?" We both nodded. "Tom, I am making Myf your responsibility, please ensure she behaves." This brought an outraged cry from Myfanwy but Nain had already left the cabin and closed the door. Myfanwy and I were left alone in the gently rocking candle light.

Myfanwy turned to me with narrowed eyes and pointed her finger at my chest. "Don't you even think about..."

I held up my hands defensively. "Myf," I said. "You can't blame me. I didn't say anything. I'm just a surfer, a schoolboy, from Australia, remember? I can't be held responsible for what one of the Nobles of Annwn said." She looked at me warily but I could see the beginnings of a smile at the corners of her mouth.

"Well, okay then," she said. "But don't start thinking you can tell me what to do." I shook my head.

"I wouldn't try," I said. "I wouldn't even want to."

She smiled at that and said, "Right answer surfer boy." She paused, and started playing with a curl of her hair. Clearly, she wanted to ask me something. After a short time she continued in a very different voice, a small, quiet voice. "Tom, what are you planning to do next year? You know, after school's finished."

"You mean, assuming that Cadell hasn't succeeded in destroying civilisation?" I asked.

She rolled her eyes. "Well, obviously!" she said. I looked at the bright patterns in the mat for some time before answering.

"I'd like to return to Australia," I said softy. "I don't really fit in London. Trouble is, I don't see how I can. You're here, Mum has her job here and Dad is in the South China Sea."I turned and looked at her. "I don't suppose you'd like to emigrate?"

She shook her head. "No, and even if I wanted to, the people of Annwn need me. Not just me, of course. They need all of us: Carwyn and Gwen as well. I want to study Arts at Aberystwyth and help Annwn to engage with the modern world." This news did not surprise me but I still found it depressing.

"Well," I said. "That leaves me with a bit of a problem." I looked at her doubtfully, waiting for her to comment but she wouldn't say anything. She just held my hand and rested her head on my shoulder. I put my arm around her and kissed her gently.

It wasn't long after this that we reached the sea. As my eyes had adjusted to the dark, I could see daylight sneaking in through gaps in the caravan's coachwork. The colour of the light changed, there was also a particular tang in the air. I knew we were beside the sea. The movement of the caravan changed about the same time: it became a swaying motion; very slow but also quite pronounced and I wondered if we were on a barge. The temptation to look out one of those chinks in the woodwork was great but I managed to put it out of my mind.

We were in the caravan for a long time. So long, in fact, that I wondered how we would have time to do anything useful and still get back in time for dinner. In the gently rocking caravan, in the candlelit dark, Myfanwy fell asleep with her head resting against my shoulder. I sat for a while, listening to her soft breaths, before I dozed off as well. We both woke when the movement of the caravan changed again. It resumed the slightly jerky motion that you expect from a horse drawn wagon. Also, the light coming through the chinks had lost its blue colour and the air had lost its salt tang. Instead, it smelt of humus and soil and I knew we were somewhere in the country.

Myfanwy was suddenly overjoyed and gave a delighted yelp. "Tom, we're in Annwn! We're in Annwn."

"How can you tell?" I asked.

"I can feel it," she said. "I can feel all the possibilities in the air!" I didn't question her certainty. Not only could Myfanwy could sense reality at a very deep level but Annwn was our proposed destination, so it made sense.

The ride began to get rough, as if we were on a track rather than a paved road, and we started to climb. Again, the temptation to look out one of the cracks was very strong but I resisted by thinking of all the ways the Council of Nobles could make my life really, really unpleasant. It wasn't long before the sunlight filtering through the cracks went dark and we could hear a stony echo of the pony's hooves. We had entered some sort of tunnel. Almost immediately, we came to a stop.

The front door of the caravan opened and Nain said, "All right you two, you can climb out now." Myfanwy laughed with happiness as we climbed out the back door of the caravan. We were in the great, arched tunnel that formed the entry to her family home. Thousands of years ago, the house had started off as a huge ring fort of solid stone, tens of meters thick. Over the years it had been added to and corridors and rooms had been tunnelled into it in a pretty unplanned manner, so that now it formed a kind of three dimensional maze with different styles and eras coming together in a very confusing manner. Only two things were constant. One was a single passageway that went all the way round through the middle of the ring and the other was the great, arched entrance which led deep into the house's interior. The trick to not getting hopelessly lost in the maze of corridors and rooms was to never stray too far from these.

Almost as soon as we stepped onto the cobbled floor of the entrance way, a small, dark haired missile of a figure came running out of the central passage way yelling: "Myfwy! Myfwy!" This was Gwyneth, Myfanwy's younger sister, who proceeded to grip Myfanwy in a limpet-like hug.

Myfanwy laughed, "Gwen," she said. "Why the big greeting? I haven't been gone long. In Annwn time, it can only have been a few days." Time in Annwn doesn't always travel at the same rate as it does in the rest of the world. Normally it's much slower. Sometimes years in the normal world will only be months in Annwn.

Gwen pulled back and shook her head. "No Myf," she said. "They said they needed time to sort something out, so they swapped it around. Time now travels really fast in Annwn and you have been gone for ages."

"You mean they reversed the time differential?" I asked.

Gwen looked at me pityingly. "I just said that. Yes, it's almost Christmas here." As she spoke I began to notice how cold it was and I realised that this would explain why Nain could be so confident that I would be home in time for dinner. Dinner in the outer world was probably days away.

As if she could read my thoughts, Nain came up behind us and said briskly, "Yes, yes. We have two weeks before we need to get you back. The Council decided that they needed time to figure out how to stop Cadell. It hasn't helped much but it does mean that we have time for a little lunch. Come on." With that she started to hustle us into the central passage way and around to the kitchen, which was at the rear of the house.

Myfanwy's mum, Helen, was in the kitchen when we got there. When she saw us, she let out a small cry of delight. "Myf! My darling girl! I wondered why Gwen had run off like that. Come over here and give me a hug, it's been far too long." As mother and daughter hugged, I couldn't help but think how much more affectionate than my own family, Myfanwy's was. My mum and dad could happily live apart, indeed on opposite sides of the globe, for months at a time and, growing up as an only child of two busy parents, I often found myself alone. As a child, I had often wished that things in my family were different but they were what they were and I had come to accept that. Helen looked up and saw me.

"Tom," she said. "How nice to see you again! But given that you are here..." She sighed. "I'm guessing that this is not a social call."

"No Helen," Nain said in a very matter of fact voice as she walked over to the door of the pantry. "These two have work to do. But first we need to see about lunch."

A short time later we all sat down to a lunch of thick vegetable soup and fresh, crusty bread. This was followed by a large mug of tea and some shortbread biscuits. While we were drinking the tea, Nain explained the situation as she saw it.

"First off. Tom, you must not be seen in Annwn. You have been banished. Unjustly, I know. But to be seen to be openly defying the will of the Council would cause too much trouble: trouble we don't need. That's why I insisted that you stay in the caravan until we were inside the precincts of the House of Pwyll. Here you are safe."

"What is the House Pwyll?" I asked.

Myfanwy answered. "Pwyll, the father of Pryderi, is my distant ancestor and this house is named for him."

"Just so," Nain said. "Here you are safe but you cannot be seen abroad in Annwn. Yet you need to speak to Friar Daffyd. I propose that you both leave before dawn tomorrow so that you are well up the Friar's Hill before sunrise. There you are unlikely to be observed and I will take further steps to ensure you are not noticed. While I am about that, do not stray from this house!" I nodded my agreement and finished my tea in silence.

That afternoon Myfanwy and I went for a walk in the kitchen garden. This was still within the precinct of the house and so was considered safe. The last time I had been here it had been spring, the trees had been in blossom and the garden had been full of newly hatched fairies. Now it was a winter garden. The trees were barren and the earth in the garden beds was bare — waiting for the first snowfall.

"All the fairies have gone," I said. Myfanwy smiled and the openness and readiness of her smile was markedly different from her normally reserved demeanor. This reminded me of the strain she was always under in the wider world. There she always had to hide who she was, to hide her power and talent. Here, in Annwn, she could be fully herself, here she smiled and laughed freely.

"Only in a sense," she said. "Another way of looking at it is that they are all here waiting to be born."She pointed at a tree and I for the first time I noticed hundreds of small, diamond like gems stuck to the underside of the branches. They glittered brightly in the winter sun. "Fairy eggs: they are clear like this at the start of winter and slowly turn green. Then in late winter or early spring they burst open like a flower and out pops a fairy. The return of the fairies is one of the ways we mark the start of spring."

"I'd like to be here sometime when that happens," I said.

"Perhaps we can arrange that," she said happily. "We only have to get rid of that silly banishment order."

Just then there was a sound like a rushing wind and a shadow passed over the garden. Myfanwy screamed and I looked up, expecting to see some sort of aircraft. What I saw was a dragon. A dragon flying low over the house. A dragon! It was bright red and the sun glinted off its scales as if they were metal. I just stood there with my mouth open in amazement. This was too much. I couldn't process it. Myfanwy grabbed my hand and started pulling me towards the house.

"Come on Tom!" she yelled. "We have to get to shelter." Following her urging, I started to run towards the house as the dragon disappeared off towards the mountains in the north. Helen and Gwen were waiting anxiously for us in the kitchen. Once we were inside, Gwen waved her hands and shutters closed across all the kitchen windows, temporarily plunging the room into darkness. The room then filled with a soft, calming light also, I assume, courtesy of Gwen. Myfanwy was shaking. She was clearly terrified.

"Mae'r dreigiau yn ôl!" she said, reverting to her native Welsh. I later learned that this means 'the dragons are back'.

"I know dear," Helen said in English. "They only appear occasionally and they haven't done anything yet, but they have been threatening the whole of Annwn for the last month." I was still coming to terms with seeing a dragon but I managed to notice what she had said.

"They? There are more of them?" I asked.

"Yes," Helen replied. "There are at least six, although you normally only see one at a time." By this time, Myfanwy had calmed down. She sat down at the table and Gwen sat next to her. When she looked at me, her face was solemn with fear.

"Tom, you once wondered what this house was built to defend against, why we needed so much stone. Well, you just saw the reason. When the dragons attacked in the past it took all of our people's skill and resources to defend ourselves. Only, then there were many more of us. Now we are so few that we could not do what we once did. If the dragons attack again, it could be the end of our people."

We had supper early that night and it was a subdued affair. Myfanwy was still coming to terms with the return of the dragons and I was still trying to accept that they were real. Gwen spent most of the time updating Myfanwy on the day to day happenings in Annwn. These were essentially the same as the goings on in any small, rural community except that mythical creatures such as pixies, water nymphs and selkies featured prominently. Perhaps sensing the depths of

Myfanwy's unease, Gwen didn't mention the dragons at all. Her unique talent for sensing people's thoughts and feelings was clearly in play.

Over the desert of bread and butter pudding, I asked her: "When you came out to meet us today, was that because you could sense Myfanwy's presence?"

She nodded and said, "Yes, but I still couldn't sense you at all." She stared at me intently. "Your mind is still all hard and shiny, like polished steel. I can't sense anything." She continued to stare at me for a while but then she smiled, a mischievous smile which reminded me very much of her sister. "You're still scary but not as scary as you were before." I took that to be a good thing, an indication that I was being accepted.

Chapter 13
Friar Daffyd's Congregation

It was biting cold and our breath hung in a cloud before our faces, when Myfanwy and I met early the next morning. The world was dark but we were surrounded by a soft sphere of light. Nain addressed us in a brisk, business-like voice, which I think covered the fact that she was quite worried about today's adventure.

"Tom, you must not be seen. Remember that: you must not be seen. Myfanwy, I suggest you teleport with Tom directly to the base of Friar's Hill and walk as rapidly as you can up the path. Make as little noise as you can and don't show any light. That should keep you from being observed. However, just to make sure; Tom I would like you to wear this." She held out a black, hooded cloak."I have cast an inattention spell on it so that you will be protected from casual observation. Even if someone does notice you, if you keep the hood down they will not be able to identify you. I will go and visit my fellow council members. That should distract them enough to make your detection unlikely. Also, I don't think the dragons would be interested in two people out for a walk. When they decide to cause trouble, they will be after bigger targets." She stopped and then said in a softer voice, "Good luck". At that, Myfanwy took my hand and suddenly we were at the bottom of Friar's Hill. Above us, the stars burned brightly in a clear and frosty sky. I pulled the hooded cloak tight around me.

"Okay surfer boy, here we go," Myfanwy said. "Hang onto me, I know the way better than you." Myfanwy did know the way but even so the way was difficult. The path was rough and it was dark. However, as we pushed on up the hill, the sky began to lighten with the coming dawn and the going got easier. Eventually the tops of the mountains began to burn with the brightness of the morning sun, even while the rest of the land was in deep shadow. Slowly, the light seemed to flow from these mountain tops and the deep shadows began to shrink until we were walking in the clear light of morning.

We were still a fair way from the top, the way was steep and the cloak was heavy. It wasn't long before I was grateful for the cold wind that was blowing in off the sea. As we got near to the top, Myfanwy stopped and looked out across Annwn. It was a patchwork of forest and hedgerow bounded fields with the river winding through it like a silver thread.

Myfanwy sighed, "Isn't it beautiful," she said. "There was a time when I dreamt only of getting away from this place. Not now. Now, this is where I belong. This is my home." I also looked out across Annwn. Yes, it was beautiful and it was special to me but it wasn't my home. My home was on the other side of the world and suddenly, even though Myfanwy was there, I felt lost and alone.

After a short rest, we made our way around the hedge that surrounded the top of the hill. It was a hedge of apple tree and roses, yew and oak, and blackberries. These were all bare now in winter, giving the hedge the appearance of some giant basket work. We followed the hedge around to the far side of the hill, where the view of tended fields gave way to deep forest and snow covered mountains. There we came to an opening and a wicker gate which led into an avenue of hedge, spiralling into the enclosure and to a second gate.

The feeling of being lost vanished as soon as I walked into the grounds of the hermitage. Here the fruit trees were now bare but the chooks were still scratching around their roots, the goat was still chewing contentedly and smoke still rose from the chimney in the friar's hut. Here I felt at home. I know, of course, that it wasn't just me, that any lost soul who found their way here would have the same sense of homecoming but it good, nonetheless, to see the stone chapel, the vegetable beds, and the friar's hut all gathered around the still pool in the centre – just as I remembered them.

Very soon after we arrived, Friar Daffyd came out of his small chapel carrying three baskets of flat, unleavened bread. "Myfanwy! My dear child. It's so very good to see you." He looked across at me. "And you too Tom. You can take off that cloak now. No one will see you here."

I pulled back the hood smiling. "How did you know it was me?"

"Don't be silly," he said dismissively. "I knew you would be coming since before you left London. Come, I have just finished mass and I have breakfast prepared." As soon as he said this I became aware of how hungry I was and quickly decided that further questions could wait. The inside of his hut was as I remembered it: spartan but warm and with a stark beauty in its simplicity, from the earthen floor to the undressed, stone walls. He put the three baskets of bread on a shelf near the door. He saw me watching him.

"This is the eulogia," he explained. "What the Greeks call Antidoron: bread that is blessed during mass but not consecrated. It is for those who cannot receive the Eucharist. I believe the custom has passed in your world but I still maintain it. I will deliver this to the poor souls of my congregation at noonday prayer." This surprised me. Given that he was a hermit, I didn't think that Friar Daffyd would have had a congregation. Friar Daffyd urged us to sit down and we were soon eating a breakfast of fried eggs and a kind of patty made from potatoes and leeks, washed down with a large mug of hot, milky tea.

While we were eating I asked, "Friar Daffyd, how much do you know of the troubles in the outside world?"

"I have seen it," he said. "Volcanoes, earthquakes, tsunamis...it is all terrible. Cadell is playing with forces he doesn't understand and can't hope to control. Once woken, the dragons will not obey him...nor anyone else."

"Not even Merlin?" Myfanwy asked.

"Not even Merlin," Friar Daffyd replied. "Although Myrddin Emrys might be able to put them back to sleep."

I looked ay both of them, puzzeled. "What have the dragons got to do with anything?"

"The dragons are the cause of all the troubles," Friar Daffyd answered. "But hold now, serious matters can be left till after breakfast. Tell me now, how is your schoolwork going?" The rest of breakfast passed discussing the trivia of teachers capabilities, students lives and the complexity of Yeats' poetry. After breakfast, Friar Daffyd took us down to sit beside the still, dark pond at the centre of the hermitage.

"Friar Daffyd," Myfanwy said in a serious and urgent voice. "We need to know about the dragons."

Friar Daffyd sighed. "It is a long story but I will shorten its telling. Do not ask me how I come to know it since it comes from a time before time was counted. Then it came about that there were two great dragons: a mother and a daughter. Hatched deep in the earth, they escaped and devastated the land, threatening everything that lived." While he was speaking, an image of two giant dragons, one fiery red and the other silver white, bursting out of the earth and surrounded with fire, appeared in the pond. "But, as is often the way with mothers and their daughters, they could not stay together. Each fled to the opposite side of the world. In time, each had three daughters, lesser certainly but still terrible, to guard against the other. These new daughters faced each other warily, fitfully bursting forth in fury." The pond showed six smaller dragons, three red and three white, facing each other and occasionally breathing out searing flame. "Meanwhile, the two original dragons went into a deep sleep, finally making peace with the wind, the rain and all living things." The pond showed the giant, white dragon lying down to sleep and slowly being covered by living things, grass and then trees, until it was indistinguishable from a forest covered mountain. Friar Daffyd stopped talking and gazed into the pond. I was trying to understand the meaning of the story.

I asked my question slowly and thoughtfully. "Friar, these dragons are mythological expressions of reality, right? They would also have a mundane expression?" Friar Daffyd nodded.

"What about the dragon we saw yesterday?" Myfanwy asked.

"The dragons in Annwn are a manifestation of what is happening in the other world. They have woken in Annwn because they are waking on the outside. When they attack on the outside they will attack in Annwn and Annwn will be devastated." The friar's voice was calm but deeply sad. "Even this sacred hermitage may be destroyed." While they were talking I was going over all that I knew about the current disasters. I kept asking myself: what were the dragons symbols of? Suddenly, it hit me. I remembered what Mr. Chester had told us in geography and it all made sense.

"They're supervolcanos!" I said. "The dragons are all supervolcanos." Myfanwy and the friar looked at me puzzled.

"What's a supervolcano?" Myfanwy asked.

"A supervolcano is a huge volcano," I explained, "one that has more than ten times the destructive power of even the biggest normal volcano. There aren't many of them and they erupt only rarely. In fact, there hasn't been such an eruption in recorded history but Yellowstone, Lake Taupo, Sumatra...from a geological perspective, these are all recent supervolcanos. If one of these erupted now, tens of millions would die. If all six erupted together, billions would die and the few survivors would be driven back to the stone age."

Myfanwy gave a grim smile and her voice was urgent and anxious, "And in a society of struggling and traumatised survivors, a powerful magic user might well be able to take control. We need to know how to stop Cadell! Friar Daffyd, you said that Merlin might be able to put the dragons back to sleep. Well, Tom and I have been looking for him and we have no credible clue as to where he might be. We were hoping you might be able to help."

Friar Daffyd shook his head. "I'm afraid I have no idea where Myrradin Emrys might lie," he said.

"Nain said something about an artefact connected to Merlin," I suggested. He looked thoughtful for a moment and the pool showed an image of the mountains deep in Annwn.

"That may be another approach," he agreed. "It would be dangerous, even for you two, but I can help a little. The artefact is so powerful that it was hidden for safety's sake, shortly after Annwn was formed. It is hidden deep in the mountains and is very well protected. Even if you could find it, I don't know that anyone would be able to wield it. Still, it may have the power to stop Cadell." We both looked at him expectantly as he paused. He seemed to be considering the wisdom of what he was about to say. Eventually he sighed and said, "I can show you where to find Merlin's staff."

I was surprised. I had never seen any of Myfanwy's people used a staff, or a wand, or anything like that. Generally, they only made small gestures with their hands, if that.

"Merlin had a staff?" I asked.

"Oh yes," Friar Daffyd said. "He used it to discipline and contain his prodigious power. It was what Nimue stole from him when she sealed him in the earth. Afterwards, she was so shocked by the violence that her actions precipitated that she used the staff to help separate Annwn and allow our people to withdraw from the world. She then hid it so that such power could not be used again. Few even know it exists, fewer still where it might be."

"But you know, you can tell us where it is?" Myfanwy asked eagerly.

The friar looked up at the sky. "Yes I can," he said, "but not now. Now I'm afraid I must get ready for noonday prayer." He got up and started to walk towards the chapel but looked back over his shoulder. "If you could fetch the eulogia bread from my hut I would be most grateful, then you may come and meet my congregation." We had no choice but to curb our impatience and do as he asked us. We retrieved the baskets of bread from the hut and Friar Daffyd emerged from the chapel wearing his heavily embroidered stole and carrying a large, leather bound book.

He signalled to us and said. "Come on you two, follow me," He led us out of the hermitage compound and across to a flat topped rock which faced out across the forest to the mountains. He placed the book on the rock and indicated that we should do the same with the bread. Then we stepped back as he opened the book and called out in a loud voice,

"Oramus!" I knew enough Latin to know that this meant "Let us pray." It was a call to prayer. Then out of the forest there came, scuttling, crawling and walking, on two four and six legs, the weirdest collection of the most ghastly creatures I have ever seen or heard about. They were both strange and horrible. The horrific thing was that they all had some human portion or aspect to them. There was one who looked like a snake, except that it was a human with scales from the shoulders up. There was one who appeared to be a massive pair of arms with virtually no body but a face where the arms joined. There were insect and spider-like things with human faces. There was one who was almost normal except that their skin seemed to be made of rock. The collection was so awful it made my skin crawl but it was also, somehow, pathetic and sad. Next to me, Myfanwy drew in her breath sharply and turned so pale I thought she might faint.

Friar Daffyd stood still for a while watching the forest, as if he were waiting for someone to come. When there were no further arrivals he shook his head sadly and started to chant the noonday prayer in Latin,

I turned to Myfanwy and asked, "What are they?"

"They are the mistakes," she answered in a horrified whisper. "They shouldn't be alive. Friar Daffyd should have nothing to do with them. They shouldn't be here."

I looked at her puzzled. "What do you mean 'mistakes'? Why shouldn't they be alive?"

"Tom, our people do not have children readily or quickly and sometimes they try to use magic to hasten the process. This is never a good idea but sometimes it can go disastrously wrong: so wrong that the Council decides that what has been born is not to be considered human. They are the mistakes. They are left exposed in the forest as soon as they are born." I felt a new kind of horror as I understood the meaning of what she had just said.

"You mean you just leave them to die?" Myfanwy nodded. When she saw my expression, she was instantly defensive.

"It's an ancient custom. The Romans did it all the time, sometimes just because the baby was a girl. At least we have good reasons for what we do." I shook my head.

"There are no good reasons," I said flatly. "It's just plain wrong. How could their parents do that? How could their mothers?"

"The parents are not consulted," Myfanwy said. "They are too traumatised. It would be cruel. The decision is made by the Council of Nobles."

"That's even worse," I said through gritted teeth.

We stood in stony silence while Friar Daffyd chanted the psalms. After each psalm there was a kind of noise from the collected group of horrors which, with a bit of imagination, may have been a response to the prayer. After the scripture reading, the friar even gave what seemed to be quite a long sermon, although it's a bit hard to be certain because it also was in Latin. He then blessed the grotesque congregation and gestured for us to come over and help him distribute the bread. Myfanwy stiffened and shook her head slightly.

"I can't," she said. She was pale and shaking.

I just grunted, angry at what I thought was her refusal to see the need, and strode off to help the friar distribute the bread. Just as I picked up one of the baskets,

Gwen came around the hedge and stopped suddenly, clearly shocked by the collection of horrors in front of her. I expected her to have the same sort of reaction that Myfanwy had had but she just looked at the gathered collection and said, "Oh you poor things!"

Then she hurried over to help with the distribution. This wasn't easy. I'll happily admit that I was so repulsed by some of the members of this 'congregation' that I was physically shaking and that the way many of them devoured the bread made my stomach turn, but I kept at my place by the friar's side until all the bread was gone. The friar then gave a final blessing and the bizarre congregation scuttled, crawled, slithered and ran back into the forest.

Friar Daffyd put his arms around Gwen and me and said, "Do you not think that holy Francis would be happy with my congregation? They are the poorest and most rejected of all God's creatures." I nodded absently but turned to look over at Myfanwy who was standing, still as a statue, watching us.

She shook her head and said in a shaky voice, "Friar, how could you give them blessed bread? They're not human!"

"How do you know they're not human?" I challenged, angry at her reaction. "They had human parents. What else could they be?" A lot of things got jumbled up inside me then: my fears about the future, my feelings of alienation in Annwn, as well as my genuine revulsion at this practice. I'm afraid I was a little more aggressive than I intended to be.

"The Council decided..." she started but I interrupted her.

"The Council of Nobles does not get to decide who is human!" I yelled, really angry now. "They do not get to decide who should live and who should die."

"Is your world any better?" she threw back at me. "It happens there too. Oh sure, it happens in a nice clean hospital and it's a doctor in a white coat who decides, but it still happens. At least we only leave them to die, we don't deliberately kill them. So don't you get on your high horse and judge us!" She was yelling now and there were tears in her eyes. "Don't you dare judge me!" Then she turned and ran off around the hedge. I turned to look at the friar and Gwen. Gwen was looking concerned but Friar Daffyd was devastated.

"This is my fault" he said. "I must apologise, both to her and to you. I have misjudged badly. I forced her to face the darkness of Annwn before she was ready." He turned and looked into the forest. "I am so used to them that I had forgotten how confronting my congregation can be. I thought, I hoped, that she would cope and grow. I was wrong and now I have caused a rift between the two of you. I am so sorry."

"Leaving babies out in the forest to die is wrong!" I said defiantly. "It's just wrong!"

The friar gave a sad smile. "I know Tom," he said. "But you must be gentle with our Myf. She is a child of her people and she is right in saying that it is not for you to sit in judgement of others."

Gwen just smiled at me and took my hand. "It will be alright," she said softly, "You know how I said yesterday that you were not as scary as you once were? Well, it's because now when I look at you, I can see echoes and images of Myfanwy. Your friendship with Myfanwy is clear and strong. It's only because she cares so much about you, that she is so upset. If it were anyone else, she would just politely disagree." I looked at her in surprise. All the little-girlishness had gone from her voice and I had the strangest feeling that I was talking to the adult she would become.

Then she smiled and the little girl was back. "And Mam told me to tell you not to come home until after dark. The white lady knows that Nain has returned to Annwn and she's suspicious." I looked to where Myfanwy had disappeared. "Oh don't worry about Myf," she said. "She can look after herself. It's you we were worried about." She laughed as she waved goodbye to the friar and me and ran off after Myfanwy.

As we walked back into the hermitage, Friar Daffyd said, "Tom, you and Myfanwy must return here as early as you can tomorrow morning. Come prepared for a long and dangerous journey, a journey that may take several days. I can help you a little but mostly this is something the two of you must do on your own." A grim thought crossed my mind: this would be much harder with Myfanwy not speaking to me.

I spent the rest of the afternoon helping Friar Daffyd prune his fruit trees and dig his vegetable beds. Then, after evening prayer and a simple supper of bread, cheese and vegetable soup, I pulled the cloak about me and set off down the hill in the dark.

As I was walking down the hill, a voice called out in the dark, "Thomas O'Malley! I know it's you. Why is it that you are walking in the dark without Myfanwy Ferchwyn to guide you? Don't bother to try and hide. It takes more than a clever cloak to fool Apple!" I peered into the gloom and could just make out a diminutive figure by the side of the path. It was Apple the pixie, the very personification of country village wisdom and nosiness.

"Apple, could you please keep your voice down?" I whispered. "There are those who would not be pleased to know that I am in Annwn. I must ask you to keep my presence a secret." The small figure drew itself up to its full height.

"You have my word of honour as a pixie," he said. I had read enough about pixies in fairy tales to take very little comfort in this. "I keep many secrets. I know many things that others do not know," Apple continued. "For example, I know that soon you will be going into the mountains and I have some advice for you:

> Remember that an apple is a dangerous thing.
> Remember that an apple is a mighty weapon.
> Remember also that you must fall,
> Before you can fly."

This made no sense to me at all but Apple had done me a service in the past, so I bowed to the small figure. "Thank you Apple," I said. "As always, I value your advice."

"Really?" he said, surprised. "In that case, I noticed the daughters of Owyn ap Rhys hurrying by before. I assume the tears were because you had offended one or both of them. Now…"

"Forget it, Apple," I said. "I will not apologise for being right."

"Ah, there's many the relationship that has foundered on the rock of those words."

"Good night Apple," I said firmly. The little figure vanished but his voice answered from the darkness.

"Good night indeed!"

Chapter 14
A Flight to the Mountains

The next morning was a carbon copy of the one before except that the silence between Myfanwy and me was like a physical weight. She had met me at the foot of Friar's Hill the night before and transported me back to the house without saying a word. She had remained silent as I debriefed Nain and Helen about the dragons and the possibility of finding Merlin's staff. Neither of us mentioned the friar's strange congregation and I could see Nain and Helen exchanging looks, wondering what was wrong. I didn't feel like enlightening them.

Helen had been upset about us going alone but Myfanwy had broken her silence to persuade her that it was necessary and that we wouldn't take any risks. Nain had only said that she couldn't be involved in any way; the political position within the Council of Nobles was too delicate. So it was that the two of us set off on our own.

The pre-dawn sky was clear, with the stars sharp and hard, when we left. We walked up Friar's Hill in the dark and in silence. I was carrying Declan's staff and a pack equipped for a couple of days travel. We didn't know what to expect.

We arrived at the hermitage just as dawn was breaking and Friar Daffyd was waiting for us outside his chapel.

"I'm afraid there's not much time for breakfast," he said. "Your rides are almost here." He pointed upwards and as I looked up I saw what seemed at first to be two giant birds soaring above the hermitage: one white as hope and the other dark as dreaming. As they circled lower, however, I could see that there was something strange about these birds. A long time after my eyes could see it, my mind refused to make the interpretation. Beside me, Myfanwy gave a small gasp of wonder and finally even I had to accept the truth of what I could see. They were not giant birds – they were flying horses!

They flew with their front legs tucked up under them, with their wings outstretched, and with their mane and tail streaming in the wind. Bathed in the morning sunlight, they were a sight of heart stopping beauty. Eventually they swooped low and landed at a trot on the grass in front of the chapel. They immediately folded their wings and started to graze. With a start, I realised that I was standing there with my mouth open, barely breathing. Every time I thought I was getting used to Annwn, it would throw up something beyond my expectations.

"Oh Tom," Myfanwy whispered beside me, our differences put aside in the wonder of the moment. "I never thought I would see them this close. They are so rare! I have seen them occasionally, soaring over the mountains but now…here they are." It is hard to convey the effect of these creatures. They seemed to be the very epitome of dignity and freedom.

"A Pegasus," I breathed softly. "Two of them; what's the plural? Pegasi?"

"Tom, you are unique," Friar Daffyd said laughing. "Rare indeed are those who would be concerned with grammar when first meeting one of these. Actually, they would more correctly be called pterippi. The Pegasus of Greek myth was only one example of a pterippus or winged horse. Still, I suppose pegasi would be acceptable in common usage." Friar Daffyd walked over to them and held out his hands. The pegasi behaved just like normal horses. They looked up curiously, then walked over, sniffed at his hands, and started to eat whatever it was he was holding. The friar looked across at us and smiled.

"Come on over," he said. "I will introduce you." Myfanwy and I walked over slowly.

"Now hold out your hands." As I held out my hands the friar poured oats into them and the black Pegasus started to eat from my hand. Myfanwy had somehow arranged her own supply of oats and was feeding the white pegasus. "Now, I have summoned these because they can take you part of your way into the mountains both quickly and without being seen. When you get to their nesting site, you must follow the river deeper into the mountains. You will come to a cliff and a waterfall. You must climb the cliff. At the top you will find another waterfall beside a deep pool and beyond that I can guide you no further except to give you an old poem. It's better in the Welsh but here is a rough English translation:

> Silver falls and pools are shining
> Dark into the rock are hiding
> Doom of Emrys, doom defying."

"What does it mean?" I asked.

The friar shrugged his shoulders. "I'm afraid I have no idea. I can only trust that you will be able to work it out when you are on the spot. Now, slide in behind their wings and climb up onto their backs." I dropped the rest of the oats on the ground and stuck Declan's staff trough my belt, so that it hung at my side like a sword. Then, with some difficulty – it was a big horse - did as the friar suggested. Fortunately, the pegasus was too interested in seeking out the oats I had dropped to worry about what I was doing. Myfanwy, of course, had no difficulty teleporting herself onto her pegasus' back.

"If you are nervous, then hang onto the mane, but they will not let you fall," Friar Daffyd said. "Now, go with my blessing." He stepped back and traced the sign of the cross in the air. The pegasi reared up and then leapt into the sky, their wings stretching out with a swift down beat. I could feel the powerful shoulder muscles ripple with effort as we rose higher into the air. At first I was too caught up in the joy of it to be worried, but then I looked down, saw how high we were, and quickly gripped my horse's mane.

We banked gracefully to turn towards the mountains and then started to speed up. Soon we were going so fast that I had to grab my cloak or it would have been torn off by the airstream and it was hard to breath in the ice cold air. Below us the forest passed swiftly away and the snow-capped mountains ahead grew closer. I don't know how long we flew but it seemed like a long time and my hands were cramped with cold when we finally started a spiralling descent. We were headed towards a narrow spur that stood out from a steep, rocky hillside. Next to this, the river Sabrina fell in a riotous cascade to the valley below.

In the middle of the spur there was a green field and it was there that we landed. Both Myfanwy and I rolled off our mounts, stiff with cold and weary from the long ride.

"Hold out your hand," Myfanwy said. When I held out my hand it magically filled with oats which my mount proceeded to eat gratefully. I looked across at Myfanwy.

"Thank you," I said. She just shrugged and turned away. Evidently the truce brought about by the arrival of the pegasi had evaporated during the long, weary flight. When my pegasus had finished the oats Myfanwy had made available, I made a half-mocking bow. To my surprise the horse returned the bow in utter seriousness and trotted over to join its mate in grazing. I turned to Myfanwy.

"I feel a bit like my name should be Digory," I said lightly. Myfanwy looked at me blankly. "You know, Digory and Polly from "The Magician's Nephew" – one of the Narnia books."

She looked at me; her face hard and her eyes cold. "Is that another reference to the books of your world? Are you trying to show me how odd I am? How much I don't fit in?"

I looked at her in surprise. "No!" I said. "No, I…" Actually I didn't know what to say next. This had never occurred to me. Myfanwy turned away to stroke her horses neck and wing. I frowned but then pushed her snub from my mind. The day was well advanced and we had a lot to do. I looked around to find a way out of the field. The field was circular and slightly bowl shaped. It was completely surrounded by a rampart of earth with old tree trunks and branches. It was too untidy and chaotic to have been manmade and I realised that it had been made by the pegasi themselves; pushing and kicking things to the side. We were, in fact, in a nest: the kind of nest that a horse would build. It had soft, green grass in the centre and a protective wall around the outside. Obviously, because the pegasi could fly, there was no ground level way out. We would have to climb.

Myfanwy and I walked over to the river side of the rampart. There was no easy way over: the rampart was a tangle of old logs and tree branches. It wasn't going to be hard for me to climb but it would be nearly impossible for someone as small as Myfanwy.

"Don't worry Myf, I'll help you up," I said, holding out my hand. She looked at me with an expression of utter scorn.

"I'm the witch girl, remember?" she said. She then teleported herself to the top of a large tree trunk about half way to the top. There she sat and looked down at me. I sighed and started climbing. I didn't care how long she stayed mad at me. I wasn't going to apologise for being right. It didn't take me long to reach her log. I paused for a rest.

"You know, this would go a lot faster if you would teleport me as well," I said.

"Oh no," she said mockingly. "I couldn't do that to you. I know how much you hate traveling by magic. You'd better get going. We have only a couple of hours of light left." I didn't say anything further but just started climbing again. As I reached the top, Myfanwy teleported herself to the top of a large branch nearby. This time, however, the branch looked much larger from below than it actually was and, as soon as she materialised, she lost her footing. Fortunately I was able to catch her before she fell. We were now at the top of the rampart and could see the river, the forest and the mountains filling all the world. For a moment she relaxed as I held her, then she drew back and said, "Thank you but you can let go of me now. I have my balance."

As soon as I let go of her, she teleported herself down to the river bank on the outside of the rampart. I didn't know how long she was going to keep up the cold shoulder treatment but it was starting to get tiresome. I began to climb down and had almost finished when I put my trust in a solid looking branch that proved to be rotten. It broke in my hand and I started to fall.

I heard Myfanwy call out my name before I hit the ground. Fortunately I knew how to land. I broke my fall and rolled to my feet. Apart from a few incipient bruises on my back and having the breath knocked out of me, I was okay. Myfanwy ran across to me but stopped a few feet away. She looked at me with anxious eyes.

"I'm okay," I said. "I didn't fall that far and the ground here is soft." She bit her lower lip and her whole body seemed to tremble. "Really," I said. "I'm fine." It was as if a blind came down and she was once again distant and unreadable.

"Good," she said, "Because I need you to lead the way into the forest." I shrugged, pulled out Declan's staff and walked up the river bank and into the forest. Myfanwy followed a few paces behind.

I didn't walk close to the river bank because the undergrowth there was too thick. However, a little way in from the river we were able to make good progress through a forest of pine and fir; the ground soft with fallen needles. After we had been moving steadily uphill for about an hour, I stopped suddenly at the top of a small rise.

"Myf," I called back, without looking around. "You know how you said that thing which chased us in the Savernake Forest looked nothing like a real troll?"

"Yes," she said uncertainly.

"Well, does a real troll look like a really ugly, potbellied man about eight feet tall with large tusks growing out of the lower and upper jaw?"

"Yes, with warty, yellow skin," Myfanwy answered. "You're looking at one now aren't you?"

"At five actually," I said. The creatures looked at me uncertainly, before snarling and starting to advance towards me. Declan's staff shivered with blue light and formed itself into a fighting spear with a large leaf shaped head and a weighted butt. One of the trolls had broken into a lumbering run and came at me well before the others. It was carrying a crude club and swung this viciously at my legs. I jumped over the stroke and thrust my spear into the creature's armpit. It howled, dropped the club and fell back. I could hear Myfanwy coming up behind me.

"No," I called. "Stay back!" The other trolls had formed a line and were coming at me four abreast. "Move around towards the river. The heavier undergrowth will make it harder for them to move." I wasn't going to let all four get to me at the same time, so I moved to the extreme left, where the first troll was still moaning and gripping its wounded shoulder. The troll at that end of the line of four tried to hit me with a vertical smash of its fist. I stepped aside and ran my spear up its arm. The razor sharp head sliced through the thick skin and the troll reeled back, screaming in pain. I swung around and smashed the weighted butt of the spear into the face of the second troll. The third troll lunged at me with a primitive spear. I parried this and thrust directly at its face, taking out an eye. The fourth troll then pushed this one out of the way and swung at me with a tree branch it was using as a club. I stepped inside the swing and drove the butt of my spear into its ribs, using the motion of its own turn to send it sprawling. I was now standing between the trolls and the river with Myfanwy behind me. For a moment all was still and I began to relax, thinking that they might just give up and go away. However, I soon found myself facing five very angry trolls, three of which were covered with a black, oozing syrup which I assumed was troll blood.

"Myf," I yelled. "If you can do anything, anything at all, now would be a good time."

"I'm not sure what I can do," Myfanwy replied with an edge of panic in her voice. "Trolls are mythical creatures and very resistant to magic." The trolls were coming at me in a heavy trot and I took an overhead guard with my spear. Suddenly, everything stopped and the whole world went silent. Myfanwy had stopped time. I only relaxed a little. This might give us an edge but I knew she couldn't keep doing it for long.

"Tom, I can see the other side of the river and I have an idea. I'm coming up to you. Please don't slice me open with that spear." I stood watching the frozen trolls while Myfanwy came up behind me and grabbed me around the waist. Suddenly we were on the other river bank and time started to flow again. The trolls howled in frustration at our apparent disappearance. Then they spotted us. They roared and started to run down towards the river. Myfanwy knelt down beside the river and called into the water,

"Sabrina, we need your help." Sabrina was the spirit of the river and an old childhood friend of Myfanwy's: to the extent that you can be friends with a nature spirit whose mood largely depends on the climate and who has no power of speech. By this time, two of the trolls were starting to wade into the river. Sabrina appeared in the water. It was interesting. Downstream, she appeared as a mature woman with her long hair formed by green water weed. Here, where the river was more energetic, she appeared as a teenager and her tresses were formed by streams of white foam. Myfanwy simply pointed to the trolls. Sabrina smiled and merged back into the water. The flow in the river started to increase. Soon the river was in full, violent flood and the two trolls who were wading across were swept away. A third just managed to struggle back to the bank. The spear in my hand flashed blue and turned back into a staff. The threat was over. On the opposite bank, the remaining trolls soon lost interest and disappeared into the forest, fighting amongst themselves.

Myfanwy and I sat quietly on the bank as the river subsided back to its normal flow. After a while Myfanwy turned to me and asked aggressively, "What gave you the idea that you could fight five fully grown trolls?"

"Didn't have much choice," I said.

"Yes you did," she countered. "You could have run away. It's a great option that you never seem to consider."

"No, I couldn't," I said.

"Why not?"

"Because it's my job to protect you," I said fiercely. "Don't ask me how or why, it just is. And don't give me any of that feminist stuff about not asking for protection. I know all that and it doesn't change anything." I picked up my pack. "Come on, we still have a long way to go and it will be dark soon." I turned to head off into the forest again but Myfanwy wasn't finished.

"Tom, those trolls would have killed you. How would that protect me?"

"I said it was my job. I didn't say I was good at it." Myfanwy grabbed me by the shoulders and turned me round to face her. For a long time she just stood there looking at me, her expression hard to read.

Eventually she said, "You took on five trolls singlehandedly and you left them bloodied and bruised…I think you'll do." I didn't know what to say so I just shrugged and turned to lead the way into the forest. At least she was speaking to me again.

We only walked about another hour before we came to the first cliff and waterfall. It was getting too dark to think about climbing the cliff, so we decided to camp beside the pool at the foot of the waterfall.

Myfanwy walked around for a while. When she came back she said, "I've made it so that it's most improbable that anyone or anything will notice that we're here. You can relax and get a good night's sleep." I had gathered some wood for a fire and Myfanwy set it alight. It burned strongly even though some of the wood was damp. As I have said before, having a magical girlfriend can be very useful. We had a supper of pasties filled with a sweet curry of lamb, raisins and apple and I made some sweet billy tea. All of this could have been very companionable except that there was still a lot of tension and very few words between us.

I had laid out our sleeping gear on opposite sides of the fire so that each of us could stay as close as possible to the heat. It was going to be a cold night. After a while staring into the fire, Myfanwy moved over to her sleeping bag.

Just before she got into it she turned to me and said, "I know you think I've been unreasonable but it's not just about the friar's congregation. Sometimes you're difficult to get on with. You are all hard decisions with sharp edges that don't yield at all. I wanted so much for you to love Annwn as much as I do. I wanted you to see its beauty but all you saw was ugliness and darkness. You ruined everything." Then she climbed into her sleeping bag and turned her back to me.

Around us the pine trees clustered close and dark while the pool and waterfall glowed white with a faint phosphorescence. Above us, the northern stars, which were still strange to me, shone brightly from a clear and frosty sky. I sat by the fire and watched the sparks drift up into the sky, dancing red among the strange stars.

"I do love Annwn," I said softly. "I think it's beautiful and just being here has changed me, deep down. I am far more at home here than I am in London. Still, if something is wrong, how can I not say that? I know that the other world is no better. I know that there evil often walks around with a lot of money, in respectable suits and with laws and lawyers to protect it, but that doesn't change things. What is wrong is always wrong." Myfanwy had her back turned to me and gave no indication that she had heard. She might have been asleep. I looked across at the pool and there was Sabrina, leaning on her elbows, her hair formed from wild swirls of foam. She had a pitying expression on her face and she shook her head as if to say 'You are here alone in the forest with your beautiful girlfriend and that's the best you can come up with?' I pulled a face at her. She smiled mischievously and merged back into the water.

I climbed into my sleeping bag and for a while everything was quiet. Then softly, almost too softly to hear, came Myfanwy's voice, "Actually, I have read all of the Narnia books and I loved them. I know what you mean about Digory and Polly." I smiled. I figured that was as close as I was going to get to an apology. Still, as I was drifting off to sleep, the thought came: Why should I have to live my life in Annwn? It was beautiful and special but it wasn't home. Why didn't I get to choose?

Chapter 15
An Apple is a Dangerous Thing

After breakfast the next morning, we examined the cliff we had to climb. The spray from the waterfall made the rock slippery and the morning sun shone on it obliquely so that parts of it were still in deep shadow. It looked as if it was not going to be an easy climb.

"Maybe you could teleport us to the top," I suggested. Myfanwy shook her head.

"Sorry, but I can't see it well enough. It would be dangerous."

"Well, nothing for it then," I said. "Stay behind me and I'll find the way." Myfanwy started to look rebellious but I insisted. "Look, I have longer arms and legs and a much greater reach. I can climb more easily and from above, I can help you."

The logic was unassailable and so Myfanwy gave a wry half grin and shrugged. "Off you go then," she said. I tied Declan's staff securely behind my back and started climbing. It turned out that the climb was not as difficult as it first appeared. I decided to climb well away from the worst of the spray and there were hand holds and small ledges on the way up. Still, we had to work together. There were times when I had to help or even lift Myfanwy up and she often directed my feet to the best footholds. It was good to be working as a team again.

When we got to the top, we found ourselves looking out over an open moor. There were still a few struggling pine trees but they were widely scattered and the ground was covered with tussocks of brownish grass. There were, in places, patches of snow. Here the river was a swiftly flowing mountain stream that cut deeply into the moor. Ahead of us a massive cliff rose at least a thousand feet into the sky and the river leapt over this in a spectacular waterfall. We set off for the pool that would lie at its base.

It was midday when we arrived and we tried to figure out our next move over lunch. The water fall was very high and in fell into a plunge pool of foaming water with a tremendous roar. When the sun was out the water shone a brilliant silver and rainbows filled the spray. Most of the area surrounding the pool was bare rock: a dark, sharp slate. I chewed on my cheese roll and grew progressively more unhappy. Myfanwy handed me a bottle of ginger beer.

"Here you go," she said, "Just like in your book, lashings of ginger beer!"

"What did that poem say again?" I asked. Myfanwy recited the clue in a singsong voice.

"Silver falls and pools are shining
Dark into the rock are hiding
Doom of Emrys, doom defying."

"Hmm…the most obvious answer would seem to be that the staff lies at the bottom of that pool," I said thoughtfully. "It is cut deep into dark rock and the water fall and the pool certainly hide whatever is at the bottom."

Myfanwy looked doubtful. "That seems too simple," she said.

"Still," I said, standing up and starting to strip off, "we're going to have to try it. Since I'm easily the best swimmer, it's up to me to see what we can find." I stood shivering in my shorts and I looked at the turbulent water of the pool with real dread. Every instinct I had was telling me that this was a bad idea but I didn't see that I had any choice. I took a deep breath and dived in.

The cold of the water cut through me like a knife. The river must have come straight off a glacier up in the mountains. The shock was much greater than I had expected and I found my limbs already sluggish and tired. The current took hold of me and carried me deep. I was running short of air and I was no longer concerned with finding the staff. All I was concerned with was trying to survive. Fortunately I had grown up swimming in the surf and my body knew by instinct not to try and swim against the current but to swim across it. I reached to wall of the pool and was able to swim towards the surface. As I got close enough to see, Myfanwy pulled me from the water by magic and dumped me on some dry heather. I was cold; bone cold and numb. When Myfanwy pointed, one of the sleeping bags unpacked itself and wrapped itself around me. Myfanwy handed me a mug of hot chocolate as she sat beside me. She pulled the sleeping bag around her shoulders as well.

"Body warmth," was all she said. When I started to shiver uncontrollably, she steadied my hands with hers and helped me to drink. It wasn't long before I felt almost normal again.

"It's no good Myf," I said. "If it's at the bottom of that pool, it's lost. You couldn't recover it without a drysuit and professional diving equipment and even then - only with great difficulty."

Myfanwy nodded glumly. "Hard to do with magic too," she said. "You'd need to keep yourself warm and fight the current as well as supply yourself with oxygen and light. Some of the fisherfolk might be able to do it, they are talented in that area, but I doubt that I could." She frowned. "Anyway, it's not really the style of my people. That is more what your people would do: protect a treasure with a really powerful physical barrier. We tend to be more subtle." She looked thoughtfully at the waterfall. "Stay here and get dressed. I'll be back in a minute." As I put my clothes back on, she walked over to the waterfall, stared around blankly for a minute and then came back.

"No, I was wrong," she said. "I thought the answer might have been a cave behind the waterfall. That too would have been in dark rock and the waterfall and the pool would have been protecting it."

"That's a really good idea," I said enthusiastically. "So why did you come back without looking?"

"There's no point. I could see that there's nothing there, only rock."

"How can you know? You didn't look properly."

"I looked well enough to see that it's pointless. It's just a waste of time." This was very strange. She had only given the area the most cursory and passing of glances. If Sydney Central Station was behind that waterfall, she wouldn't have seen it. Then I remembered that magic people were just as prone to magic as anyone else. I stowed everything in the pack and, given my recent experience, I tried to make everything watertight.

Then I said, "Myf, come with me." She looked doubtful but I insisted. "Come on, just trust me." She continued to protest but she followed me. As we got closer to the waterfall, she hesitated. I took her hand and led her to the edge of the curtain of water. From here I could see an opening in the dark rock; not a cave but a tunnel. Myfanwy was still insisting that there was nothing there and that this was a waste of time.

"Myf, close your eyes and hold onto me," I said. Trust me." To her credit, she did just that and followed me as I walked behind the curtain of icy water and turned into the tunnel. I felt the now familiar 'pop' sensation as I walked through a magic barrier and I heard Myfanwy gasp in surprise as she opened her eyes.

"You couldn't see it because it was enchanted," I said.

"And you could because the spell didn't effect you," she said. "Good, I'm glad my search theory worked."

"Yes, but your theory had you detecting the presence of magic and you didn't detect the magic at all," I pointed out. "In fact, you tried to stop me from investigating."

"I did detect it," she said haughtily, "by being effected by the inattention spell when you weren't."

"Okay, canary person," I said grinning. "Let's get going." I started to pull a small LED torch out of my pocket but Myfanwy contemptuously waved her hand and the whole tunnel filled with light. The tunnel had a flat floor and an arched roof of dressed stone. It was large enough for two trucks to drive down side by side — or one dragon I thought nervously. We followed the tunnel as it sloped down into the hill. After we had been walking for about half an hour, the tunnel levelled out and made a sharp turn to the left. Here Myfanwy stopped.

"Why are you stopping?" I asked.

"Because we've come to a dead end, of course," she replied. Then she looked at me closely. "It's not a dead end is it?" I shook my head. "The tunnel keeps going?" I nodded. "Okay," she sighed. "Lead on surfer boy." She closed her eyes and put her hand on my shoulder. As soon as she closed her eyes, all the light vanished from the tunnel and I was left in total darkness. Fortunately, I still had the small LED torch in my pocket and, by its bluish light, I was able to lead us around the corner. As soon as I did, I could see a faint light up ahead. When Myafnwy opened her eyes again, the tunnel was once more flooded with light. We hurried on and quickly came to the end of the tunnel without incident.

The tunnel ended in a great ornamented archway which seemed to lead outside and into an apple grove. This was impossible. We were now deep under the mountain. Yet all about us it seemed to be a foggy morning with bright sunlight and shining mist – as if the fog was just about to be burned off by the sun. The apple trees were in bloom, their scent was heavy in the air and the ground had a lush covering of green. The strange thing was that even though the trees were in blossom, there was ripe fruit hanging from the branches. The branches were also in leaf: some the bright green of spring and some the yellow/brown of autumn. I instantly didn't trust the place and Apple's warning came back to me clearly, "Remember that an apple is a dangerous thing."

Myfanwy, however, I suppose because she was more used to magic, had no such qualms. She walked over and reached up to take an apple from one of the trees.

"No Myf! Don't!" I yelled. She looked at me puzzled.

"Why not?" she asked. I cast around for a reason. I couldn't mention Apple because, like all her people, Myfanwy would take no notice of the advice of a pixie. Then I noticed something lying at the base of the tree next to her.

"Look across to the tree on your right," I said. She looked and for a while didn't notice anything amiss. Then she screamed. At the base of the tree was a skeleton with grass growing through its bones and the ragged remains of clothes. Strangely, the apple that had rolled from the bony hand was still fresh and sweet. It had only one bite taken from it. Clearly, in these mountains an apple was a dangerous thing indeed.

Myfanwy stood frozen in place, contemplating what very nearly was. She had turned as pale as the white lady. "I think the apple put him to sleep," she whispered, "and he didn't wake up, even as he died of starvation and thirst."

I walked over and put my arm around her. "Come on," I said. "There's nothing we can do for him now and we still have a job to do." She came with me quietly, hanging on my arm, as we walked deeper into the mists of the apple grove. There was no way to take a bearing but I made sure that we left an obvious trail in the grass: a trail that we could keep more or less straight.

As we moved deeper the sweet apple smell became heavier and heavier until it was nauseating. Then it suddenly stopped and we stepped out of the apple trees and into a cleared space. Here the bright mist was even thicker and we couldn't see more than a few feet ahead. We had walked about 300 meters into the mist when we came to a stone platform of polished red marble. As we stepped onto this, the mist cleared enough for us to see a structure at the centre of the platform. It was round, raised up two steps from the rest of the platform and built like a small, Greek temple. It was open sided, with four ionic columns holding up a simple dome: all made of pure, dazzlingly white marble. There, hanging suspended in air at the centre of the temple was what appeared to be a thick, wooden staff. I started to walk towards it. Myfanwy let go of my arm.

"Be careful, Tom" she said. "You might be able to break the protective spells but the power of that staff may be too great even for you." Somehow I didn't think so. As far as I could tell, there were no protective spells and the staff in the temple looked like the one Gandalf carried in the Lord of the Ring movies. In fact, it looked exactly like the one Gandalf had carried in the Lord of the Ring movies.

I walked up the steps and into the temple structure. As I grabbed hold of the staff, I knew that what I had been both dreading and expecting was true. I turned the staff over in my hands and found what I knew would be there. Without any hesitation I took the staff out of the temple and carried it over to where Myfanwy was standing. I offered it to her but she stepped back in fear of its power.

"Don't worry," I said. "This isn't Merlin's staff. At least, not unless his staff was made out of plastic and manufactured in China." Myfanwy looked totally confused as I handed her the staff and pointed out the 'Made in China' imprint.

"I don't understand," she said.

"I do," I replied. "Myf, this is a toy. It's a piece of movie spin-off merchandise. Cadell got here before us and he has the real staff. He left this as a kind of joke. He would see this as a mockery of his power: that the outside world has replaced real magic with fictional magic. So, he replaces the real staff with a mock staff and uses this mockery to help destroy the world that mocked him. In his own twisted, psychotic sort of way, Cadell is actually quite clever." Myfanwy gave a chocked scream and started to look about wildly, desperately.

"Don't worry," I said. "He won't be here now. He'll be long gone." Myfanwy shook her head.

"No, Tom," she cried, "Look!" I looked around. The mist had cleared back to the apple trees. This was enough to show that the platform was surrounded by six dragons, alternating red and white, each one as big as a small airliner. They were awake and their gaze was fixed steadily on us.

"Perhaps they would go back to sleep if we returned the staff," Myfanwy suggested.

"I don't think so," I said. "Perhaps the real staff was keeping them asleep but I don't think this toy was doing anything much. Maybe if we just walk quietly away, they'll ignore us." This didn't work. As soon as we stepped off the platform, all the dragons got to their feet and the two closest to us started to move towards us. We hurriedly stepped back onto the platform and they settled down again. I looked into the eyes of the nearest dragon and I knew that this wasn't safety. This was the kind of game a cat plays with a mouse before the kill.

We had to get out of there. Almost without thinking, I reached behind me to feel for Declan's staff.

Myfanwy noticed. "Don't you even think of trying to fight six dragons. There must be a limit even to your idiocy." It seemed that Declan's staff agreed. It was still a walking stick. Apparently it couldn't come up with any weapon which would be useful in the current circumstance. As I thought about it though, I could. Apple had been right once before, maybe he would be again. It was a crazy weapon but one which might just be effective if only we could get to it. I turned to Myfanwy and said grimly,

"If we stay here we are going to die. We need to move. I have a plan. It's desperate and might end in disaster but it's all I can come up with. Unless you have any ideas?" Myfanwy shook her head. "Right, what I need you to do is to teleport us back along our trail as far as you can and then to stop time for as long as you can. Okay?"

"Okay," she said. "But I don't really know this place, so I can't teleport us any further than I can see. That would put us back at the edge of the clearing, almost between that red dragon's claws. Also, I can't guarantee how long I will be able to stop time. These are big creatures. Stopping their energy will take a lot of effort."

"I understand but you need to try. I think this is the only way. Do it on the count of three. One, two, three..."

Chapter 16
You Must Fall Before You Can Fly

Suddenly we were on the edge of the clearing; almost between the dragon's claws and with its head and jaws looming over us. For a moment the dragon reacted. It started to lift its front claw and open its jaws. Then everything was still. The dragon froze, the swirling mist froze and the world had that deep, deep silence it has when Myfanwy stops time.

"Come on!" I said. I took her by the hand and we ran into the apple grove. As I ran, I started to pick as many apples as I could, stuffing them in all the pockets of my coat and pants.

"Tom," Myfanwy called. "I can't hold them for long and its gets harder as we move further away." I looked at Myfanwy and she was clearly getting tired.

"Don't exhaust yourself," I said. "We have a long way to go. Let them come and start picking apples."

"Why?" she asked.

"You'll see...hopefully," I replied. I watched the strain go from her face and almost immediately heard an earth shattering roar that could only be the howl of a dragon. Not long after that, there came the sound of crashing apple trees as the dragon made its way towards us. We couldn't out run it, so I decided to stand and wait. Myfanwy stood beside me.

The red dragon that was closest to us came crashing through the mist with the two white dragons that were either side of him coming in on diagonal tracks. As it got close to us it opened its mouth to roar again. I started to run towards it, throwing apples. It was huge and its jaws opened as wide as a house. I couldn't miss. After the first few apples had landed in its mouth it stopped running, closed its mouth, fell down and went to sleep. Myfanwy caught on immediately and started running towards one of the white dragons.

"You take the right. I'll take the left," she called. The same pattern repeated itself. After a few apples had landed in the dragon's mouths, they lay down and went to sleep. We could hear the other dragons coming behind these ones and we started to run towards the entrance. We got further than we expected because the last three dragons stopped to investigate what had happened to the others. We were nearly within sight of the tunnel when the two remaining red dragons caught up with us. They separated and attacked us one on one. Clearly, they had figured out what had happened to their sisters because they kept their mouths tightly shut and came at us with their claws. These were huge and razor sharp; they sliced through the apple trees like butter.

However, this swiping with their front claws was clearly not their natural mode of attack and they were clumsy. I was able to dodge, to duck, to fall flat, to jump and generally to avoid being hit and sliced, although every moment threatened to be my last. I knew that I couldn't keep this up for long, eventually I would make a mistake and be hit. The dragon, however, proved to have less patience than I had stamina and it opened its mouth to hiss at me in anger: a big mistake. I had three apples in its mouth before it realised its error and closed its mouth with a snap. Then it rolled over and went to sleep.

Meanwhile, Myfanwy had been teleporting herself around randomly, giving her dragon no proper target. When it saw its sister fall and me coming to Myfanwy's help, it simply couldn't resist roaring in frustration. Myfanwy gestured and a whole stream of apples flew into its mouth. It simply dropped where it was and was asleep.

Once again we started to run towards the entrance. We were almost there when we found out what had happened to the last dragon. There it was, all white and silver, sitting between us and the tunnel. I pulled the last of the apples out of my pockets and hefted them in my hands. I could swear that it was smiling as it shook its great head. It was not going to get caught that way.

"Tom," Myfanwy said, "I can see the tunnel entrance."

"I know," I said in frustration. "We can see it but we can't get to it."

"Oh, you idiot!" She said as she took my hand. Instantly we were in the tunnel and behind the dragon.

"Run!" she yelled, somewhat unnecessarily. We both started to run up the tunnel. Myfanwy was clearly tired and I had to stop repeatedly to help her. It didn't take the dragon long to figure out what had happened and come after us. Fortunately the confines of the tunnel slowed it down a lot and it had particular trouble getting around the sharp turn. As a result, when we ran out of the tunnel it was still a long way behind us. However, we were both out of breath and tired and there was a long stretch of open country in front of us.

"Myf, can you teleport us back home?" I asked hopefully. She shook her head.

"No. It's too far and I'm too tired," she said. I knew it wouldn't be that simple.

"To the pegasi nest?" I suggested. Again she shook her head. "Perhaps to the flat rock where we climbed out next to the waterfall, can you remember the place well enough?" She nodded, took my hand and we were standing kilometres away at the top of the first waterfall.

"Tom, I'm tired. We can't travel that way anymore," she said, "and I just can't climb or run. I just can't" At that moment the dragon came out of the tunnel and stretched its wings in the sun. We were running out of time and options. Again I thought of Apple and began to formulate a crazy plan.

"Alright," I said, "this is a bit desperate but you're going to have to trust me." I took my pack off and strapped it onto her backwards, so that it sat on her chest. I made the straps as tight as I could. Then I took her to the very edge of the waterfall. The dragon was now flying in circles, looking for us. Myfanwy looked over the edge of the cliff.

"Tom, what are you going to do?" she asked in a panicked voice.

"Don't worry," I said. "The water is cold but it's deep and that pack will float." Then I grabbed her as I jumped over the waterfall, taking her with me. She screamed as she fell.

I tried to hold onto her but lost my grip at the shock of hitting the water. Here the water was still as bone-chillingly cold as it had been at the other waterfall but this time I was ready for it. I was pulled down by the current but I knew that the strong down current under the waterfall would be replaced by an equally strong up current on the downstream edge of the plunge pool. I swam strongly downstream but I don't think it made much difference. The current had me in its grip. Soon enough it carried me to the surface and I found myself gasping for air in a torrent of wild water. I had, however, failed to take into account the thick, woollen cloak and this dragged me back down. I was saved by Declan's walking stick which was still strapped to my back. This changed into a thick plank of some very light wood; the buoyancy carried me to the surface. There I desperately searched for Myfanwy but could see no sign of her.

"Myf! Myf!" I called. Ahead of me, the teenage Sabrina formed herself from the swirling water. "Myf!" I cried desperately. "Where is Myfanwy?" Sabrina smiled and merged back into the water. I found myself caught in a cross current and then a powerful counter current that carried me to a still pool close to the river bank. Here I found Myfanwy sitting on the riverbank, having only just dragged herself from the river. She was blue and shivering with cold. When she saw me, she glared.

"This is how you protect me? You throw me off a cliff and try to drown me...or was it freeze me?"

"Better than being eaten by a dragon," I answered shortly. I couldn't tell her of the wild, soul tearing panic I had felt when I thought I might have lost her. "Come on, we need to get you warm," was all I said. I pulled the pack out of the river where Myfanwy had dropped it. When I opened it I found, as I had hoped, that the sleeping bags were still dry. I laid one out deep under the cover of a pine tree where the dragon would not be able to spy us. Then I went back to get Myfanwy. She was still sitting and shivering by the river. The teenage Sabrina was sitting next to her, looking worried. She was listless and silent as I led her to the sleeping bag and got her in. Then I took off the cloak and my coat and, even though it was a bit of a squeeze, climbed in with her. I was uncomfortably aware that I was now closer to her than I had ever been to anyone in my life. If we hadn't been so cold and wet it would have been very awkward. As it was, she was like ice to the touch.

"Hey! What are you doing?" she complained.

"We both need body heat," I said. "Especially you, you're smaller than I am and you're tired from all your magical excursions. This really is the recommended first aid for suspected hypothermia."

"Okay, but just don't get any ideas surfer boy. I'm still not sure that I forgive you." She was talking, this was good. As long as she was talking, she was okay and it was good. It didn't matter what she said. I wanted to keep her talking.

"Could you tell me about Annwn?" I asked. "When you were growing up, what were your favourite things?" She was quiet for a while and I started to get worried.

Then she said, "I think maybe it was Christmas, when we had snow on the ground and great log fires in the house, or maybe the night of the summer festival, when all the community had this great party around the meeting tree..." she kept on talking about Annwn, about all the little things that a child notices and remembers. I started to appreciate how deeply she loved this place and its people. In the end, I was the one who drifted off to sleep, listening to her talking.

When I woke it was dark and I was alone in the sleeping bag. A little way off, Myfanwy had a fire going. She had changed and was drying her wet clothes.

"Myf, the fire, the dragon is searching for us!" I called anxiously.

"Don't worry," she said. "Dragons hunt by sight. I don't think this one will be flying around at night." She paused. "Are you sure it was only my hypothermia you were thinking of when you climbed into that sleeping bag with me?" I reacted with mock outrage.

"My Lady!" I said. "I assure you that my intentions were purely honourable."

She gave me a wry grin. "Hmm...Maybe," she said doubtfully. "I just hope that my mother doesn't get to hear of it." I climbed out of the sleeping bag and went to stand by the fire. Myfanwy handed me another of Nain's pasties. It was hot and there in the forest it tasted really good. It was washed down with a mug of hot, milky tea. Myfanwy threw me some dry clothes and I retreated into the dark of the forest to get changed.

"If dragons don't fly at night, perhaps we should move out and spend the night travelling," I suggested.

Myfanwy raised an eyebrow. "Really? You want to spend the night wandering in the dark through a troll infested forest."

"Good point," I said as I returned to the fire light. "How about we sleep here tonight and start out in the morning."

"Good thinking, surfer boy. Your sleeping bag is over there," she said firmly, "and mine is over here." I smiled; clearly she had her strength back. Later, when I was almost at the edge of sleep, I heard a whisper from the other side of the fire.

"Thank you Tom. I know you did what you needed to do to protect me and I don't think there's many who would've been able to do what you did."

In the morning the sky was grey and there was a cold wind coming from the mountains. We packed quickly. I started to set off through the forest but Myfanwy put out her hand to stop me.

"Walking will be too slow," she said. "The dragon will be up soon and we would be hunted down." She looked thoughtfully into the distance. "I don't think I can teleport us as far as home. Nor even as far as Friar's Hill. They are too far and I am too unsure of the relationship between here and there. I can see the possibilities but they are small and hard to reach." I started to anxiously scan the sky. "I can, however, easily get us to the nest of the pegasi. We can ask them for help." She reached out and took both my hands and stared very directly into my eyes: her own green eyes full of mischief and hidden purpose. "Do you want to travel with me, Thomas O'Malley?" she asked.

"Yes," I said nervously, unsure because she seemed to be giving those words a significance I didn't understand. "I need you to..." We were at the pegasi nest.

"Good," she said. "Just as long as you know that you need me." I shook my head in confusion. Sometimes this whole girl thing could get very confusing - at least it did with Myfanwy.

The two pegasi were standing very still. They were ignoring us but paying close attention to something off in the mountains. I followed their gaze and saw the white dragon circling high in the sky. It was a thing of great beauty with its wings shining silver in the morning sun. It was clearly searching for us or for our bodies.

I walked over to the black pegasus. As I did so, Myfanwy whispered loudly; "in your pocket". I reached into my coat pocket and there found a carrot. Magic girlfriends are handy for things like that. I held out the carrot as I got to the pegasus. He looked at me, looked at the carrot and then looked back at the dragon. Somehow, I knew that this was a question and I nodded in answer. Yes, the dragon was looking for us and it would come after us. There was intelligence in the dark eyes of the horse as it considered the situation. Then it nodded once and took the carrot. Next it spread its wings and knelt to make it easier for me to mount. As soon as I had scrambled onto its back, it leapt into the sky with Myfanwy following on the white horse not far behind.

The dragon spotted us almost immediately and flew towards us like an arrow. It was much faster than the pegasi and it quickly caught up with us. There then followed a kind of deadly aerial ballet. The dragon was faster than the pegasi but it was far less agile. As the dragon got close to either horse they would swerve away in a tight turn that the dragon couldn't match, or dive under, or soar above or sometimes even, terrifyingly, loop over the dragon, so that the dragon was left searching and frustrated. At times they would fly into the cloud and lose it that way. The pegasi certainly proved more than a match for the dragon in the air. I was reminded of two small birds harrying a larger bird away from their nest. All the time we were moving closer to the coast.

This went on for a long time and the day became a blur of dizzying aerial manoeuvres and great vistas of the forests of Annwn. The pegasi were expert at riding the currents of the wind and I had the feeling that this flight tired the dragon more than the pegasi. There were longer and longer periods where the pegasi could fly straight and true while the dragon gathered its strength for another attack.

It was about mid-afternoon when my tired mind registered that the two pegasi were flying side by side and coming closer to the ground. They were clearly on what pilots call final approach and preparing to land. I sat up and started to pay attention again. We were approaching the field in front of Myfanwy's family house and the dragon was closing rapidly from some distance behind.

The two pegasi landed at a gallop and came to a halt in front of the entrance to the house. As soon as we slid off their backs they were gone, climbing swiftly into the sky. The dragon ignored them and continued to fly towards us; setting what could only be described as an attack run.

Both Myfanwy and I bolted for the great arched entrance to the house. As soon as we were inside, Myfanwy turned and spread her arms wide.

"Gwarchodwch y tŷ!" (Guard the house!) she yelled. Massive steel doors that I didn't know existed slammed shut across the entrance, with huge bolts locking them in place. All around the house I could hear steel shutters closing over all the crazy windows in this crazy house until it was once again a fortress of stone and steel. Then the dragon did something at the end of its attack run that it had not done before: it breathed fire. The great steel doors shook and glowed red hot at the assault of the dragon fire – but they held. There was a pause, presumably as the dragon circled round, but it wasn't long before the dragon attacked again. Once again the doors glowed red hot and Myfanwy held up her hands in a warding gesture – reinforcing them with magic. They held. Then it all went quiet and stayed quiet. The dragon had gone.

Chapter 17
Back to London

Myfanwy turned to me and said, "This house was built to defend against dragons but I don't think we could hold out against a concerted attack."

A bare moment after this, Gwyneth came running out of the central house passage and gripped Myfanwy in a great hug. It was almost a repeat of our arrival except that now there were tears instead of cries of joy,

"Myfwy! Myfwy! I could feel that thing coming after you," she sobbed. "Then you closed the house and I knew you were safe."

Myfanwy stroked Gwen's hair. "It's okay Gwen," she said. "The dragon's gone now."

"I know," Gwen replied, disengaging herself. "I made it feel too tired to stay." We both looked at her puzzled.

"Well," she explained, "I tried to do what I could to protect you, so I reached out to its mind..." She paused, looking thoughtful. "Only it doesn't really have a mind. It's intelligent but it's all passion, anger and pent up power. It was also tired. So I tried to intensify those feelings of tiredness and remind it of how far away the mountains were and of how late in the day it was. It must have worked because it flew away." We both looked at her in amazement. She just looked like a young, simple girl, vulnerable and in need of protection and yet...

"Gwen, you drove off a dragon attack!" I exclaimed. She smiled broadly and suddenly as if just realising for the first time what she had done.

"Yes, I guess I did. That was good wasn't it?"

Myfanwy simply hugged her and said, "Oh Gwen, you are amazing. You are just amazing."

As we were speaking, Nain and Helen arrived, I then stood back as the normal family interactions took place, mostly in Welsh. Two other figures also emerged from the house. They were an unlikely pairing. One was Friar Daffyd in his Franciscan habit and the other was Declan of the Irish Tuatha de Dannan. Declan was the De Dannan's ambassador to Annwn. He was resplendent in his brightly coloured cloak, fastened with a large gold brooch, and an immaculately white tunic. I walked over to them.

"Now Tom," Declan said. "Why is it that I'm not surprised to see you here as the house is attacked by dragons?" He looked across at the group of mother, daughters and Nain. "I'll say this for the House of Pwyll, a visit here is never dull. Potentially hazardous? Oh yes, most certainly - but never dull."

"Hi Declan," I said. "What brings you to Annwn?"

"Oh, I just needed to get an update on the situation in the Council of Nobles from Nain. The High King is concerned that the Council is becoming dysfunctional and that Annwn is being left essentially ungoverned. Personally Tom, I am pleased to see you but your presence does reinforce the point…"

"And yet there are more important matters in play," Friar Daffyd said softly. I could only agree. "I must leave you now," he said. "I need to say evening prayer and give thanks for your safety. I will see you at dinner."

After a while Myfanwy released the house and all the steel shutters vanished back to wherever they were before. The massive steel doors also unbolted themselves, opened and vanished. The field outside the house had been blasted black by dragon fire and around the edges, here and there, a few small fires were still burning. Fortunately, the sheep and cattle had been moved to their winter shelter some time ago and were safe. It had been threatening to rain all day and as we were looking, the first drops of rain fell. Soon it was raining heavily. The grass would grow back.

Dinner that night was an informal affair. We sat in the kitchen, kept warm by the heat of the wood fired stove, and listened to the rain beat against the windows. Nain had disappeared on business of her own and Helen prepared a thick lamb stew and warmed up some crusty bread. It was only after Nain arrived back, in time for mugs of tea, that Myfanwy and I told a suitably edited version of our story. Helen was distressed and angry by the danger her daughter had been exposed to and she glared at Nain, clearly blaming her and the Council of Nobles.

When we came to the fake staff and our escape from the dragons she exclaimed, "So you went through all of this - and for nothing!"

"No," I said quietly. "Not at all. We now know what Cadell is doing and that he's using Merlin's staff to do it. Knowing this, we're closer to stopping him."

"There is this also," said Friar Daffyd, who had been very quiet since the dragon attack. "You put those dragons to sleep in the mountains. This will have an effect. I think that as long as their mythological manifestations sleep in Annwn, their mundane manifestations will be quiet in the outside world. You will have put a major delay into Cadell's plans and may well have saved many lives." Nain took no notice of Helen's outrage, instead giving her own report on how the events had been perceived in Annwn.

"Your flight with the dragon was widely observed," she said. "As was the attack on the house. Luckily, no one seems to have been able to identify the character in the black cloak and they have all assumed that it was Carwyn. The story seems to be that the children of Owain ap Rhys have decided to take on the dragons before they attack Annwn and that they didn't ask the Council of Nobles for permission." She gave a wry smile. "There's enough truth in that to leave it stand but it is a nightmare for some members of the Council. I think they would prefer Tom." Through all of this Declan was sitting relaxed and at ease, sipping his tea. Of course Declan was always relaxed and at ease, even though, with his archaic finery, he looked quite out of place in the simple kitchen setting. When he spoke it was clearly out of simple curiosity.

"What I don't understand," he said, "is why you were going after Merlin's staff. Why not seek out Merlin himself?" I could have screamed in frustration and in a very exasperated voice I told him of how we had tried and how all our leads turned out to be dead ends. He raised an eyebrow only when I got to Drumelzier and Merlin Caledonensis.

"Oh, I know him," he said. "At least I met him once I think; when I was very, very young."

Nain nodded. "So he was one of you," she said. "We thought he might be. We could never discover his origins."

Declan nodded casually. "Yes, he was one of us although…" Here he paused, considering his next words carefully. "He wasn't the sharpest sword in the armoury if you understand my meaning. He was a gentle soul and he had the basics of the power but he never really developed any talent, except perhaps a great empathy with other living things: hardly useful. He couldn't ride, wouldn't hunt and literally couldn't throw a spear or use a sword to save his life. We sent him to study under Myrddin Emrys or Merlin Ambrosius as the Romans knew him. He came back when the political situation in Britain became too unstable. I was told that he hadn't learnt much. You must remember that this all happened when I was very, very young." I looked at Declan's ageless face and considered that this happened over fifteen hundred years ago. A shiver went down my spine.

"How did he end up getting murdered three times in Drumelzier?" I asked.

Declan shrugged and answered in a soft, thoughtful voice. "Well, he was one of the Tuatha de Dannan so he would have been hard to kill, but he also wasn't very talented, so it wouldn't have been impossible. Also, as I said, he was one of those souls who feel great empathy for others. He wouldn't fight and he wouldn't even eat meat: didn't fit in to Tyr na nOg at all. I think that maybe he didn't defend himself when they came to kill him."

"Yes, but why did he go back to Britain and why was he in Drumelzier at all?" I asked. Declan seemed to be looking deep into the mug that held his tea.

"Those are very good questions," he said at last, "and I think that now may be a very good time to find the answers."

At that point, Friar Daffyd got up and bowed deeply to Helen. "Thank you very much for your hospitality my lady, but it's time and past time for me to return to the hermitage. I have much to think and pray about. Do not trouble yourself to get up, I know the way." As he left the room I also excused myself from the table and got up to follow him. I caught up with him in the passage and we talked as we walked towards the entrance.

"Friar Daffyd," I asked, "Could I ask you some questions about your congregation?"

"Certainly Tom," he answered. "What is it you wish to know?"

"A lot of things really," I said. "Like…are any of your congregation able to speak and what about their magical ability? Do they have any?"

"Some of them can speak, yes. Many more, of course, do not. Just the same with magic. The magic will sometimes express itself in them in strange and powerful ways: ways they often can't control."

"Are they Christians?" I asked urgently. "Do you baptise them?" He looked at me curiously. "I mean, do they have names?"

"Yes, I baptise them," he replied, "If they show me some sign that they want me to. I use a conditional formula; 'If thou art human then I baptise thee…' And of course they have names. I name each one of them after one of the saints. Why are you suddenly so curious about my congregation? I would have thought you would have had other things on your mind."

I didn't want to tell him my real reasons; they were too vague and uncertain. So I said,

"I'm just trying to understand Annwn society and its processes. Do you always get the same crowd or do some go missing?" Friar Daffyd looked down at the floor. When he looked up again, his face was both deeply sad and quietly angry.

"Mostly they come back. They come because they find something that goes to the very core of their humanity. Their humanity! A humanity so often denied. Yet they do sometimes go missing. If the hunters find any of them in the forest they kill them without question or hesitation. So yes, they go missing. In fact I am currently very concerned about one of my congregation. He is special: intelligent and gentle. He hasn't been coming for a while now." There was a sharp intake of breath behind us and we turned to see Myfanwy standing there. She was clearly angry.

"Why?" she asked. "Why not ask about the good and beautiful things in Annwn? Why do you keep coming back to this? Why can't you leave it alone?"

"Myf, I'm just trying…"

"No! There's no reason, is there? You're just doing this to annoy me!"

"Don't be silly…"

"It's just plain mean: to keep bringing this up; to keep throwing this in my face." I reached out to her. "Don't touch me!" she said and ran past us down the passage.

"Myf!" I called after her. "That's not fair. I didn't even know you were there!" I turned to the friar, pleading for support, but by then she was gone.

Friar Daffyd smiled and held out his hands in a gesture of helplessness, "I'm a Franciscan hermit Tom; have been since my youth. I'm afraid I can't give you much advice about courting a young lady." He turned and continued to walk towards the entrance. "Instead, walk with me and I'll tell you about something I do know. I'll tell you about St. Francis. Francis was a great lover of beauty. He saw in it a reflection of God. However, this caused him a problem. He was repulsed by lepers. He knew he was called to love all people but the ugliness of the disease horrified him. After much struggle, it was St. Clair, his closest friend in all the world, who led him to see the beauty of the person beyond the ugliness of the disease. Eventually, he was able to love, to tenderly kiss, a dying leper. It was a moment of great liberation." I looked at him puzzled. I couldn't see what this had to do with Myfanwy and me.

He sighed. "All I'm saying is: be patient with our Myfanwy, be gentle. You may not know it but you're asking for a great act of courage from her. It may take time but do not doubt the strength of her spirit." By this time we had reached the main entrance. Outside it was night. The rain clouds had cleared away in front of a strong westerly wind and the sky was on fire with starlight.

"Sorry I wasn't able to offer you any advice," he said smiling. "But I have no experience in romantic matters." Then he stepped into the dark and vanished. When I returned to the kitchen, Nain was the only one still there.

She said, "Pack up your things tonight Tom. We leave straight after breakfast. I have to get you home in time for dinner." I went to my room unsettled. There were a thousand thoughts in my head and it wasn't just the situation with Myfanwy that bothered me.

When I got to the kitchen the next morning, Declan had already left on business of his own. There was a new air of great excitement around the table. The reason soon became clear, both Helen and Gwyneth would be coming with us to London. The exhibition of paintings and photographs made by Helen and my mother during their stay in Australia was opening the following week and Helen had decided to come over and assist mum with the preparations. So, after a quick breakfast of ham and eggs, we climbed into the back of Nain's gypsy caravan. Before we left, Myfanwy again closed all the shutters and doors around the house again, leaving an impenetrable ring of stone and steel. Then she joined us in the caravan and Nain headed off. All the windows and doors in the caravan were closed as well, so that my presence could not be detected.

It was an awkward trip home, at least for me. Helen and Gwyneth were chatting happily about all the things they would do in London. Myfanwy occasionally joined in but generally she was quiet. She sat next to me on the bed, stiff and upright. Helen and Gwyneth eventually ran out of conversation as we were crossing the sea and they dozed off with their heads on the table. I leaned over and whispered in Myfanwy's ear.

"Myf, I had good reasons for asking about the congregation. It wasn't directed at you. I didn't even know you were there."

Myfanwy gave a slight nod of her head. "I know I may have over reacted," she whispered back. "I just don't want to talk about it, okay?" I nodded. I could live with that. Gwyneth opened one eye. She looked at us and had a fit of giggles.

"You are both so funny," was all she would say.

It was early evening when we arrived back at my house in London. Mum was very surprised when Helen and Gwyneth also climbed out of the back of the caravan. She rushed over and hugged Helen.

"Hello Helen. It's so good to see you. This is a wonderful surprise. Are you staying for the exhibition?"

"Thank you, my dear," Helen said. "Yes, we will be staying in Cadfan's house." Professor Rhys owned a house next door to ours. "I didn't think it would be fair to leave all the work to you again."

Mum turned to me and said, "You young man, have been in Annwn and you didn't tell me you were going. I would have liked to have come." I shrugged. The thought of Mum being in a house attacked by a dragon was not a happy one. That night we had pizza for dinner, much to the delight of Gwyneth who had had pizza for the first time during her stay in Australia Then we watched TV, another rare experience for those from Annwn.

That night, after our guests had left, Mum asked me, "So, how was your day in Annwn?"

"Good," I said.

"You and Myfanwy seemed a bit quiet tonight, anything wrong?"

"No, not really," I lied.

Chapter 18
A House Break In

The previous exhibition that Mum had held with Helen had been small. Mum had primarily been known as a fashion photographer and Helen hadn't been known at all, at least not in this century. However, it had been a great success and this time their exhibition was being hosted by a major gallery. Last time I had to help with the setting up. This time that was all done by the gallery staff. This meant that we had four days of the break to explore London with Gwen. We went to see the Houses of Parliament and Buckingham Palace. We took a ride on the London Eye and visited the Tower of London. Then I suggested the British Museum and the girls suggested Harrods's. After this a pattern started to emerge. I would suggest a visit to someplace; the girls would decide to go shopping. The only time I won out was when I suggested we watch a parade by one of the mounted guard units. What is it with girls and shopping? Half the time they didn't even buy anything! It did emphasise the bizarre contrast I found myself in. In Annwn I would fight trolls and dragons. In London I would go shopping.

During all this time the earth was quiet: there were no earthquakes or volcanic eruptions. It was a relief to see the newspaper headlines dominated by some footballer's affair with a minor member of the Royal Family. Also, in Gwen's presence Myfanwy started to thaw. There were still issues between us, issues I didn't really understand, but at base we were still friends and really enjoyed each other's company.

The opening night of the exhibition was a big gala affair and I had to get dressed up in a suit and tie. Prof Rhys came to pick us up in his Rolls. When Myfanwy appeared, she had her hair tied back from her face and she was wearing a simple dress of silver grey with a green sash around her waist and a kind of green shawl thing, embroided with silver thread, fastened across her shoulders. It fitted her perfectly and she looked more beautiful than ever. Once again I was left speechless and awkward. I didn't know how she could still do this to me. Helen came up beside me.

"There are some forms of magic you are not immune to, Tom." She said. "My daughter is magical, don't you agree?" I could only nod in agreement. Nain and I were the last to get in the car. Just before we did, I noticed something in the park. It was as if one of the boulders they used in the landscaping had come to life. It moved across the lawn towards our house, then it rose up; tall and threatening. This only lasted a moment before it disappeared into the bushes. There was, however, no doubt. This was the creature we had been threatened by in the Savernake Forest. I looked across at Nain. She was staring intently into the park.

"Yes boy, I saw it," She said, her eyes never shifting their focus. "I just don't recognise it. It was clearly some kind of mythical creature, but I don't know the mythology it comes from or what it's doing in London. That's the problem with having an empire. You import mythologies from all over the world. All fine in stories but a worry when they start to take on substance." It was a good analysis but it turned out to be wrong. As I have said before, anyone can make a mistake.

The opening reception was pretty much as you would expect it to be. There were a lot of dressed up people, soft music and drinks being handed out by silent waiters. There were also some formal speeches about the complimentary visions of photography and paint. One of these was given by a fat and florid little man who was the art critic for one of the major papers. Afterwards, he came over and dragged me away from Myfanwy to discuss my mother's art. He kept asking me what I wanted to do when I finished school and saying how he hoped I had inherited my mother's talent. When I told him I was more interested in Science, he seemed shocked.

"But your mother is an artist!" he exclaimed.

"Yes," I replied, "but my father's a petroleum production engineer." Just then a woman in a long red dress came up to speak to him and I was able to make my excuses and escape. As I left, I overheard him whisper,

"What a pity, it seems the apple has fallen from the wrong tree."

I found Myfanwy over in front of one of her mother's paintings. It showed Angle River entering a stormy sea, with high cliffs in the background and a sky full of storm clouds. She was talking to a thin, young man dressed in black, with very skinny jeans and pointed, patent leather shoes. At least, she was listening while he talked. He kept putting his hand on her shoulder as he pointed to features in the painting. Each time he did, I could see Myfanwy stiffen and step back.

I found one of the waiters and took two glasses from his tray. Then I walked over to Myfanwy. As I approached, I could hear him saying, "…Yes, I suppose it could be taken as a metaphor for social and environmental conflict but I feel it is too tied to the outdated archetype of beauty to speak in a modern context."

I walked up and said, "Here's your drink Myfanwy." She gave me a big, bright and most relieved smile.

"Thank You Tom," she said. She turned to the guy in black. "Tremaine…It was Tremaine wasn't it?..This is my boyfriend, Tom. Tom, this is Tremaine." I stuck out my hand and said in the broadest Australian accent I could manage,

"G'day Mate. 'ow ye goin?" He took my hand as if it were coated with poison.

"How do you do," he said. "Um…Excuse me." Then he wandered off.

"Thanks for coming to rescue me," Myfanwy said.

"No problem, that's what I do." I said in a casual voice.

She looked at me with a sly smile. "You were jealous, weren't you?" She said.

I replied in my most offended voice. "No, of course not! I just didn't like the way that creep kept touching you."

She smiled warmly and took my hand. "There was no need," she said. She looked across to where Tremaine had gone and shuddered. "Believe me, there was no need at all."

"At least you can still introduce me as your boyfriend," I said.

She looked at me with a pitying expression. "Tom," she said. "You are my best friend and you are a boy. So of course I can call you my boyfriend. Anything more is up to you." This just left me confused but I stayed close to Myfanwy for the rest of the night.

We got home to our place around midnight and could immediately see that something awful had happened. The front door was smashed and lying on the steps, even the door frame was broken, and half of the heavy dining room table was protruding through the front window. Mum gave a little gasp and immediately started to call the police. I made to go inside but Nain stopped me.

"Leave it, Tom," she said. "There's nothing to be gained by you going in there. Leave it to the police." She turned to Professor Rhys and said, "Cadfan, get the girls to safety. I will stay with Elizabeth." Professor Rhys nodded and got into the car to drive off. Myfanwy protested but I shook my head and gestured for her to go.

It didn't take long for the police to arrive and then for more police to arrive. After they had checked that the house was empty, we were asked to see what had been stolen; nothing had. The heavy dining room table had been thrown through the front window, the TV had been thrown across the room and had shattered, the solid kitchen table had been broken to matchwood, the refrigerator had been thrown through the rear window and into the back garden, every chair in the place was upended or broken. Anything that could be wrecked was wrecked, but nothing was stolen. Even the stairs were broken, smashed as if someone had used a sledge hammer on them. This made it hard to check the upstairs rooms but when we did we found they were untouched. The police concluded that some sort of message was being sent and the gang involved simply couldn't be bothered climbing the stairs. They could do all they needed to do down stairs I had another explanation, one that I didn't share with the police. It seemed likely to me that whatever did this was simply too heavy and too large to climb the stairs - and so it smashed them instead

It was well after two am when the police finally left. Mum stood in the middle of the dining room, looked at the mess around her, and started to cry. At first I didn't know what to do, but then I had a sudden inspiration and I called my dad. Where he was it was the middle of the day. I didn't call him that often so he immediately knew that something was wrong. I explained to him what had happened and he asked to speak to Mum. I left them to talk and went into the lounge room. There Nain and I started to clean up as much as we could, right the furniture and clear up the broken fragments of just about everything else. Eventually Mum came into the lounge. She seemed calmer but when she saw the mess she just shook her head.

"What are we going to do?" she asked. "This place isn't liveable anymore."

"You will stay in Cadfan's house next door," Nain said firmly. She took mum by the arm. "Come on dear, let's go into the kitchen and see how much of your crockery we can rescue." After they left, I continued to do what I could to establish some sort of order in the room.

I had not been at this long when I heard a polite knock at what was left of the front door and call of, "Excuse me Tom, but we really need to talk to you." I recognised the voice. I went out to find Dr. Jones and Sergeant Fisher as well as Director Smith standing there. I noticed two other DIAP agents taking guard at our front gate. I invited them in. Mum came out of the kitchen with Nain behind her and was surprised to find a crowd of strange men barging into her ruined hallway. Director Smith came forward to greet Mum.

"Hello Mrs. O'Malley, I'm Director Smith, Director of…well… never mind. I'm sorry for the intrusion but we really need to speak to you about this incident." Mum gestured rather uncertainly to the lounge room. The director bowed his thanks and went in. Dr Jones followed.

"Nice to meet you again Mrs O'Malley," he said as he passed. Sergeant Fisher would have gone in without saying anything but Mum stopped him.

"I know you," she said. "You were that British policeman in Australia."

"Yes ma'am, I was," he said quietly as he walked in.

The director and Dr. Jones sat on the couch. Sergeant Fisher remained standing near the fireplace while Mum and I sat on the chairs with Nain standing behind us. The Director looked grave.

"It's good to see you back, Director," I said.

"Thank you, Tom. I have almost fully recovered. I wish this could be a social call but we obviously have a problem. The police can't make sense of this as a normal crime. The best they can come up with is that it was a warning intended for an organised crime boss that somehow went to the wrong address. Given your connections to a certain community, I think that unlikely. These are dangerous times, Tom. We need to know what is going on." I spread my hands out helplessly, trying to express all my fear and frustration.

"I wish I knew," I said.

Dr Jones leaned forward, "The other theory the police have is that it is connected to your earlier abduction and this is another attempt to put pressure on Professor Rhys. Is this possible?"

I shrugged. "I guess so," I said.

"In that case Tom, we need to know the whereabouts of Professor Rhys and his family."

I shook my head. "They are safe," was all I would say.

"Tom, we know the family owns a castle on the Norfolk coast..."

"Oh, Aelred Abbey," my Mum interrupted. "Yes, it's a lovely place. We stayed there for the weekend once."

Dr. Jones looked at her surprised. "Then you are indeed lucky Mrs O'Malley. Whenever we try to send operatives to check it out they always seem to get lost and find themselves wandering in Wales or Scotland or somewhere."

"Perhaps if your men had asked, rather than sneaking around like criminals," Nain said. "They could also have entered as guests." All the DIAP people looked at her in surprise. The English still have a remarkable ability to ignore anyone they consider a servant and Nain, even in her best floral dress, looked very much like a servant.

"Touché madam," the Director said with a slight bow of his head. Then he turned back to me. "Is it possible that the criminal gang who did this could find a way in?"

"I don't think so," I said. "From what Myfanwy has told me, it's very well defended. You could attack it with an army and still not get in."

"What about this psycho magic user, Cadell?" the Director asked. "Could he get in?" I shook my head.

"I don't think even Cadell could breach the defences of Aelred Abbey," I said. "But if he had, you would already know about it. The battle would have destroyed half of Norfolk." This news did not make either the Director or Dr. Jones look any happier. Just then there was a yell from one of the agents outside the house.

"Contact! Contact in the park!" Sergeant Fisher left the room with amazing speed and then everything went quiet. Sergeant Fisher returned a few minutes later and spoke quietly to the Director.

"I can't figure out where it went, sir, and I don't know what it was, but it was big. It was also weird enough to badly spook the men and none of my men are easily spooked." The director nodded.

"We continue as planned," he said. "Good night Mrs O'Malley. I'm sorry to be so abrupt but, as I said before, these are dangerous times." After they had left, Mum remained sitting in her chair, looking a little stunned.

"Well, that was... disturbing," she said. She looked at me and I could see that she had been crying. "I know you don't always tell me everything you do and that what you do is probably important, but please be careful

Thomas. There are other people who love you too, you know. You also need to think of them."

The next day it was raining and we had to get emergency builders in to secure the front door and the windows. We had slept in Professor Rhys' house, I had overslept. So it was mid-morning when I looked out on the park from the Professor's front lounge. The homeless guy, Michael, was there again, with the same faded jeans and old army coat. He was sitting on the same garden seat in the falling rain, staring fixedly at our house.

I was kept busy till lunch time moving clothes and personal effects from our ruined house to our rooms in the Professor's place. After lunch I found Nain in the front room, studying the homeless guy who was still sitting out in the rain.

"He's the one I told you about," I said. "Always on the same bench, always looking at our house." We stood and watched him for a while. He didn't move. "He must be cold," I said. "I think I'll go and offer him some lunch. "

"Good," Nain said. "Engage with him as often as you can. There is something here I don't understand, something that makes me nervous." I took a mug of the pumpkin soup and a warm bread bun that Nan had prepared for lunch and brought them over to him in the park.

"Salve," I said. "Accipite et manducate." (Take and eat – my Latin was still stilted).

"Thank you," he said, taking the soup and bread eagerly but with a kind of reverence.

"So, you've learned to speak English," I observed.

"A little," he said. He didn't add anything further so we sat in silence for a while as he ate the food, after a while I asked, "Did you see what happened to our house last night?" He nodded.

"Can you tell the police anything about it?" He shook his head. Then he handed back the empty mug.

"Fugite!" he said urgently. He was staring at me with an almost insane intensity. "Fly! Fly from this place. Fly to somewhere he cannot find you." Then he got up and walked swiftly away.

Chapter 19
Conflict and Reconciliation

It was soon enough that school started again and I got up early to meet Myfanwy at the Aelred Abbey gate near the school. When Myfanwy found me waiting for her, she hugged me and held me tight for a long moment.

"I am so glad to see you. I was worried," she said as she released me. "How is your mother?"

"Busy," I said as we turned to walk down the street. "She's been talking to the insurance company people at the same time as trying to run the exhibition. She's coping but I think she wishes my dad were here. What about Gwen and your mum?"

"Given the dragon attack, it was decided that they would be safer at Aelred Abbey. Uncle Cadfan and some of the local people are holding the fort at the house. It's good to be living with my mum." I nodded and we held hands until we got to the big bus interchange, which was crowded with students. School was much as it always was. An assembly was followed by homeroom and homeroom by English. English and homeroom were the only periods that Myfanwy and I now had in common. In English we were still considering the modern poets and we returned to the poem 'The Second Coming' by William Butler Yeats. Again I was struck by the lines:

"And what rough beast, its hour come round at last,

Slouches towards Bethlehem to be born?"

I knew the rough beast, I had seen it in the Park and in Savernake Forest, but where was Bethlehem for this creature, when was its hour and what would happen when it was born?

Still, the Earth was quiet and the days fell into a pattern. I did not always get up early enough to greet Myfanwy in the morning but I did walk her home each night and often visit Helen and Gwen at the Abbey. Even though we enjoyed being with each other again, the tension of unresolved questions remained. After a week or so, Mum and I were able to move back into our own house. The repairs was still under way but it was liveable again. Mum and Helen's exhibition had again been a great success and Mum, who was growing tired of the high stress world of fashion photography, was thinking that she might make a career as a landscape photographer, especially considering how dangerous London was proving to be. She would have long phone calls with Dad late at night. The fact that this would probably mean a return to Australia and I didn't know how to raise the possibility with Myfanwy, only added to the stress in our relationship. Things came to a head one lunchtime, when Gabriella started to discuss a project she was doing on the fall of the Roman Empire.

"Did you know that if a baby looked sickly or week, the Romans would just leave it out in the fields to die?" The rest of the table just kept on eating lunch. It was clear that everybody already knew that and nobody was particularly interested. "Well, the Christians put a stop to that because they thought it was tantamount to murder, and in this book I read, this guy thinks that this weakened the Roman race and led to the fall of the

Empire. So that, by stopping something they thought was evil, they caused the death of a people." This was greeted with general derision. Everyone knew only too well where ideas about racial strength and purity could lead.

I kept quiet through most of this but eventually Rachael asked. "What do you think Tom?"

"I think his reasoning sucks," I said. "Firstly, there was never really any such thing as 'the Roman Race'. Rome was always very cosmopolitan. Secondly, what's wrong is wrong. We can never know all possible outcomes, but a child has a right to protection from its parents. Any society whose survival depends on the death of its children deserves to die." It was only when Myfanwy got up suddenly from the table and walked away that I realised how she might interpret what I had said.

"Myfanwy," I called after her. "I didn't mean it that way!" She walked out of the dining room without turning around. Rachael watched her intently as she left.

"What is it with you two lately?" she asked. "Ever since you came back from the break, you have been tiptoeing around each other. You've been so careful with each other it's like you're each afraid that the other will explode."

I shrugged. "We just have a difference of opinion, that's all," I said.

"Ah! Well that's how it starts," she said knowingly. I looked at her quizzically.

"At first you think the other person is perfect," she explained. "Then you start to notice little things that annoy you. Eventually you have a really big argument and all those minor problems become major. Then you come to the denial stage, when the relationship has no future but neither party wants to be the one to call it off."

"Have you been reading another one of those pop psychology books over the break?" Wilson interjected sarcastically, "because that worked out so well last time." This was the first time I had heard him express bitterness about the ending of his relationship with Rachael. Rachael ignored him and looked directly at me.

"Don't think of this as an ending Tom. Think of it as a new beginning, as an opening up of new possibilities."

"You mean like Susan Cavendish," I suggested.

"Her, yes, but there would be others if only you would look."

I shook my head. "No Rachael," I said firmly. "Firstly, Myfanwy and I are people, not puppets of psycho/social theory. As I said, not all outcomes are known. Secondly, I choose to be with Myfanwy in spite of our differences. It is my choice just as it is hers." Rachael gave a self-satisfied smile.

"In time you will change your mind," she said. "It's only natural. You're too young to form a stable lasting relationship." I just rolled my eyes in disbelief. Wilson got up from the table.

"Come on Tom," he said. "We'll be late for physics and I want to ask Mr. Robertson about gravity waves." This was clearly a pretext to leave. Wilson already knew far more about gravity waves than Mr. Robertson ever would.

As we walked away I heard Gabriella laugh and whisper to Rachael, "There would be others if only you would look!? Why not be obvious." She was clearly being sarcastic but I didn't understand the subject of her sarcasm.

That evening, Myfanwy left school early, while I was still in Chemistry and I caught the bus home. There was an accident somewhere and the bus was delayed for over an hour in traffic. As a result, I missed multiple connections and it was dark when I got to the park in front of my home. I decided not to cut across the park, as I normally did, but to walk around it. I was thinking about Myfanwy and not really concentrating on where I was going when the creature landed like a falling boulder on the footpath in front of me. Out of instinct I jumped back and a massive, rock-like fist missed me by millimetres. I turned and ran, not backwards but sideways, across the street. Behind me a fist slammed into the pavement, sending fragments of concrete flying. I ran down the footpath as fast as I could but there was no further sound of pursuit. I paused when I got to the front door of my house and turned to see if the creature was following. It had vanished. I walked up the steps and let myself in, locking the door behind me. It could easily have killed me but it didn't. It could have chased me but it didn't. Once again I felt that I was like a mouse being played with by a cat. Only this time I didn't have any clever plan to escape the game and I knew that home could offer no security.

The next morning I got up early to greet Myfanwy at the gate near the school. However, as soon as she opened the gate and saw me, she closed the gate again and, instead of a path through the birch wood, I was left staring at a blank wall. I wasn't going to give up that easily. I just stayed there facing the wall. I was prepared to stay there all day if necessary. As it turned out, it wasn't necessary. About ten minutes later the gate opened again, only it wasn't Myfanwy who opened it. It was Gwen.

"Oh, hello Gwen," I said in surprise. "I wasn't expecting you."

"Hello Tom," she said brightly. "Did you think that Myf was the only one who could open the gate? She's up in her bedroom by the way. She's very upset, has been all night. I think you two need to talk." She gestured for me to step through the gate.

"Thanks," I said. "I want to talk to her. I'm just not sure she'll listen."

"She'll listen to you," Gwen said in a softer voice. "She might not admit it but she'll listen. You'd better hurry or you'll end up really late for school." I dropped my school bag and ran down through the wood and across the causeway. The main doors opened for me and I ran up the stairs two at a time.

However, when I got to the first landing there was an extra door; a door that would lead into the ruined monastery. I paused. I was anxious to explain myself to Myfanwy but I also knew that this was a rare invitation that shouldn't be passed up. I sighed and turned aside to open the door. Once again, I found myself in the familiar, long, high-ceilinged room. It was empty, so I went and sat on the wooden bench to wait. It wasn't long before the familiar figure of Brother Theophane rushed into the room.

"I am sorry to keep thee waiting, Sir Thomas, but the Abbot was a bit long winded at Chapter this morning." He sat down next to me and smiled. "Now, how may I help thee?"

I explained to him about Friar Daffyd's congregation, about the practice of exposing the newborn 'mistakes' to die and about Myfanwy's reaction to it all. He shook his head in sadness and said,

"'Tis a foul practice indeed but not unknown. There are worse things done. The holy friar is doing good and noble work but 'tis oft times difficult for those who belong to a community to see evil that is mayhap endorsed by long custom. I believe 'twas a mistake to confront thy lady in this way." I nodded ruefully and went on to explain the stress that this had caused in the relationship between Myfanwy and me. I also explained how I had made things worse by speaking carelessly at lunch. Brother Theophane didn't speak. He just sat looking at me with a slight smile on his face, waiting for me to go on. Eventually I was able to say what really bothered me; to ask what I really needed to know.

"But Brother," I said pleadingly. "What's wrong is wrong, isn't it? I don't understand how I can support Myfanwy, how I can stop offending her, and yet still tell the truth. I can't pretend that what's wrong is right just to be nice. I just can't."

"Nor would I ask that of thee," he replied. "Thy honour would not allow it, or at least it should not. Speak the truth indeed but speak it from the heart of thy love. Indeed, it is only ever in love that the truth can be spoken. 'Tis not for thee to judge another soul struggling to live in the right: nor even a people. Remember that in this fallen world, no society is truly ordered wholly to the good. Look into thy own heart also and know that thine own soul is only saved by grace. Thy righteousness is not thine own." I looked at him, still not understanding what to do. He smiled gently.

"Explain thee first thy love and thy lady mayst then come to hear thy truth. Be patient and have compassion for the struggle of her heart. In this thou mayst even learn the struggle of thine own heart. Now go, she is waiting for thee." I stood and bowed to the elderly monk and went to take my leave. Just as I got to the door, he called out to me.

"Oh, Sir Thomas. About the other matter, do not fear. The force arrayed against thee is strong indeed but there is, all unseen and unknown, a yet greater force to help thee. All will be well." I bowed again and went to face Myfanwy.

Myfanwy's room was on the top floor of the castle; on the eastern side with a view along the coast. Her door wasn't locked so I opened it and stood in the doorway. Myfanwy was sitting on her bed with her back to me, looking out the windows. She didn't turn around.

"You shouldn't barge into my room uninvited," she said. "It's just rude."

"Myfanwy, we need to talk," I said. She turned to face me and her anger was clear.

"You can keep your polite, conventional apology," she said. "I know you won't change your mind, so it would just be empty words. Don't cheapen yourself by saying them." I stood in her doorway, almost like a soldier standing at attention.

"No, it's not like that," I said. "Myfanwy, I love Annwn. It's a place of wonder and beauty. How could I not love the culture and people that produced you? If you ever need to fight to preserve Annwn, or its people, or its culture, know that I will be alongside you with all my strength and will. Yesterday I spoke flippantly and carelessly. I didn't think about how those words would sound to you. I hurt you and for that I am truly sorry. Look, this is not an apology driven by convention or politeness. There is no Apple here to say: 'apologise to her anyway'. This is just me, hurting because I hurt you. Please don't turn me away."

"Have you changed your mind about the other thing then?" she asked cautiously.

I shook my head. "No," I said. "What's wrong is wrong and I can't deny that. I still believe exposing the 'mistakes', as you call them, to die is evil and I will always oppose it but I oppose it from a place of love – of wanting Annwn to be perfect. Also, I'm not going to set myself up as judge and jury. I'm in no position to do that." She looked at me thoughtfully for a while, then she gave me her little half smile.

"If you had said anything else, I would have known you were lying," she said. "I'm not going to try and change you Tom. I don't really want to. Apology accepted – you can come in if you like." I came and sat on the bed next to her.

"Tom, what are we going to do?" she asked. "I know you want to go back to Australia and I understand that, but Annwn is such a long way from Angle Creek and they're such very different places. Yet Annwn is the only place where I can relax and be myself, where I don't have to always watch how I use my talent, where I don't have to be forever careful. Also, they need me. Annwn is slowly dying. They need me to be there." Listening to the hopelessness in her voice I finally understood the root cause of the tension between us: she was afraid I would make her choose between Annwn and me. She laid her head on my shoulder and we sat in silence for a while, looking out the long, narrow windows. I knew that this was not a time to keep secrets.

"Myf," I said softly. "My Mum is thinking of developing her career as a landscape photographer. If she does, she'll almost certainly move back to Australia." Myfanwy sighed deeply. Clearly, she was not surprised by this news.

"Tom, what are we going to do?" she asked again. I put my arm around her and held her to me.

"I don't know," I said honestly. "But distance isn't everything and we can't see the future. I think something'll turn up. We just have to have faith. One thing I do know, I will never ask you to abandon Annwn. I just won't do it." She lifted her face towards mine...

"Ahem," said a voice from the doorway. We both turned to see Gwyneth standing there holding my bag. "You two do realise that unless you get a move on you're going to be very, very late for school."

One advantage of having a magical girlfriend is that when you need to get somewhere in a hurry, they can get you there very quickly. However, even using the gate and teleporting, we were still late. We arrived in the middle of Mrs Brown's homeroom period and she was not happy. Most of the girls in the class had a great time, however, gossiping and laughing about what we might have been doing together. Rachael didn't look up from her desk.

I guess it was because she was annoyed that we had been late that she picked on us in English class. The class was meant to have familiarised themselves with some of the poems of William Butler Yeats and Mrs Brown decided to test this by calling Myfanwy out the front of the class to read her favourite poem and give a brief breakdown of its meaning. Myfanwy, of course, was one of the few students who actually did know the poems and could do this with a fair amount of ease and grace. She choose the poem 'Aedh Wishes for the Cloths of Heaven' and when she got to the last two lines, she looked directly at me.

"…I have spread my dreams beneath your feet
Tread softly because you tread on my dreams.

I choose this poem mostly because of its beautiful imagery," she said. "It is a love poem and it talks about how loves means that you open yourself up and give yourself to another person. To love is to make yourself vulnerable. The romantic poets all talked about the experience of love. This goes deeper. This talks about the cost of love." All the time she was saying this, she was looking directly at me and this fact wasn't missed by the rest of the class. There was a lot of whispering, especially among the 'in girls' down the back.

"Thank you Miss Ferchwyn. That was very well done," Mrs. Brown said. "Perhaps our other late comer would like to share a poem and his thoughts." I had known this was coming. I didn't know the poems anywhere near as well as Myfanwy but there was one poem that had stood out for me because it spoke to me of Annwn. I decided to use it and I recited it with pretended confidence. The poem was 'The Lake Isle of Innisfree", one of Yeats best known poems. I took a leaf out of Myfanwy's book and looked directly at her as I recited the last few lines.

"...I hear lake water lapping with low sound by the shore

While I stand on the roadway or on the pavements grey

I hear it in the deep heart's core."

I kept looking at her as I talked about the poem. I wanted her to know that this explanation was for her.

"The poem speaks of the beauty of simple things, away from the complications of modern life. It proposes a magical, mystical place where the values of beauty and simplicity can be honoured. This is clearly a dream for the poet but it is important to him. In a way, this magical place is more important and more real than the world of roadways and pavement." Myfanwy smiled a small, shy smile and I knew that she understood. At the back of the class, one of the 'in girls' was sticking her fingers down her throat and making gagging noises. Her friends seemed to think this was very funny but I really didn't care.

That lunchtime, Rachael was in a very bad mood. She didn't say much but scowled at the world in general. When Myfanwy laughed at a joke I made about Mrs. Brown picking on us in English, she said forcefully, "I just don't get you two. One day you aren't speaking to each other and the next you're so cutsey sweet it makes me want to throw up. I wish you'd both just grow up!" Then she got up from the table and walked quickly out of the dining room. Myfanwy and I looked at Gabriella.

"What's up with her?" I asked. Gabriella started to laugh.

"Nothing you'd notice or care about," she said.

I walked home to the gate with Myfanwy that evening. I paused at the gate.

"Myf, the Australian Ballet is performing their version of Swan Lake at Covent Garden next week. Would you like to go with me on Friday? It would show you that not all Australians are no-culture surfers." Myfanwy gave me one of her brightest smiles.

"Thomas O'Malley, are you asking me out on a date?" I nodded silently. "Well it's about time," she said. "Of course I'd love to come and you are a very cultured person. You have a poet's soul, you just don't listen to it very often." She then reached up and kissed me on the cheek and we walked, holding hands, across the causeway to the abbey.

Chapter 20
A Date Gone Badly Wrong

All the next week I kept making arrangements for the big date. I arranged for a taxi to pick us up from my house to take us to a pre-theatre dinner within walking distance of the ballet. At school, our lunch time group soon heard of the upcoming date.

"Well, I'm just glad you're doing something normal for a change," Gabriella said. "You two have been together for ages but I think this is the first time you've ever gone out together."

"Yes," Phil agreed, "but to the ballet? On a first date?"

"Phil, if you suggest a soccer match as a better choice, I'm going to thump you," I said.

Phil pretended to be highly offended. "I was going to suggest a rock concert," he retorted. He then went on to suggest half a dozen bands, none of whose music I liked.

"Let them be," Wilson said as the bell rang. "There are already far too many people concerned with what is normal."

That Friday, Myfanwy and I came straight home from school using the gates as a short cut: gate through to the birch wood forest and then gate back to the street near my house. Myfanwy went next door to the professor's house to change.

After I had changed out of my school uniform, I went next door to collect Myfanwy. She met me in the hall, dressed in a royal blue dress with a short dark blue cape. The dress was tight about her upper body but fell loosely from her waist. She looked stunning. I just stood there looking at her.

She raised her eyebrows and asked, "Aren't we meant to be going somewhere?"

I got hold of myself. "Um…You look… terrific," I said weakly.

She gave me a quirky smile and said, "Thank you, but can we go and eat now?" As I opened the door for her, I saw the others at the back of the hall. Nain was looking like the whole thing was a very bad idea; Helen and Mum were sharing amused smiles and Gwyneth was laughing openly. I had made a goose of myself again.

The taxi was waiting for us, the traffic was relatively light and, after a quick dinner, we got to the theatre well before the start of the ballet. Our seats were high up on one wing but they were good and the ballet and the orchestra were great. It was a perfect night. That is, until we came to leave the theatre.

As we came to the curb, Myfanwy slumped against me. I grabbed her before she fell to the ground but she was already unconscious. I looked around me desperately and cried out for help. No one seemed to hear me and it was then that I felt a prick in my own arm. Everything started to go dark and someone took Myfanwy from me. Ahead of me a car door opened and the last thing I remember was someone pushing me towards it. Then all was black.

I woke up with a head that felt like there was a jack hammer on the inside. I was tied to a chair and my arms were tied tight behind me. When I opened my eyes the bright light sent stabbing pains through my head.

"Good, you are awake. Now we can talk." I couldn't see the speaker clearly because he was sitting behind two very bright lights. I didn't recognise the voice either but it belonged to an adult male with a cultured accent.

"Who are you?" I demanded.

"No, you don't seem to understand," he replied. "The way this will work is that I ask the questions and you answer them. If you don't answer to my satisfaction, I will hurt your little girl friend." Myfanwy! I looked around me desperately. The room I was in was large but it was dark. There were other figures in the room beside the speaker but they stayed back in the shadows and did not speak. I saw Myfanwy lying on a table about three feet to my right. She was unconscious but she was not tied down and she seemed to have been injured.

"Don't worry," the voice said. "She has not been harmed – yet. But I think we'll keep her asleep for a while longer." I tried to stretch the ropes that held me but they were so tight that they were painful. "You'll find that your restraints are very secure. My colleagues were all good boy scouts." This brought muffled laughter from some of the others in the room. "Oh! and the GPS trackers that you were wearing around your necks are now on their way to the South of France aboard a very fast train. A nice young couple are wearing them. I'm afraid all this will look to the police like a young couple running away together. No one will come looking for you."

"Wrong!" I said. "No one will believe that."

"Are you sure?" he replied. "After all, I understand that you have done that before. Anyway, even if they do come looking for you, they will have no way to trace you. Now, can we get down to business." He leaned forward in his seat but I still couldn't see his face. "You have caused a significant delay in my Master's plans. Nothing too problematic of course, the processes he has set in place are now irreversible, but he would like to know how you did it. You will tell me. In particular, you will tell me if you have found Merlin's resting place and if any of your girlfriend's family have found a way to use his power or lore."

I looked at the shadowy figure behind the lights. "No I won't," I said. "But you have just told me something. You have told me that your master doesn't know what is going on, that he has lost control and is worried. You're on the losing side."

"Nonsense!" the figure said, his voice now agitated. "Britain will rise again! The Empire will be re-established. They will all bow and they will be glad to do it. Even your upstart nation will once again offer its mother country due obedience." Who were these guys? That rant bordered on the insane.

"You're mad," I said. "If Cadell has his way, there won't be enough left of the world to forge any sort of empire!"

"Yes, the world will be in ashes," he replied, "but from those ashes will rise a glorious phoenix," Just then Myfanwy started to stir. "Fools! Inject her again!" he demanded. "She must not wake up!"

One of the other figures came forward out of the shadows. He was a young man with a shaven head and wearing some kind of grey uniform. In his hand he was carrying a syringe. As he came close to inject Myfanwy, I braced my feet on the ground and then managed to topple my chair directly into him. We both fell heavily to the floor. Fortunately, I was on top.

He got up quickly and yelled in a thick London accent, "You bastard!" He underlined his displeasure by kicking me in the ribs.

"Never mind him, find the syringe," the man behind the lights said urgently. "She must not wake up!" At that point I could do nothing further to help. I was still tied to the chair and lying on the floor. The young man gave me another kick and then went looking for the syringe.

He bent down in a corner and called out, "I found it!"

There was a loud crash as the door to the room was kicked in. I was expecting a swat team, instead eleven guys dressed in blue and gold tracksuits and carrying hockey sticks rushed into the room. They were, however, clearly all expert in the martial arts and in their hands the hockey sticks were formidable weapons. They were outnumbered but it was quickly obvious that they were more than a match for the guys in the grey uniforms. The one with the syringe was soon unconscious and the bodies of his comrades started to pile up around the room.

"Enough! Put down your weapons!" The guy who had been questioning me stepped from the shadows into the light. He was thin, grey and balding. He was also dressed in what looked like a World War II German SS officer's uniform and was carrying an automatic assault rifle in his hands. "You will put your weapons down or I will shoot the boy and girl. Then I will shoot you." Myfanwy! I was meant to protect her but there was nothing I could do. I looked up at her hopelessly only to find a pair of brilliant green eyes looking back at me. She was awake! The guy in the SS uniform was continuing to give orders. "You will sit along the back wall with your hands on your head and then we will decide what to do with you."

Myfanwy winked at me and sat up. The guy in the SS uniform suddenly found himself holding a hockey stick. He dropped it in surprise and stood looking at it as if it were a poisonous snake. The leader of the tracksuit brigade, on the other hand, found himself holding an automatic assault rifle. His only reaction was to check that it was cocked and loaded and point it at the SS guy.

"No, I don't think so," he said in a French accent. "I think it is you who will put your hands on your head and sit with your backs to the wall. Now!" I knew that voice. It was Captain Pierre Gauthier of the Swiss Guard, special operations unit.

The ropes tying me to the chair undid themselves as Myfanwy hopped off the table and helped me to my feet. We hugged each other tightly and for a long time. Eventually there was a polite cough behind us. We turned around and Myfanwy went over to Pierre and kissed him on the cheek.

"Thank you Captain, I am in your debt," she said.

Pierre smiled and bowed. "No, no," he said. "To rescue a beautiful maiden, the debt is mine." There was some quiet laughter from his men at this comment.

I walked over and held out my hand. "My thanks also Captain," I said as he shook my hand. "But - what are you doing here posing as hockey players?"

Pierre stood very straight with an offended look on his face. "We are not posing," he said. "We are very good hockey players." Then he relaxed and smiled. "Of course, it is far easier for a hockey team to move around England than a foreign military unit. As to why we are here, I would like to say that we are here to look after you but that is not so. There has been an infestation of… What do you call them? Little green creatures: bald head, pointy ears, sharp teeth and very nasty attitude."

"Goblins," Myfanwy said.

"Yes, just so." Pierre agreed. "There has been an infestation of goblins in southern Scotland and we are on our way to sort it out. While we were in London, we thought it would be a good idea to check up on you and the Lady Myfanwy." He bowed to Myfanwy. "It was just fortuitous that one of my men saw you kidnapped and was able to follow you here." He looked with distaste at the prisoners, who were all sitting quietly with their backs against the wall with the exception of those who were lying bleeding or groaning on the floor. "Who are these men and what are we to do with them?"

"I have no idea who they are," I said, "but I do have a good idea of what to do with them. First, I need to call home." I was feeling in my pockets. "My mobile phone seems to be missing but I'll bet he has a phone I can borrow." I pointed to the leader in the SS uniform who was sitting with the rest of the prisoners. Myfanwy gestured and a phone flew out of the top pocket of his jacket. I caught it and smiled at the balding guy.

"Thank you," I said sarcastically. I then called my Mum. At first it was hard to get a word in against the flow of panicky questions but eventually I was able to assure her that we were both alright and still in London. I told her that we were with Captain Gauthier and his men and that Nain could explain who that was. I also suggested that Professor Rhys come around and pick us up. I got the address off Pierre and gave it to her. I didn't say much about the kidnapping. I thought the details could wait until she could see that we were alright. I then called DIAP, using the number I had been given during the fight with Apophis.

"Good evening, Prometheus Research Service. How can we help you?" DIAP hides behind a series of cover identities so you could never be sure who you are actually talking to. I just had to push on and trust that I was, in fact, talking to DIAP. To be safe, I decided to play along with the cover story.

"Hello, this is Thomas O'Malley. I'm researching the Welsh heroine Myfanwy, but I've been on a bit of an enforced field trip and I have..." I counted the prisoners. "...thirteen large parcels that need to be collected and handled with care."

"Please wait one moment sir," came the reply. There was a brief period of silence then the receptionist was back on the line.

"It seems that some aspects of the problem you refer to are already known and some consultants are now on their way to your location."

"Thank you," I said.

Pierre bowed deeply to Myfanwy. "My lady," he said. "It is time for us to take our leave. No government has known of our unit's existence for over a thousand years. We would like to keep it that way." He looked at the prisoners with a worried expression. "I do not know how to secure these men and also, it would be best if they did not remember we were here. I do not like to impose my lady..."

Myfanwy smiled. "Do not worry yourself Captain." She waved her hand. "They are paralysed until

I say they can move and they will remember nothing of your existence." She gave a mischievous smile. "Although, you may well haunt their nightmares." The Captain bowed once more and then he and his men disappeared through the broken door.

DIAP arrived about five minutes later in the form of Sergeant Fisher and about ten of his men. As soon as they arrived, the head prisoner started yelling and insisting on his right to see a lawyer.

Sergeant Fisher looked at him with disgust. "Neo-Nazis, I hate those guys. Tom, they didn't talk to you about any terrorist activity did they?"

"Actually," I said. "They seemed to be planning some attacks involving weapons of mass destruction."

Sergeant Fisher put on an expression of mock sadness. "Well, I'm afraid that puts you all under the jurisdiction of the military according to the Terrorism Prevention and Investigation Measures Act of 2011. No lawyers for you just yet."

One of his men called out, "Sarge, some of these men need hospital treatment."

Sergeant Fisher looked at me curiously. "Tom, what happened here?"

"Myfanwy and I were kidnapped coming out of the ballet using that," I said, pointing to the syringe lying near the table. "They tied me up and questioned me when I woke up. I couldn't do much but I was just able to stop them injecting Myf a second time. She woke up and that didn't go well for them." Sergeant Fisher looked impressed. Myfanwy gave her sweetest and most innocent smile.

Professor Rhys arrived very shortly after that and managed to extract us from DIAP. He drove me home and then took Myfanwy and her family to Aelred Abbey where they would be safe. Mum and Nain spent the rest of Saturday going over and over what had happened. As a first date, I'd have to say it was pretty interesting. There were two distressing news items that arrived in the period following the kidnapping. The first was relayed to me via Sergeant Fisher (aka Mr. Black) a week later. All the healthy prisoners from that day escaped from within locked cells in the most secure gaol in Britain. Those who were too injured to move had been murdered in their hospital beds. The second was in the newspaper the next morning. There had been a mass die off of fish at Lake Taupo in New Zealand. The lake was now too hot and too acidic to support life. It seemed that magic apples can only keep a dragon asleep for a short time. Soon the others would also be waking up.

Chapter 21
The Creature

There was no mention of our kidnapping in the press. This was probably because of DIAP's obsession with secrecy. It did, however, make it kind of hard to answer questions like 'How did the big date go?' If we said it was great, we were not being entirely honest. If we said that we were kidnapped and held prisoner by neo-Nazi terrorists, no one would believe us and we would be considered really, really weird. As it turned out, we both independently decided to answer 'interesting'. This less than glowing response led everyone to believe that the date had not gone well. That lunchtime Myfanwy again had to leave early to go to French and I faced a barrage of questions and advice.

"Are you going to try again? You should. You know, if at first..." said Gabriella.

"Yes, but only if you do it properly this time - none of that stupid ballet stuff," said Phil.

"This relationship seems like a lot of work. Are you sure it's worth it?" asked Rachael.

Only Wilson really stopped to think about what we had said. He looked at me thoughtfully and asked, "Tom, what are you both hiding? Something happened that you're not talking about."

"Yes, we were kidnapped by aliens." I said sarcastically. "Look Myf and I...' I thought of how we had held each other when Pierre's men had rescued us, when holding Myfanwy seemed like the most important thing my aching arms could do. "We go well together." This brought raised eyebrows from Gabriella and a disgusted snort from Rachael. Then the bell rang and we hurried off to our classes.

We did try again. Not as a big production number but just spending time with each other for no purpose other than to be with each other. Every Friday after school we would go to the movies or maybe get milkshakes at the big shopping centre near the bus interchange. There was no need for formal theatrics. It just felt normal for us to be together, although every now and then I would stop and catch my breath at how beautiful Myfanwy was. In all of this Nain watched over us like a hawk

In the meantime, life went on and planning started for my 18th birthday party. Mum wanted it to be a big production at a restaurant. I wanted it to be small and at home. In the end we compromised: Mum could call in the caterers and have a grand five course meal and I could choose a small enough guest list to have the party at home. We have gone through a similar process every year, ever since my sixth birthday when I refused to have a clown.

So it was that on November 23, ten of us squeezed around our dining room table. Myfanwy and Mum of course, and Helen and Gwen were there, along with Professor Rhys and Nain. Of the normal school lunch group, only Rachael was a no show. The meal was really good, although the portions were a bit smaller than I would have liked. We had appetisers of crusty toast with tomato and some sort of seafood; an entree of smoked salmon and a main course of roast beef with mashed potato and a sort of Greek salad. Instead of a traditional birthday cake, I had a lemon and passion fruit tart and this was followed by a cheese and fruit platter. The party went really well I think, until, that is, all our guests were leaving.

Mum had ordered taxis to take everybody home and, while we were waiting for them to arrive, the creature appeared. It loomed out of the darkness of the park like some monstrous shadow. Phil was the first to notice it.

"What's that?" he asked uncertainly. The creature started to lumber towards us. Hints of its rough, rock like skin started to be seen.

"It's some kind of trick," Wilson said, looking at me accusingly. "It's got to be." The creature raised its fist and smashed the park bench where Michael normally sat to splinters. It grabbed a large branch and ripped it off the tree and threw it towards our house. The branch flew through a front window, smashing into the room where we had just eaten. People screamed and even Wilson looked terrified and confused. Nain, however, stepped forward and raised her hands in a warding gesture. A shield of blue energy, like a translucent soap bubble, started to form but it collapsed almost immediately. Nain staggered back and Myfanwy and Professor Rhys rushed over to support her. This time all three raised their hands in concert and the blue shield started to form strongly and spread across the front of the house. Then it paused, seemed to waver, and collapsed in a great flash of light. All three magic users looked shocked and frightened. I think it was the fear that I saw in Nain's face, something I thought I would never see, that drove me to do what I did next. I had had enough of being threatened and chased. Now it threatened Myfanwy. This had to stop. I was angry, so angry that I didn't have room to be afraid. I walked out and stood in the centre of the road. The creature stood still in the dark of the park and watched me.

"Come on!" I said. "You want me? Well, here I am. All you need to do is to come out of those shadows and get me. But don't go terrorising people who have nothing to do with this. It's between you and me." The creature reared up to its full height, well over eight feet tall. In the dark, it was a grotesque and bulbous shadow, full of threat. It stretched out its arm like a bizarre imitation of a Christian cross.

"I'm not afraid of you!" I yelled. Apart from anger fuelled bravado, this was a blatant and obvious lie but it seemed like the thing to say at the time. Surprisingly, the creature hesitated. Then it turned and moved back into the shadows and was gone. I stood and looked at the shadows in the park. Again, it could have killed me but it didn't. Maybe, I thought, that wasn't its aim. Maybe it was only trying to scare me. That would make sense of its actions. But why?

As I turned I could see my school friends all frozen in place, shocked and white faced. Mum and Helen were clearly terrified while the three magic users were looking at me; worried and confused. Only Gwen stood apart, her gaze never leaving the park.

"Oh, the poor thing," she said. "The poor, poor thing." We should have listened to her but we didn't. After all, she was only a little girl. A fraction of a second later Myfanwy rushed over and caught me in a crushing hug.

"You stupid, stupid boy," she said sobbing. "Why must it always be you? Why can't you just back away?"

Professor Rhys looked across at Nain. "Holly, what was that thing?" he asked.

Nain shook her head. "I don't know," she replied. "I have never seen anything like it before." That was not what I wanted to hear.

Something clearly needed to be done about my party guests: Gabriella was sobbing, Wilson was standing frozen in shock and Phil was sitting on the front step; as pale as a ghost and holding his head in his hands. Nain looked at them and then said,

"Cadfan, if you could look after the youngsters, I'll fix up the window." Professor Rhys nodded. He walked over and seemed to touch each of them consolingly on the head. At the same time, Nain pointed at the shattered front window. The tree branch flew back into the park and the window repaired itself. Nain walked over to Mum, who was sobbing and being comforted by Helen.

"Helen dear," she said. "I don't think there's much point in getting the police involved, I doubt that they would be able to help." Mum and Helen both agreed and started to get up and get organised.

It was then that the reaction set in and the rest of the night is a bit of a blurr. I didn't collapse or get a fit of the shakes or anything. I just sat on the step and stared into the park. The taxis came and everyone left but all I could feel was terror and, every time I closed my eyes, all I could see was the creature, raised to its full height and with its arms stretched out like a monstrous cross. Eventually, Myfanwy and her family went next door to the Professor's house and Mum took me up to my bedroom. As she walked out, without any trace of irony, she said, "Happy birthday Tom."

That night I don't remember going to sleep. My waking visions blurred into my nightmares and my strongest memory is of feeling an overwhelming, irrational fear. Something I didn't feel when I was actually facing the creature. Fragments of my dream still clung to my mind the next morning as I waited for Myfanwy outside the Professor's house. As I waited, Michael walked up and looked at the smashed remains of his of his usual seat. Then he looked across at me and shrugged in a kind of hopeless resignation, as if this was just one of the bad things he expected to happen. Then he walked away with his head bowed and his shoulders slumped.

It was only about a minute later that Myfanwy came out and we walked to school together, using the gates to get there quickly. In the birch wood, Myfanwy took both my hands and looked at me with the same worried and confused expression she had worn the night before.

"What's going on Tom?" she asked. "You're not telling me everything."

I shrugged. "I really don't know much more than what you've seen," I said. "The thing has threatened me before, but I don't know why and I certainly have no idea what it is." Myfanwy gave a wry smile and hugged me. I could smell the sweet soap she had used to wash her hair.

"Do all your social events have such dramatic endings?" she asked. I laughed. Perhaps I laughed a bit too loudly, a bit too long and perhaps my laughter was a bit hysterical, because the comment wasn't really that funny, but as I laughed the shadows of my nightmares faded from my memory and I was free. I was with

Myfanwy, the sun was shining and the wind was carrying the scent of the sea. Just then it was really good to be alive.

In English that morning, we were finishing up on Yeats before moving on to T.S. Eliot.

"In summary, can anyone tell me what the main theme of the poem is?" Mrs Brown asked. A mousey haired girl, whose name I could never remember, answered.

"Everything he knew was coming to an end and he was afraid of what was coming next," she said.

Mrs Brown nodded. "Essentially, yes," she said. "Remember that this was written in the aftermath of the first world war and the Russian revolution. Yeats had this idea of cycles in history and he thought one cycle was coming to an end. He thought the Christian ideals that had held civilisation together were falling apart. Something would replace them but he was afraid of what that 'something' might be." I had a different insight into the 'rough beast', an altogether more concrete conception but not a conception I could share with the class.

At lunch that day, Wilson lost no time in telling Rachael the story that Professor Rhys had planted in his memory.

"There was this group of hooligans vandalising the park opposite Tom's house. They wrecked a park bench and tore a branch off a tree. So, what does Tom do? He goes out and confronts them! Tells them to shove off." I had to admit that Professor Rhys was good at covering up the tracks of uncanny events. That story was reasonable and quite close to the truth. It would have required minimum intrusion. Wilson looked at me with his most serious expression. "Tom, you know you really shouldn't have done that. If those guys had turned on you, you could've been badly hurt."

"Yeah,' Phil chimed in. "You may think your martial arts skill makes you invulnerable but it really doesn't. They were big, there were a lot of them and they were mean. You're not Bruce Lee. You could've been in serious trouble."

"And yet it backed away," Myfanwy said. She quickly corrected herself. "They, I mean...They backed away." She gave me a bright smile full of affection. "I think you're wasting your time. He won't change. If he was in a fairytale, he'd be that character who'd charge five trolls holding only a stick."

Rachael gave an exasperated sigh. "Messiah complex," she said. "He thinks he's on a mission from God to save the world. Look Tom, just relax and be a normal teenager. You're not some crusading medieval knight errant. You're a school boy in the twenty first century – act like it."

I shrugged. "I can only be me," I said. I looked across at Myfanwy. "Five trolls? That would be silly. Four – not a problem." Rachael groaned and the bell went for class.

Nain remained in London for the rest of the term. She was determined to find out what the creature in the Park had been and stayed in the Professor's house to investigate. She couldn't understand how any mythical being could exist in a very rational and mundane London. She also didn't know what it was and I think this puzzled her most of all. This was very upsetting because anything that Nain found strange must be very strange indeed. Each day she would go to look at the remains of the park bench. Unfortunately, these told her nothing and Michael didn't return.

The newspapers were now beginning to be dominated by stories of relatively minor earthquakes, volcanic eruptions and strange phenomena. The sea started to boil off the coast of Sicily and a lake in Siberia became so acidic that it ate through the hulls of aluminium boats. There were floods in New Zealand as the supposedly permanent snow fields and glaciers on Mt Ruapehu melted. Large swaths of rainforest in Northern Sumatra died as the ground became too hot to walk on and volcanic gasses seeped from the soil. There was panic in the south of China as a major tremor hit in the area already devastated by the tsunami. In the United States, rangers started to quietly evacuate and close Yellowstone National Park. The dragons were well and truly waking up.

The possibility of a connection between all these events did not go uncommented on. They were all centred on six former, but relatively recent, super-volcanoes and I was not the only one to notice. Reports started to appear which connected these events to the super-volcanoes underneath them. Opinion articles were written and disaster shows started to appear on TV, All of this, however, was amateur speculation. No expert commentary was available. This was because all the university geology and geophysics departments and research institutes had been placed under military security and all the staff, even the senior students, had been made to sign the official secrets act. This wasn't confined to the United Kingdom. All across the world, similar things were happening – sometimes brutally. Governments had obviously noticed the super-volcano connection and had asked their experts what would happen if all six erupted at the same time. The answer had clearly frightened them badly.

Still, nothing of this was certain and the dangers of mass panic were well known. Until they could understand and manage the situation, all the governments could do was to try to control the information flow. So, armed guards appeared outside geology departments. Seismic institutes found that their data were classified and aged professors, who had spent their adult lives teaching and researching in obscurity, were bemused to find themselves consultants on top secret government projects. The trouble was that none of the experts knew why this was happening. They could only have talked about statistical probability, coincidences and random chance. They didn't know that Cadell had stolen Merlin's staff and was somehow stirring the dragons into action.

All through this I felt the same old frustration. I knew what was going on but didn't know what to do about it. We still had no leads on where Merlin might be, Cadell was well hidden, and it was unlikely that the dragons would fall for the apple trick again. Things came to a head for me on the Thursday before the last week of term. There was a huge forest fire in Yellowstone National Park that was started by a small volcanic eruption. The forest was dry, even in winter, because the ground was so hot. Escaping volcanic gases meant that even some of the surrounding areas had to be evacuated and it had been weeks since anybody had heard from parts of Eastern Siberia. Things were getting worse and I knew that I couldn't just stand by and let Cadell destroy the world. I had to do something and, at last, I had an idea of what that 'something' might be. The next day, I met Myfanwy early at the gate near the school.

"We have to go to Drumelzier," I said.

Myfanwy nodded.

"I know. I've been thinking about it myself. It's the only place on our list that has a real, solid connection to Merlin. His disciple went there and chose to live there. We need to know why."

Chapter 22
The Battle of Drumelzier

Getting to Drumelzier proved to be easier said than done. The easiest way I could find on the web still involved a train and two buses and took over seven hours. This would mean some very difficult negotiations with both Nain and Mum about Myfanwy and me spending at least one night away together. Even if they could be made to believe in our mission, which was doubtful, I didn't think that idea was going to fly. All the recent violence had made them both very protective.

I spent the first few days of the break trying to come up with an argument that would convince them. I had to get it right because I wouldn't get a second chance. Now that school had finished, Aelred Abbey's lack of electronic communication was also a very real problem since it meant that I couldn't coordinate with Myfanwy.

Complicating all of this was the fact that Christmas was coming and I had to think about buying Christmas presents. Unfortunately, this meant shopping. In spite of the weather being consistently cold and rainy, which matched my mood, the shops were filled with a false, commercial happiness which only made me more irritable. Age old, sacred carols were robbed of any meaning by overproduced, upbeat, modern performances and then turned into a kind of background noise. To make matters worse, some has been rock star, whose voice had failed many years ago, had put out a dreadful, sentimental dirge of a Christmas ballad and this was played almost continuously. Don't get me wrong, I love Christmas. I just hate Christmas shopping.

Mum and Dad were easy. I got them books; more imaginative than socks but only just. Myfanwy, however, was nightmare. She was magic, rich and probably had access to jewellery and stuff that would make anything I bought look lame. Nain was no help and Mum didn't seem to comprehend the seriousness of the problem. After a long and frustrating day I chanced to walk past one of those shops which sell pointless but expensive ornaments. There in the window was the only real possibility I had seen all day. I spent virtually all of my money buying it and was happy as I left the shop. As I stepped into the crowded street, the woman in front of me collapsed. I bent down to help her and the guy behind me collapsed. It was then that I noticed the dart sticking out of the woman's arm. People started yelling and running; someone else went down. I decided to make myself scarce. I was getting really sick of this. I merged into the crowd and took a roundabout way home, hoping that that would be the last I heard of the incident.

This was not to be. When I got home there was a large, black car parked outside our house and two large and very alert looking men standing either side of my front door. They waved me inside. Director Smith was waiting for me in the lounge room. He was showing my mum a video loop on the television. It was from a security camera in a store and it showed me walking away as a crowd gathered around some people lying unconscious on the ground.

"I had nothing to do with that," I said. "It just happened around me."

"I know, Tom," the Director said, "The police have arrested two Neo-Nazi thugs armed with a tranquiliser gun and darts. The two of them were escaped prisoners. They had previously been arrested when you and Miss Ferchwyn were kidnapped." He looked at me with an intense and determined expression. "These people are still hunting you. Why?" I shrugged and decided to come clean.

"They think I can help them find Merlin," I said. "They want to kill him. He is quite safe, however, because I have absolutely no idea where he is." The Director showed no reaction. He turned to my mother.

"These people will not give up Mrs. O'Malley. You and Tom need to go somewhere you can be protected. London is not safe. We can arrange a safe house but even that might not be sufficient."

"That won't be necessary," Mum said. "We've been invited to spend Christmas at Aelred Abbey. We'll be safe there."

The Director nodded grimly. "Then I suggest you go there as soon as possible," he said. "Rest assured that we will continue to hunt those responsible but we cannot guarantee your safety." He rose to leave. "Good evening... and happy Christmas." He walked out the door to the waiting car. As he left, so did any chance of persuading Mum to let me go off with Myfanwy.

Mum's only reaction to the visit was to turn to me and say, "You need to go and pack young man. Nain came around today with an invitation to Myfanwy's birthday. We leave for Aelred Abbey tomorrow morning." I looked at her in horror. I had forgotten Myfanwy's birthday!

"Mum, when is Myfanwy's birthday?"

She looked at me with an exasperated expression. "It's tomorrow. Don't tell me you forgot."

"No, of course not," I lied. "I was just checking the arrangements."

"Well, I got you a card anyway, just in case it had slipped your mind." I took it but dinner was not a happy meal, not for me at least. I had no present for Myfanwy. It was her birthday and all I had to give her was a card chosen by my mother. It was when I was in my room, thinking of what to write in the card, that I had an inspiration. It took me until early in the morning but eventually I had a poem that I was halfway happy with.

My Lady is Passing Fair

My lady is passing fair
With eyes as green
As the forest deep
Where once we walked.

My lady is passing fair
With skin as white
As the mountain snow
Where once we climbed.

My lady is passing fair
With hair as dark
As the fire warm night
Where soft we slept.

My lady is passing fair
Her laughter my joy.
All my thought, my longing.
Is my lady Myfanwy.

I printed it out and pasted it over the routine greeting in the card. At least I would have something to give. I just hoped she wouldn't laugh or think it was weird.

The professor picked us up the next morning and took us by car to Aelred Abbey. At Mum's insistence we packed for an extended stay. When we arrived at the abbey, the whole family was there, Carwyn having flown in from his school in Ireland. It was only after we had settled in that Myfanwy and I managed to get some time alone together, walking in the ruins of the abbey. It was there that I gave her the card.

She read it without any change of expression but when she had finished there were tears in her eyes. She flung herself at me and hugged me tightly.

"Thank you, Tom," she said. "That's just perfect." That was clearly an exaggeration. Her emotions were getting the better of her but I would take it. As we left the ruined abbey, we were coloured by the light from long vanished stained glass windows and accompanied by the monks chanting God's praises.

Myfanwy's party that evening was a strange combination of formal feast and family celebration. Mum and I were the only outsiders invited. It was soon clear why. Dishes would appear and disappear with the changing courses, glasses always remained filled and the candles on the birthday cake happily lit themselves. It would all have been very strange to someone who knew nothing of magic. It also made clear how isolated Myfanwy must have felt at school: never to be able to have friends home, invite them to a party, or even talk to them on Facebook or mobile phone. I couldn't help but wonder how much of her affection for me was simply a reaction to her own loneliness.

The evening ended with Carwyn giving Myfanwy his gift. It was a ball of dark crystal that was somehow connected to a part of a concert hall in London. When Myfanwy took hold of the ball, one whole wall of the dining room faded and it was as if we had the most magnificent seats in the hall. That evening we sat and listened to a performance of Saint-Saens' third symphony. I'll say this for Carwyn, he's got style.

It was after breakfast the next morning that I told Myfanwy of the difficulties in getting to Drumelzier. She just gave me that same pitying look she gives me when I say something stupid.

"Go and get Declan's stick and a warm coat and meet me in the kitchen,' she said. She promptly disappeared, leaving me to walk up the stairs the old fashioned way. When I came down to the kitchen a few minutes later, Myfanwy was filling a backpack with some left-overs from last night's party and trying to convince her Mum that it would be alright for us to go for a walk and a picnic.

"It will only be a short walk and we'll be home by mid-afternoon. No one knows where we are and we will be very careful. At the first sign of trouble, the first hint, I'll teleport us back here."

Helen looked doubtful. "I don't know," she said. "It would be safer to stay in the house."

"Mam, we are both eighteen," she pointed out. "Anyway, Tom is carrying Declan's walking stick. He can even fight trolls with that thing and there are no trolls in Norfolk." Helen looked across at my Mum, who shrugged. Helen finally gave in.

"I suppose it will be alright," she said. "Just be careful." Myfanwy went across and gave her a kiss on the cheek.

"We will Mam. We'll be back soon."

As we were walking across the causeway to the birch wood, I said, "Myf, much as I would like to have a picnic with you, I don't see how this is going to get us any closer to Drumelzier."

She laughed. "Silly boy, just you wait and see."

When we went through the gate, we didn't step out into the country lane but into a dark and musty corridor. Cobwebs hung heavily from the ceiling.

"Ugh!" said Myfanwy. "I'll need to tell Uncle Cadfan to get this place cleaned more often."

"Where are we?" I asked.

"This is a house that Uncle Cadfan uses when he has business in the north," Myfanwy said. "We should be able to get to Drumelzier from here." She led the way down the corridor and out through the front door onto the street. The house behind us was small, narrow and grey and we were standing on a cobblestoned street. I looked around in amazement.

"We're in Edinburgh," I said.

"Oh, well spotted!" Myfanwy replied sarcastically. "What was it gave it away? The big castle on the hill?" Actually it was but I didn't answer. I pulled out my mobile phone to get directions to Drumelzier. Even from here, we still had to catch two buses but fortunately the bus stop was close by and, whether by Myfanwy's magic or happenstance, the first bus came quickly.

After changing buses, it was just before noon when we finally got to Drumelzier. There was nothing much to see. It was more a rural district than a town. It also covered quite a large area. There was a shop, a ruined castle and the meeting of two rivers. We walked around for a while with Myfanwy transporting us quickly to important vantage points. At each point I looked carefully but I didn't see anything unusual and Myfanwy had no sense of magic being used. Eventually, we sat down under a hawthorn tree to have lunch. A sign said that this was the tree under which Merlin Caledonensis was buried but it was clearly a tourist committee lie. The tree was far too young.

"Well this was a complete waste of time," I said, after finishing a lunch of cold chicken and apple juice. "We can cross this place off our list and we're back to where we started. We need to get back if we're going to make it to Aelred Abbey without raising suspicions."

Myfanwy nodded glumly. "We also need to get back before that hits," she said, pointing to the dark clouds of a storm that was rolling in from the north. "I'll transport us back to the house in Edinburgh. And we'll be back in plenty of time."

Just then the chattering started. I call it chattering because I can't think of the word that properly describes it. It was like a lot of people gossiping all at once in high pitched voices only there were no words and it was clear that this sound did not come from a human voice. It started softly and rapidly increased in volume. It was as distracting as trying to listen to a half of conversation and had the same annoyance factor is finger nails down a blackboard. Myfanwy went very still as soon as the sound started.

"What is that?" I asked as blue fire raced down Declan's staff and transformed it into a thick cudgel - what my grandfather would have called shillelagh.

"Goblins!" Myfanwy said. "We have to leave here quickly." As she said this, the first of the creatures began to emerge from the hedge row in front of us. They were small, about two feet high and coloured green. They were bald with large eyes and pointed ears. When they opened their mouths you could see a large collection of very sharp teeth. More and more of them started to emerge. Soon we were surrounded by a crowd and the chattering was almost unbearably loud.

"Myf, there are too many of them," I said. "We need to get out of here now. Teleport us!"

Myfanwy looked at me in anguish. "No, I can't!" she yelled above the noise. "I can't concentrate. I can't think clearly enough to take us anywhere."

The sharp toothed monsters were coming closer. One of them made a run at me and I swung my shillelagh like a cricket bat, planning to hit back into the crowd. The thing exploded silently as I hit it and all that was left was a thin whisper of green smoke.

More of them came on and soon I was in full defensive mode, using all my weapons skill to keep them away from Myfanwy but there were too many of them and they were attacking from all directions.

"Tom! We have to make for the river, they can't stand running water," Myfanwy shouted. I didn't ask any questions I just attacked on the river side and tried to fight our way through. More and more of the wretched little things kept coming and it soon became clear, to me at least, that we wouldn't make it. Myfanwy still had her hands over her ears and I was getting tired but I didn't dare let my concentration drop. I was caught in this weird kind of dance and I couldn't see a way out. The afternoon was also becoming dark as the storm approached. The first drops of rain began to fall.

Just then some dark figures started to emerge from the trees near the river. They were swinging some short, hooked clubs with great efficiency and the goblins started to turn their attention away from Myfanwy and me towards this new group. The figures drove through the goblins in a disciplined wedge formation. I didn't have much time to take notice as I was still trying to keep the goblins away from Myfanwy. I didn't even realise that they had reached us until I heard Myfanwy say, "Captain Gauthier, I am very pleased to see you." I paused for a moment and turned to see our rescuers. It was indeed Captain Gauthier and his platoon or, rather, hockey team. I realised that the clubs they were using were in fact hockey sticks. Uncharacteristically, the captain spent no time on pleasantries.

'Quickly," he said. "We will have a more defensive position with the river at our backs." We placed Myfanwy in the centre of the wedge while I put took point next to the captain. We retreated back towards the river, fighting goblins all the way. For every one we killed two seemed to appear. A pall of green goblin smoke hung over the field. In the middle of all this, the bizarre nature of the battle struck me forcefully. I could see the lights of the traffic on the nearby motorway. Here I was fighting goblins while, less than a kilometre away, 21st-century life was going on as normal.

When we got to the river, we formed a defensive perimeter with the river at our back, Myfanwy in the middle and the men spread out, each a hockey sticks length from his neighbour. The captain and I held back in reserve to catch any who got through and, in the worst case scenario, to fill any gaps. Then the work began - and it was simply hard work. We had a strong position but the goblin numbers were overwhelming. Myfanwy was using her power to throw rocks from the river at the goblins. They flew hard and fast. This took some pressure off the guards and, I think, allowed our defences to hold for as long as they did. Still, more and more goblins just kept coming. If this kept up, eventually the men would grow tired, make a mistake and we would be overwhelmed.

Suddenly the goblins fell silent and drew back. They parted as a tall figure in a black, hooded cloak walked through their midst. It was almost as if they were afraid and, while it was good to have even a momentary break, it was concerning that we were now faced with someone who could make even this great mass of goblins fear. The guards gripped their hockey stick clubs tighter as the figure approached.

When the figure got to the defensive line, it clearly expected that line to break and fall back as well but the papal guard held. The figure stopped and stepped back in surprise. Then it pulled back its hood.

"Hello Tom, Lady Myfanwy," Declan said. "You must introduce me to your friends."

I gave a long sigh of relief and Myfanwy actually let out a squeal of delight and pushed through the bemused guards to greet him with a hug. She then brought him over to meet Pierre. As soon he passed inside the ring of guards the chattering started again.

"Tom, before you make the proper introductions," Declan said. "Could I borrow that staff I gave you for a moment?" I handed him the shillelagh and blue fire ran along as it turned back into a simple walking stick. He held it high with both hands and then rammed it into the earth. A wave of blue light surged out from where the stick hit the ground. It passed through the goblin hoard and there was a high pitched scream. Then they just weren't there anymore. All that was left was a thin green mist, dissipating before the approaching storm. The chattering was replaced by a sudden and deep silence. Declan handed the stick back to me.

"My people were once worshipped as gods around here," he explained. "That still gives us some mythic power. The land retains some memory of us." As Pierre's men spread out to search the field, I made the introductions.

"Declan, this is Captain Pierre Gauthier of the Swiss Pontifical Guard, Special Operations Unit. Peirre, this is Declan MhicOsin of the Tuatha de Dannan of Tyr na nOg." The two men bowed warily to each other.

"Declan of Tyr na nOg, I thank you and my men thank you," Pierre said. Declan smiled broadly.

"I am honoured to have the gratitude of the Pontifical Guard," he said. "But we need to talk about why there were so many of these things and how they came to be here."

Pierre gave a characteristic shrug of his shoulders. "These creatures are the mythological expressions of the little evils of the every day," he said. "The selfishness, the little cheating. This world is full of such things; so when these goblins manifest themselves there are always very many of them. One by one they are easy to overcome but in large numbers they are deadly." Pierre and his men were now leaning wearily on their hockey sticks.

"But why here? And why now?" Myfanwy asked. "And how is it that they could manifest themselves at all?"

"Could it be Cadell?" I asked. "Maybe he called them up and left them here to guard Merlin's tomb or, even more likely, as a diversion; causing us to concentrate on an area where he knew Merlin's tomb wasn't."

Declan shook his head. "I doubt both of those, Tom. Oh, Cadell could do it. He's a skilful and powerful magic user but I have come across these goblins elsewhere in Scotland. It's an infestation that seems random and uncontrolled. That's not Cadell's style."

"It's the staff," Myfanwy said suddenly. "Cadell has Merlin's staff. He must be searching Scotland for the tomb as well and everywhere he goes, the power of the staff calls forth these mythical creatures. He probably doesn't even know he's doing it but because he's evil he calls forth evil things. We're lucky it was only goblins."

"That may well be," Declan said. "Whatever the case, I'm afraid that Drumelzier is just another dead end to add to your list. I have been tracing stories of Merlinus Caledonensis ever since I left Annwn." He smiled and pulled back his cloak to reveal a small harp strapped to his back. "Did you know that you can do quite well as a travelling minstrel in Scotland today; going from tavern to tavern? Anyway, this is clearly where he died but it is not where he spent most of his time. He seems to have wandered all through the north and west of here, although he wasn't always known by that name. I have found many stories of a slightly mad wizard or holy man throughout the highlands. I think he came down here after he had found Merlin but was unable to reach him. He may have been trying to lead curiosity seekers away from the real resting place until he thought up his next move. It turned out to be a bad choice."

"So, Declan," Myfanwy said dryly. "All your efforts have succeeded in narrowing Merlin's resting place only to somewhere in north west Scotland." Declan pulled a theatrically disappointed face.

"Your lack of appreciation wounds me my dear. Still, I'm afraid you're right and North West Scotland is big, rugged and remote. I'm afraid Merlin is still well and truly hidden." There was a squall of wind as the storm hit in earnest and it started to rain heavily. Thunder rolled across the horizon and by now the afternoon was almost as dark as evening. Myfanwy waved her arms and we were all in a pool of bright sunlight where the rain didn't fall.

"Thank you my lady," Declan said to Myfanwy. "But I'm afraid I have nothing further to offer and I must leave. I must report back to the High King and let him know what is going on." He turned to Pierre. "Before I go, since you are attached to the Pontifical Guard, could you deliver a message to the Bishop of Rome?"

Pierre nodded cautiously. "It might be possible," he said.

"Then could you tell him that Abbot Aidan of Trinity Monastery in Tyr na nOg sends his greetings to the Bishop of Rome and wishes to inform him that the same Abbot Aidan was elected by the community following the death of Abbot Cormac, appointed by the saintly Brendan who is called the Navigator. Abbot Aidan offers his obedience and asks for Peter's blessing." Pierre raised his eyebrows. Abbot Cormac would have been appointed by Brendan over a thousand years ago.

"I will make sure your message is delivered," he said. "What the curia will make of it I cannot say but it will be delivered."

"Good. Then I must be off," Declan said. He pulled his hood over his head and vanished into the dark of the storm.

"We must leave also," Pierre said. "We have a big game to prepare for on Saturday. Our van is parked down on the road. Can we give you a ride somewhere?" By now the rain outside our bubble of sunlight had turned to sleet.

"Thank you Captain," Myfanwy said. "But we need to get back to Norfolk and I think your van would be too slow. We will make our own way."

"Goodbye then, my lady." Pierre took and kissed Myfanwy's hand to the whoops and laughter of his men. They all then turned and walked off into the storm. Myfanwy silently took my hand and we were back in the cobbled street in Edinburgh, outside the same small, grey house. Here the rain had turned to thickly falling snow. We went into the house, down the musty corridor and stepped through the rear door into the birch wood and bright sunlight. Behind us, through the gate, was the countryside of Norfolk.

Gwen met us on the causeway as we walked back to Aelred Abbey. She gave us a very disapproving look.

"You can't go in there like that. Nain is already very suspicious of this little picnic of yours." When we looked puzzled she gave Myfanwy exactly the same exasperated look that Myfanwy sometimes gives me. "You are all wet and covered in snow. It's been warm and sunny here all day."

Myfanwy smiled. "Oops!" she said and with a wave of her hand fixed the problem. We were warm and dry as we entered the hall. Still, Nain had a very stern look on her face when she met us there and it occurred to me that she was suspicious of us on many different levels.

Chapter 23
Christmas and the South China Sea

The storm came in from the north during the night and we woke the next morning to falling snow. The ground was covered and the world had that peculiar stillness that comes with snowfall. At breakfast, my Mum was very excited.

"Tom, we're going to have a white Christmas! Isn't that wonderful?" It was. This excitement may sound strange to someone from the northern hemisphere, but in Australia Christmas occurs in summer and we are far more likely to have melting bitumen on the roads than melting snow in the fields. So it was exciting. It was wonderful and it was magical.

That Christmas at Aelred Abbey stands out in my memory as a special time: a kind of 'time out' when everything was right with the world. It was a time of snow and roaring log fires; of warm bread and hot soup; of rich stews and hot chocolate. It was a time when the ghosts of Christmas past caroused through the castle and the monks chanted their advent prayers from their long ruined monastery. It was a time of playing in the snow and resting by the fire; of listening to Myfanwy talk by the fire; of watching Myfanwy in the firelight. I think it was there, watching Myfanwy in the firelight of Aelred Abbey, that the nasty little worm that Rachael had planted in my mind finally died. I knew I could be happy listening to Myfanwy for the rest of my life. I have no memory that I said anything much at all.

On Christmas Eve, we went through the gate to Belmont Abbey for midnight mass. The grounds of the Abbey were thickly covered with snow and the night was clear as crystal with the stars blazing bright. The stained glass windows of the chapel were brightly lit and we approached it across a kaleidoscope of coloured snow. Even before we entered the church, we could hear the monks as they chanted the vigil prayers. I noticed that many were familiar and I realised that I had been hearing them all week from the past-echos of the monastic ruins at Aelred Abbey. Here the same prayers were being sung by living 21st century monks dressed in their habits and cowls: past and present in one celebration.

Mass was solemn and beautiful and filled with a kind of joy that Cadell, for all his power, could never touch. After mass we went back to Aelred Abbey. As we approached, the ruins seemed whole in the moonlight and the long vanished stained glass windows were a blaze of light. A monk came out of the church carrying a statue of the Christ child and handed it to some villagers dressed in brightly coloured cloaks. Then they all vanished and the monastery was a ruin again.

"It was a local custom," Myfanwy whispered to me. "They would take the Babe back in procession to the village and put it in a manger in the centre of the village square. It was a symbol of the monks giving Christ to the world." I nodded and looked at the broken arches of the church and I thought; nothing good ever really vanishes. It stays there, unseen and unknown perhaps, but there none the less.

It was warm when we entered the keep. There were blazing fires and the hall was decorated in evergreen branches. We gathered in the dining room and had an early Christmas feast of hot, spicy pork pies and mulled wine. Gwen fell asleep and had to be carried to her room by Helen. Truth be told, the rest of us followed shortly after. As I went to sleep I thought. This is Christmas as it is meant to be: no bad music, no fake decorations, no advertising pressure to buy just one more bargain. This was Christmas as I had never known it before.

I slept late the next morning and when I went downstairs I found the kitchen full of frantic activity. Nain and Helen were at the centre of it all, directing activities while Gwen and Myfanwy were running about doing odd jobs. Even Mum was at work washing potatoes. I took one look at all the work and decided to skip breakfast and go somewhere else. I found Carwyn reading by the fire in the library and went over to join him. I was aware of the injustice in this arrangement but, since it was in my favour, decided to go along with it.

"Hi Tom," he said as I sat down. "You escaping the kitchen madhouse too?"

I nodded. "Carwyn, when does your family do Christmas presents?" I asked.

He grinned. "Getting impatient are we? We normally open them after lunch. Mind you, Christmas lunch normally takes a long time." It was then that Nain found us.

"What are you two doing in here?" She asked in a very agitated manner. "There are peas to be shelled and potatoes to be peeled. You are needed in the kitchen!" There was the rest of the morning gone.

We met formally in the dining room at 12.30 for Christmas lunch and it did indeed go on for a long time. We started with some spicy fruit tarts and then moved on to seafood. There were two main courses: pork with apple sauce and goose with gravy, potatoes and vegetables. I didn't think the goose was as good as the turkey we would normally have, but it was still good. This was followed by plum pudding and cream. The plum pudding had gold sovereigns cooked into it, which came as a bit of a surprise if you weren't expecting it and bit into one. All of this had been prepared by hand without the help of magic: apparently an important part of the Christmas tradition.

After dinner we retired to the library where all the gifts had been placed earlier. I felt a vague disappointment that all the gifts were not fabulous magical artefacts. They weren't. They were the normal sort of gifts that could have been shared by any family: books, clothes and games featured prominently. Mum's gift to me was a bit of a surprise and a very happy one. It was air tickets to Hong Kong where we were to spend a weekend with Dad. Myfanwy gave me a beautifully bound and illustrated edition of Malory's *Le Morte d'Arthur*, the most famous of the retellings of the Arthur legend, written in 1485. I wanted to hug her there and then but it was a bit hard with all her family crowded round.

"Thanks," I said. "That's absolutely fantastic."

My hands were sweating when I came to give Myfanwy her present. I had convinced myself that she would think it was corny and stupid. My heart was thudding as she opened it eagerly. It was a fancy crystal snow globe with a white pegasus, wings extended, flying over a mountain landscape. The base was a detailed base relief in ceramic and contained a clockwork music box. At first she didn't say anything. She just made the gesture she uses when she stops time. Everything, and everybody, froze around us. Even the flames in the fire were still. Then she threw her arms around me and hugged me tight. It was good to hold her close.

"Thank you Tom," she said. "That is beautiful."

"Myfanwy, I lo..." She quickly put her finger to my lips.

"Don't say it," she said. "Even with time stopped, those words have power, especially around here. Don't say it until you're absolutely sure and forever." I sighed. The moment had passed.

"I was only going to say that I liked your dress." It was indeed a nice dress; green with red trim.

Myfanwy laughed. "Oh yeah, sure you were," she said. "Don't ever get a job where you have to lie for a living. You're terrible at it." I leaned forward and kissed her. The snow globe started to play Greensleaves, which was odd because everything was supposed to be frozen. When we looked at it, the pegasus was actually flying through a storm of swirling snow, its mane flowing in an unseen wind. Myfanwwy looked at me in surprise.

"But I'm not doing that!" she said. Around us, everyone else was still frozen. Myfanwy let time flow again and the snow globe resumed its normal static self. Everyone was looking at us.

"Thank you Tom," Myfanwy said. "That's really nice." The gift giving continued and the snow globe stayed what it had been when I bought it in London. After the large lunch, no one wanted to eat much later, so supper was a very light meal and bed was very welcome. If I was given the choice, I would have had all my Christmases at Aelred Abbey.

There was nothing much else to do in the days between Christmas and New Year except read by the fire and play in the snow. Mind you, playing in the snow with Myfanwy and her siblings could be very problematic. On the day after Boxing Day, I was practicing my Tai Chi Chuan forms on the snow covered forecourt of the keep. I had Declan's staff which had conveniently turned itself into a practice spear. I was minding my own business when Myfanwy and Gwyneth decided to have a snowball fight with me. The first thing I knew about it was when a wet snow ball hit me in the back of the head. I turned around to find them both laughing.

I knew better than to try and retaliate in kind. My snowballs would have just stopped in mid-air or worse, turned around and come back at me. I did, however, dodge the next two snowballs they threw. These turned around in the air and came at me like heat seeking missiles. Declan's staff raced with blue fire and turned itself into one of those heavy sticks the Irish play Hurley with. I was able to blatter both snow balls out of existence. The girls clearly took this as a challenge and snowballs started to come at me in rapid succession and from all directions. I used all my techniques; spear fighting, my sword guard, even cricket strokes, to bat away all the snowballs as they threw them at me. After several minutes of constant attack, I was still fairly dry. Carwyn appeared at the front door.

"It looks as if he has your measure Myf," he said.

"No he hasn't," Myf answered. "They never look up." I looked up quickly and there were a large number of snowballs hanging in a cloud above my head. As soon as I saw them they all started to fall. However, even though they were directly above me, they somehow landed on Myfanwy.

"Carwyn, you rat!" Myfanwy called out, furious. Carwyn found this enormously funny and even Gwyneth had a fit of the giggles. I walked over to the house, smiling. Gwen took my hand.

"You really are very good," she said. Myfanwy put her arm around me.

"Yes he is," she said. As we turned to go into the house, I thanked Carwyn for his help.

He smiled, "No problem," he said. "Male solidarity and all that." Myfanwy let go of me and smiled sweetly at Carwyn – then, out of nowhere, a snowball hit him in the back of the head. Snowball fights in this family could get very complicated.

Ironically, sledding in the birch wood was safer, although the slope always seemed to be longer and steeper when Carwyn went down. Myfanwy watched him in growing frustration.

"I don't know how he does that," she said. "He has this peculiar ability to warp space. It can be very irritating." I didn't agree. I didn't find anything here irritating at all. I was an only child and I was simply enjoying the experience of having surrogate brothers and sisters, of sharing in the close affection all three had for each other.

After New Year, which wasn't a big celebration, Mum and I went back to London to prepare for our trip to Hong Kong. Much as I would miss Myfanwy and Aelred Abbey, I was looking forward to seeing my Dad again. It was the night we got back that the phone rang at 2.00 in the morning. I heard Mum answer and then a cry of "No!" I got out of bed and found Mum crying in the hallway, the phone still in her hand. She stopped crying when she saw me and suddenly became all business.

"Pack your things Tom," she said. "We leave as soon as possible. I want to catch the next flight."

I felt fear grip my heart. "Mum, what's wrong?"

"There has been an accident, an earthquake in the South China Sea. Your father's drilling rig has been destroyed and he's missing."

My memory of the next few hours is confused. In fact, the whole of the next week now has a dream-like quality for me. I only remember snatches, like scenes from a movie about someone else. I remember packing my things in an unnaturally calm, detached and methodical way. The drive to the airport I hardly remember at all. At the airport, Mum had to contend with airline booking staff, who kept telling her that the flights were full, and with a representative of the oil company dad worked for, who kept ringing and saying that there was no point in our coming to Hong Kong; that they could handle everything and that we would be better to stay in London. Mum faced all of them down and by 10.00 that morning we were on a flight to Hong Kong.

On the flight over I could think of nothing but the possibility that my Dad might be gone. He had never been around all the time as I was growing up, he was always off on an oil rig somewhere, but I knew he would always come back. I always knew he was there, somewhere. I couldn't face the thought that he might be gone for good. It didn't seem real.

In Hong Kong we were greeted at the airport by a representative of Dad's company and taken to a briefing.

There had been an earthquake near the rig and this had caused one of the legs to give way. The whole rig had rapidly collapsed into the sea. There were four lifeboats and three of these had been found using their emergency beacons. They had all been caught up in a tsunami that had followed the quake and had been swept well inland in Vietnam. One had been slammed into the ruins of a building and another into a rocky cliff. All the crew onboard those boats had died. Another had been found perched in a tree in the Mekong Delta. Even here there were serious injuries. Dad was not in any of these. Our only hope was that he was onboard the fourth, as yet unfound, lifeboat. But the safety beacon on this lifeboat was not functioning and, even though no one said it, we knew they thought that this boat was buried somewhere under the wreckage piled high by the tsunami.

Mum and I returned to our hotel and waited. For three days we waited. We didn't say much, we just listened to the news reports and got periodic updates from the oil company. Outwardly, Mum was dry eyed and business like but I know she cried herself to sleep every night. I prayed. I prayed the same prayer over and over again: "God save him, God keep him safe." I was able to talk to Myfanwy via Professor Rhys' university phone but they were awkward conversations. Words couldn't say what I felt and I couldn't hold her close over the phone.

On the fourth day we got the news that Dad had been found. He was well and on an American aircraft carrier in the Western Pacific. They were arranging for him to be sent to a base southern Japan. The company arranged for us to get a flight to meet him. We got a briefing on what had happened before we left. As he was about to get into the last lifeboat, Dad realised that a young geologist was missing. He went back to find her. The rig was beginning to collapse and was already listing at a large angle. He found the geologist struggling on a steeply tilting gang way and virtually lifted her to safety. In defiance of operating procedures, the crew in the lifeboat had stayed on the rig until my Dad and the geologist were on board. It was too late to launch normally and they had ridden the rig into the ocean. It was then that their emergency beacon had been torn away and their motor damaged. They never regained contact with the other boats.

The company guy who told us all this thought it was an amazing story but I wasn't surprised. My Dad went back into a collapsing oil rig to save a junior member of his crew? Of course he did, he's my Dad. His crew risked their lives to wait for him? Of course they did, he's my Dad. This is just the kind of guy he is. He would put his life on the line for his people without thinking and they would put their lives on the line for him. It's what good people do.

Ironically, their late departure may well have saved their lives. They missed getting caught up in the tsunami and were instead swept out into the Pacific where they were eventually, and accidently, found by a passing American naval battle group.

We met Dad in a bland reception room at a US air base in Okinawa. He hugged Mum tight and long and hard and then he kissed her. My eyes filled with tears which was a bit embarrassing. It was just that after all the stress of the last few days, this was right. This was how it should be. He turned and caught me up in a hug that lifted me off the floor, which was not easy to do since I was as big as he was. When he put me down, we laughed to see that we were both wiping tears from our eyes. All the strain, all the fear, was gone. Cadell had not got my Dad.

They offered Dad counselling but he said he would rather take a holiday instead. So we found ourselves back in Australia. My school wasn't happy but at that time the thing I needed most was time with my Dad and my parents needed time together. Everything else could wait: even spending time with Myfanwy, even looking for Merlin.

Our house at Angle Creek was being let for the summer holidays but that was fine because Dad said he'd had enough of looking at the ocean for a while. We went instead to a small cabin in the mountains to the north east of Melbourne: mountains of tall trees and hidden fern gullies; mountains of wilderness and a grandeur to match anything in Annwn.

They were also mountains where wild fires could be catastrophic and were an all too frequent summer occurrence. This had happened a few years ago in the area around our cabin. The small town near us had been destroyed and subsequently rebuilt. The forests, however, had recovered quickly and it was now difficult to see the scars of the fire. We spent our days walking on the trails through the mountains. These were nearly deserted as most people had gone to the coast for the summer. It was good to be able to spend time with Dad, but it was even better to be able to spend time with Mum and Dad together. Our walks always took more time than you would expect because we had to keep stopping so that Mum could set up her camera and take a picture of a tree, or a rock or a wildflower: each picture took a long, long time. It was okay though, because since the accident Mum and Dad were getting on well together. So well, in fact, that I sometimes felt like I was getting in the way.

On one of our walks I pointed out an area of forest that had been burnt but had not recovered. It was on the top of a ridge overlooking a deep ravine. The trees were still black and bare around a stone obelisk.

"Where?" Dad asked.

"Just there on the top of that ridge," I said.

"No, I can't see anything," he said. It was there in plain sight. I did not understand how he could not see it.

"There!" I said, pointing. "Mum, Can you see it? That rock with all the dead trees around it?"

She shook her head. "There's nothing there but trees," she said. They wouldn't look where I was pointing. The way they wouldn't look and didn't even know that they wouldn't look, reminded of Myfanwy and the way she wouldn't see the tunnel under the waterfall. I looked at the ridge again. Why were all those trees still black and bare and what was a stone obelisk doing on a ridge in the middle of nowhere? Magic seemed to be at work here. I didn't need to push Mum and Dad to do something they couldn't do but it was clear I would need to investigate.

That afternoon we went down into the town for some drinks and I chanced to read a tourist information sign about the adjacent National Park. It gave a simple run down on the geology of the area. Apparently, this town was on the edge of something called the Cerberean Cauldron, part of a larger structure called the Cerberean Ring: a thick and extensive pile of volcanic rocks which included a large sequence of explosive rhyodacites and andesitic basalts. I was stunned. It was so obvious and yet so unexpected that I just stood there staring at the sign. About 300 million years ago the Cerberean Cauldron was an ancient super volcano. It all came together in my head. What Friar Daffyd said of the ancient dragons, '...they could not stay together. Each fled to the opposite side of the world' he was referring to what geologists would call continental drift and the breakup of Pangaea. Pangaea was an ancient supercontinent which began to break apart around 200 million years ago, with each of the smaller continents scattering to different parts of the globe. Australia was certainly at one end of the world, so it was just possible that the ridge with the obelisk was part of one of the ancient dragons!

The next morning, when Mum and Dad said they were going into town for a coffee, I excused myself and said that I wanted to go for a run. The day promised to be blisteringly hot so I set off soon after they left. I needed to get this done in the morning, before the heat of the day took over.

I ran along a path that would take me near to the obelisk ridge but no path actually went to that particular ridge so I had to 'bush bash' my way through the forest to finally get there. As I came to the area of burnt and barren trees, I felt the now familiar buzzing sensation between my eyes that meant I was walking through, and destroying, a magic barrier. The skeletal trees moved in the hot, north wind: their bare branches sounding like dry bones as they rubbed together. Nothing grew here. There were no wildflowers, no grass – nothing. Cadell had the power to change the physical constants of our universe so that life was impossible. He had once used this power to kill Myfanwy's father. I wondered if he had done that here. If so, it was sad but somehow fitting that his great power should lead only to this place of dead and creaking bones.

I walked through a second magic barrier as I approached the obelisk, a more powerful one this time, and finally came to a cleared space around the stone itself. The obelisk was a rough standing stone about three meters high. Standing in front of it, I felt the same buzzing and itching between my eyes only at an intensity that I had never felt before. It was so intense that it was painful and it didn't go away but increased as I walked closer to the obelisk. Tentatively, I reached out with my mind. 'No magic', I thought. The buzzing only increased further. It was so bad now that I had difficulty concentrating. I stretched out my hand to touch the obelisk.

Suddenly, I found myself in two places at once. I was still standing on the ridge in the Australian mountains in the hot morning sun but I was also standing in a cold, dark, steep sided valley with snow on the mountain tops glowing under a full moon. I was being pulled apart. My mind was balanced on the very edge of sanity and the pain was intense. Across the dark valley from me there was a sheer rock face, several hundred feet high. Carved into the rock face was the image of a dragon. As I watched, its eyes glowed blue and the great head turned to look at me.

"No!" I cried in my mind and maybe with my voice also. "No magic!" The pressure became immense and there was heat and massive energy. I had never experienced anything like this before. I couldn't hold it together. I felt something break... then there was only darkness.

Chapter 24
Recovery in Australia

I woke up lying in a bed in a bright, cheerful but empty room that had the unmistakable smell of a hospital. The clock on the wall indicated that it was nine o'clock and bright morning sun was streaming in the window, so I knew I had lost at least one day. I tried to get out of bed but found I was weak, not sore and nothing seemed broken, but I was very weak. I had to sit on the side of the bed and rest. After a short time, a nurse came in.

"Oh good, you're awake," he said cheerily. "But you really must rest. There's no need for you to get out of bed. I'll call your parents to let them know you're awake."

"How did I get here? How long have I been out?" I asked. "And why am I in a hospital? What's wrong with me?" He looked at me sheepishly.

"So many questions! I think it's best if the doctor talks to you about all that," he said. "But... you've had a good long sleep."

"Then why do I still feel so weak?" I asked. He didn't answer. He just smiled and assured me that the doctor would be in soon and that he would ring my parents. I lay back on the bed. I got the feeling that I had missed more than one day. The doctor came in a short time later. He took my blood pressure and listened to my heart. Then he looked at me as if I was some sort of puzzle.

"The trouble with you Mr. O'Malley is that there is nothing wrong with you. Yet you were brought in here unconscious and you have remained that way for over a week. Then this morning you wake up and, apart from a little weakness from spending so long in bed, you're fine. As soon as your parents get here I'll discharge you but I need to know. What happened to you on that ridge?"

I shrugged. "I don't really remember," I lied. "I went for a run on the ridge and then I woke up here." He didn't look satisfied.

"Very well," he said. "I guess we will just have to put it down to heat stress and nervous exhaustion: no doubt a result of your recent trauma. You should take it easy for a while. Whatever it was that happened to you, it hit you really hard. It was as if your whole body had undergone a massive shock." He paused and looked at me intently, as if trying to see through my skin. "Yet there was absolutely no sign of any physical damage. We looked for evidence of snake bite, electrical shock, dehydration...There was nothing." He shook his head. "You are a mystery Mr. O'Malley." He prepared to leave. "Rest until your parents arrive. I'll see you before you go."

Mum and Dad came in about half an hour later. I was in hospital in a large regional town at the foot of the mountains and they were still staying up in the mountain cottage. When they came in, they wanted to know all the same things the doctor did and I told them the same lies. I didn't feel good about it but, in truth, I didn't understand what had happened well enough to tell a coherent story anyway, I was hoping they could help.

"I went for a run" I said. "How did I end up here?"

"We got worried when we came back and you were still out," Dad said. "The temperature went up over 40 degrees that afternoon. So, when you didn't come back by late afternoon, we called the police. They wanted to know where you might have gone and all I could think of was the interest you had shown in that ridge the morning before. So I told them about that. It didn't take them long to find you. You were up on the ridge in a patch of dead trees, next to a pile of broken rocks."

"You were unconscious," Mum said. "At first we thought it was heat stroke but the doctors here didn't think so and then you didn't wake up. Days went by and you still didn't wake up. The doctors just called it complete exhaustion but I don't think they really know what was wrong." She quickly looked across at my Dad, who was picking up my bags. Then she turned back to me with an even more worried expression. "Tom, what happened to you was strange, was it...you know...special? Myfanwy special?"

I shrugged. "I went for a run and I woke up here. I have no memory of the last six days. It's just a blank." That at least was true and it seemed to satisfy her.

She patted my arm and said, "Come on, we'll get you some lunch." That was good because I was very, very hungry.

Late that night, which was early in the morning London time, I got a telephone call from Myfanwy. She was calling from the phone in her uncle's university office. I had so rarely seen Myfanwy use any form of electronic communication that it was weird to hear her disembodied voice.

"Tom, I'm so sorry," she said all in a rush. "I wanted to come but they wouldn't let me. Not knowing how you were nearly drove me mad with worry. What happened to you? Are you okay?"

"I'm fine Myf, really," I said. "And it's good you didn't come out here. That would have been silly. All you could have done was sit and watch me sleep, which would have been about as interesting and useful as watching paint dry. Not even St. Agatha's is that bad."

"I suppose so," she said. "That's what they keep telling me anyway. Still, I wanted to be with you. I wanted to be there when you woke up."

"That would have been nice," I said softly. "I would choose you over the male nurse anytime. But I'm fine and I'll see you soon. Don't worry. I'll see you soon. I lo..."

"No!" she yelled. "Don't say it. Even over the phone, words have power, particularly those words. Don't say them casually." I was about to pretend to have been going to say something trivial when I stopped. A worried Myfanwy deserved more than that.

Instead I said with all the seriousness I could muster, "Don't worry, Myfanwy. When you hear me say those words, you'll know how deeply I mean them." Then Mum wanted the phone to talk to Professor Rhys about something, so we said goodbye.

The doctors had advised that I should rest before the long trip back to England. So the next day we moved back to our house in Angle Creek. The January summer holidays were over and the holiday renters had gone home. I still felt weak, too weak even to surf, but I was slowly getting stronger. Each day I would sit on the beach and watch other people ride the waves as they came in from the Southern Ocean. Each night Myfanwy would call me and tell me what had happened at school that day. I didn't much care about the gossip or T.S. Elliot's poetry but I found that I needed to hear the sound of her voice. The day she wasn't able to call was bleak for both of us.

On the morning of the eighth day after leaving the mountains, I picked up my board and joined my Dad for an early surf. There was about a two meter swell coming in as regular as clockwork. I was a bit clumsy and dropped a couple of good rides but I didn't care. I was back and I was well again.

That night, after Myfanwy's call, Mum and Dad sat me down with their serious 'we need to talk' faces. My experience of such talks is that they are nearly always extremely uncomfortable and rarely useful. This one was no exception.

"Tom, we want to talk to you about Myfanwy," Mum started.

"You know we really like her. We think she is a lovely girl," Dad added. "It's just that we don't want you to get too involved too soon. You're still very young and there's a whole world full of possibilities out there."

"Also," Mum said. "Your Dad has decided to take a job on the Penguin III production platform." This was an oil and gas platform in Bass Straight, offshore from Angle Creek. Work there would be more routine and less exciting than work on the exploration rigs but it would be close to home. "And I've decided to leave the fashion industry and work as a landscape photographer. I already have some commissions." She paused. "All this means that we will be leaving London and moving back into this house permanently. I'm afraid your relationship with Myfanwy will become a very long distance affair." This was not unexpected but it was annoying all the same. There was no discussion, just ',,, we will be leaving London..." and I had to cope with that. I didn't get too annoyed, however, both because I knew it was coming and because I also wanted to come back to Australia. I thought for a moment before replying. They were saying a lot without saying it openly.

"I have to finish school in London," I said firmly. "I would end up a year behind if I had to start Year 12 here now." Mum and Dad nodded to indicate that they accepted that point. "As for Myfanwy and me, don't worry. Neither of us are stupid and we're not irresponsible. And while I admit that I may be a bit impetuous at times," Mum rolled her eyes at what she clearly considered to be an understatement, "Myfanwy and her family aren't. Are we too young? I don't know, time will tell. How will we handle such a long distance relationship? I don't know. One thing I do know. I would never do anything to hurt or dishonour her in any way and I take my responsibility to her very seriously. You'll just have to trust me on that." There was an awkward silence then Dad slapped his hand on his knee.

"Well that's good enough for me," he said. "There's an early Star Trek on the Late Night Movie. Anyone care to join me?" Mum hesitated.

When Dad had left the room, she said, "You know a relationship with Myfanwy has more than its normal share of challenges. Are you sure?" I gave a simple nod in reply. It's strange, but sometimes you don't know the answer to a question until it's asked by another person. I was sure but I did wonder how long she had been talking to Nain and what Nain had told her. I also wondered whether Helen was having a similar conversation with Myfanwy back in England. I thought of what Br. Theophane had told me…"I have seen men thy age shoulder the burden of raising a family. I have seen men thy age lead others into battle. Aye, and die there too…" I had a strange feeling then; a feeling that my childhood was ending.

Myfanwy didn't call for the next two days and I was worried that the conversation at her end had gone badly. Then, as I finished my morning surf, she was there on the beach. We didn't speak. We just held each other tight. It was only when I was holding her that I really believed she was there. Then, to my embarrassment, I started to cry. It was okay though, Myfanwy was crying too. All the strain of the last weeks melted away.

"How did you get here?" I asked.

"We flew in this morning," she said. "But I couldn't wait for the car, so I teleported here as soon as I could. I just needed to see you."

"I'm so glad you did," I said. "It's so, so good to see you." Then I hugged her again and we walked together up to the house. Three hours later the car arrived with Helen, Carwyn and Gwyneth. Carwyn was not happy at being made to ride in the car while Myfanwy had teleported ahead, but he got over it.

On the beach that evening, during the long summer twilight, Myfanwy and I got together with her siblings to compare notes. They were here because it was now the mid-term break back in England and they had all flown out to get me. I was going to go back with them to finish school. Meanwhile, Professor Rhys and Nain were in Annwn trying to resist the dragon attacks which were becoming steadily more frequent and destructive.

They all wanted to know what had happened to me and for the first time I told the full story. Myfanwy and Gwyneth didn't know what to make of it but Carwyn looked thoughtful.

"Tom, do you know how the gates work?" he asked. I shook my head. "They are ontologically entangled. You know about quantum entanglement? How sub-atomic particles can be entangled, so that what happens to one happens to the other - at the same time, no matter what the distance between them?" I nodded. "Well, the gates are like that only at a more complete level. It's like they are the same gate existing in different places. They are a lot of work to construct but once they're built they need little or no energy to operate and distance is irrelevant. I think what you encountered was like that only it was two places being forced to exist in the same space and your mind reacted against the impossibility of that."

"Why?" Myfanwy asked. "Why would anyone do that?"

"I think I know," I said. "I was investigating the ridge because I thought the Cerberean Ring might be one of the ancient dragons in Friar Daffyd's story. 300 million years ago it was a super-volcano. In the story, the mother and daughter had to go to opposite sides of the world. Well, what if Cadell forced them back together; forced them to occupy the same space? They are long dead but the strain could wake their daughters."

"If that's true," Carwyn said. "Then the energy running between those two sites would be immense. What you did was like trying to unplug the power by grabbing a high voltage cable. I'm not surprised you ended up in hospital. I'm just surprised that you're still alive."

"What about the obelisk?" I asked. "That was reduced to rubble. Does that mean the link has been broken?"

"Maybe," Carwyn said. "You would need to go to the other site to be sure. The obelisks were there as a focus. To do this entanglement you need objects to entangle. There will be, or would have been, an obelisk at the other end. What I don't understand is the dragon. What has that got to do with anything?"

"I think I know," Myfanwy said. "It's Merlin's tomb. It's got to be! A carving like that in a cliff face - it must be hidden by magic. If it weren't it would be famous and we would all know about it. It's exactly the kind of thing we were looking for. Tom can see it but no one else can."

"Maybe not even Cadell," I said thoughtfully. "I think that maybe Cadell's link and Merlin's tomb are both there for the same reason - it's the heart of the dragon. I don't think Cadell even knows Merlin's tomb is there. It's just as hidden from him as it is from everybody else."

"But we know it's there. So all we need to do is find Cadell's link and we've found Merlin's tomb," Gwen said brightly.

"Yes." Myfanwy said. "But we don't know where Cadell's link is, so that doesn't help us very much."

As we walked back to the house, I thought about the valley I had seen. It was dark, with a bright moon high in the sky so it was late at night. It was a broad valley with steep sides, cold with snow on the mountain tops. All of this was consistent with North West Scotland which was already out target area. I just needed to find that same valley.

Over the next week there was increasing volcanic activity across the world but all was quiet at Angle Creek. It was a week of warm summer days, an open beach and waves rolling in from the Southern Ocean. At the end of it we packed up to fly back to England. Mum was coming with me, to wind up all her London affairs.

We were all booked on the same flight although not all of us travelled by car. Helen and Gwen came with us while Myfanwy and Carwyn went their own, much faster, way. Dad came to see us off and said a very long goodbye to Mum. As we waited to get on the plane, I dreaded the boredom of the long flight. Spending 24 hours in a cramped metal tube did not please Carwyn either.

"There's got to be a better way to do this," he grumbled. No one could think of one, however, so the plane it was going to have to be.

About thirty hours later we arrived in London. This time there was no one to meet us and our trip back to our London address was uneventful. From there Myfanwyy and her family used the gate to go to Aelred Abbey. The next day was Sunday. It started with the news that over a thousand people had died in Japan as a long dormant volcano suddenly erupted. I spent a lot of the day in Westminster Cathedral praying to be able to bring this to an end.

Chapter 25
Strange Encounters

Going back to school the next day was a bit of a shock after being so long away. The shock was that so little had changed. I met Myfanwy at the gate and as we walked to St. Agatha's she filled me in on what had happened in English in the first part of the term. It had mostly been an introduction to T.S. Eliot and I had read a long review essay on him so I was pretty confident I could keep up. As it turned out, we didn't have English that morning. It was replaced by a special memorial service for all those killed in the volcanic disasters plaguing the world: some of whom had been past pupils of St. Agatha's.

The service was run by a nice lady vicar from the local Church of England parish. Apparently she was the school's chaplain although I don't think anyone had seen her at the school before this. The service was pretty bland, as all these types of service must be, but at least it was better run and more prayerful than the Headmaster's efforts. In the face of suffering on such a massive scale, even those who would normally not darken the door of a church seemed to accept that prayer might not be such a bad idea.

I had a free period after that and I met Wilson in the library for a catch up on the science and maths subjects. He gave me a copy of his notes which, as I've said before, were much better than my own and went through them with me. Even so, in the maths period that followed I really struggled to follow what was going on.

That lunch time there was a girl with wavy, brown hair sitting at our usual table. She had a clear complexion without any make up. I sat down prepared to introduce myself.

She said, "Hello Tom, Glad to see you back." It was only then that I realized that it was Rachael.

"Rachael, you've changed!" I said. She smiled and that was another shock. I don't think I'd seen Rachael smile until that moment. It changed her whole face, and for the better. The girl in front of me looked nothing like the wannabe goth that I had said farewell to before Christmas.

"I decided to try a new style," she said. "I believe in the infinite possibilities of self-reinvention. Do you like it?"

I nodded readily. "Yeah, sure," I said. "It really suits you." She seemed pleased. Just then Wilson and Phil joined us.

"How do you like the new Rachael?" Wilson asked.

"I think she looks great," I said. It was about that time that Myfanwy sat down and I couldn't help but notice a certain coolness at the table. Myfanwy made no mention of Rachael's new look. The conversation soon shifted to the chaplain that no one knew we had. We all agreed she was nice and it turned out that she had only recently been appointed to her parish. There were also a number of new hook ups among the students.

One of the blond 'in girls' had gained temporary fame by going out with a guitarist from a B-Grade rock band. It didn't last long. Apparently Gabriella wouldn't be joining us. She was now spending all her time with a timid, long haired classical guitarist from the IB stream.

"I wish people would stop swapping and just settle down," Phil complained. "It's really confusing."

"No!" Rachael said in an exasperated voice. "This is normal for our age. This is the time when we all explore who we are and who we might be: experience our different possible selves. Change is a constant." She looked across at Myfanwy and me. "Except for the two of you, of course," she said somewhat sarcastically. "You two never change."

I raised my eyebrows at her and said, "Given that we're approaching the end of our last year of school, I think we'll soon have all the change we can handle."

All the rest of that term we were getting ready for our final exams and starting to consider where we would go next: what it was we wanted to do. There was far less general discussion and a lot more concentrated study: study of what we really needed to know. After Easter there would be very little except exam preparation and, of course, the exams themselves. All this time I was looking at pictures of Scottish valleys, trying to find the one I had seen. The trouble was that there were a lot of wild, steep sided valleys in Scotland and I had only seen mine in the dark and under stress.

All the time, the volcanic activity was getting more violent and frequent. Large areas were now evacuated but if all the super-volcanoes erupted at the same time, there would simply be nowhere to go. Meanwhile, life at school went on with only a few hiccups. Myfanwy and I made a habit of meeting up and going to lunch together. This was just as well because one such lunchtime, we walked into the dining hall to find a whole crowd of students either frozen in fear at their tables or huddled in the corners as elegant ladies and gentlemen from the 18th century danced around them. In fact, just as we got there one girl screamed as a couple danced through her. Instinctively, Myfanwy froze time. The students froze but the couples kept dancing. I looked questioningly at Myfanwy.

She shrugged. "I froze our time not theirs," she said. As she was speaking, the past shadows faded but Myfanwy kept time frozen.

"Tom, I don't know what to do. There are too many of them and the experience is too intense. Maybe Uncle Cadfan could take all these memories away but I don't think I can." As I looked at the time frozen students, they looked like they were asleep and that gave me an idea.

"Myfanwy, put them to sleep,"

"What good would that do?" She asked. "They will have to wake up eventually."

"Yes, but you could just slightly alter their memories so that they became like dream memories. Just alter how they're being stored in the brain. Then they will wake up all having had the same dream. It will be really, really weird… but not terrifying."

Myfanwy nodded. "I think I can do that," she said. Then she smiled. "Actually it's quite clever. I must mention this to Uncle Cadfan." She let time flow again and then, straight away, all the students went to sleep. A few moments later they started to wake up. They were uncertain, puzzled and really weirded out, but they were calm. For them, it had been an odd dream when they had strangely fallen asleep in the middle of the day: nothing more.

The other interesting thing was that even though Rachael now looked more normal, her behavior just became stranger. She seemed to take it as a personal insult that Myfanwy and I were not breaking up. She kept returning again and again to the theme of trying new possible versions of yourself and the natural instability of romantic relationships. She took objection to the strangest things.

One lunch time, for example, Roland Greensmith, who was the last of Horace's henchmen remaining, came and stood threateningly over Myfanwy, his hands balled into fists. When he spoke his voice was slurred with anger.

"You and all your people, they're all bastards! You know that?" Myfanwy looked at him, more surprised than frightened. "You sit there all toffy and posh. You slum it with an Australian boyfriend but you're too good to talk to us. Well to hell with you! Real people have to work for a living. You don't know what that means do you? You don't have a clue!" By this time he was yelling and his posture was very intimidating. Myfanwy was starting to get worried. Everyone else was just nonplussed. What had brought all this on? I moved up next to Myfanwy, in part to protect Roland from whatever Myfanwy might do.

Roland snarled. "What's this? Skippy to the rescue! Well, you don't worry me, mate. I can take you."

"No, you can't," I said.

"I can. I've been training since we last met," He directed a reverse punch at my diaphragm and it was clear that he had indeed been training. He was balanced, his technique was pretty good and there was real power behind the blow. However, he signaled his move, his timing was off and he lacked focus. I easily deflected the blow and placed my hand on his shoulder. I didn't hurt him or hit him but the message was clear: the only reason you're not hurting now is that I choose not to hurt you. He got the message and stepped back, his body stiff with suppressed anger.

"It isn't fair," he yelled. "My dad has worked hard all his life and now he's lost his business because of you."

"What are you talking about?" Myfanwy said, exasperated. "I don't even know what your dad's business is."

"You and all your kind," he replied. "Your uncle works in finance. I read it in the paper. Well, the banks, the stock brokers, the traders, all of them, they just shut down my Dad's business. Now I'm going to have to leave school... It isn't fair!" I was shocked to see that there were tears in his eyes.

Myfanwy moved in front of me. "No Roland, it isn't fair," she said. "But neither I nor my family had anything to do with it." She leaned forward and whispered, "I can arrange it so that you don't have to leave school."

"I don't want charity from you," he whispered back savagely.

"It's not charity, it's influence, "she said quietly. "My family donates a scholarship each term to the school. I can pull some strings and make sure it goes to you."

He looked at her uncertainly. "You would do that?" he asked. "Even after I called you witch girl and... all that." Myfanwy nodded. Now he was openly crying.

"Thank you," he said in a choked voice and turned and hurried from the dining hall. I looked at her suspiciously.

"I didn't know your family donated a scholarship to the school," I said.

Myfanwy shrugged. "We do now," was all she said.

The strangest thing about this whole incident was Rachael's response. She had observed everything from the table and when we sat down she started to harangue us.

"You two are hopeless," she said. "You live in some kind of fantasy." Phil and Wilson sat down at the table. Rachael ignored them. "You act like the noble lady and her knight protector. I'm surprised you're not wearing her favour on your arm, Tom. This is the 21st century, not the 14th. That kind of romance is completely out of date. There is no happy ever after. There's only happy while it lasts and then goodbye. No one sticks to things when they go bad anymore. When something doesn't work, you walk away and try something new."

"Try telling the Aston Villa supporters that," Phil said. "They haven't won a premiership since the early eighties but their supports still follow them. You don't change your football team just because they're going bad." Rachael looked daggers at him.

"Change is growth, stability is death," she said.

"Actually, you put that around the wrong way," Wilson said. "It would be more accurate to say that growth is change but growth also implies continuity and stability can be the result of commitment. Commitment is what gives you direction and purpose, without it you are just like a leaf being blown about by the wind." He looked at Rachael, his expression hard to read.

"Commitment requires discipline and self-sacrifice but it's the only way you can achieve anything," he said. "You should leave Tom and Myfanwy alone. It's the idea that you can have love without commitment that's the real fantasy."

This speech proved to be a bit of a conversation killer and the rest of lunch was a bit awkward. Rachael remained sitting at the table as we left. Wilson turned to look at her as we left the dining room. She was still sitting alone at the table: a sad and lost figure. Wilson watched her for a while, a strange expression on his face. Still watching her he softly whispered, "What I didn't say was that commitment is love and sometimes love can hurt like the hell." Then he turned and walked off quickly.

Through all of this, and my catch-up study, I kept exploring Scotland on the internet through every web page I could come across. Scotland, however, is a big place and it has a very large web presence. It wasn't until near the end of term that I found a travel blog detailing some guy's recent walks through the valleys of Scotland. He was an incompetent photographer and his pictures were dark and poorly focused. However, it was precisely these features which enabled me to recognize the area I had seen at night and under great stress. The carved dragon and the obelisk were missing from the photograph but the rest of it was there: the same steep sided valley and snow covered hills. I quickly researched the location and it made sense. It was in Glencoe, and 400 million years ago Glencoe had been a super-volcano.

I had found the other ancient dragon and Merlin's resting place!

Chapter 26
Michael's Choice

It was too late and too dark to set out that night but I started to put all the things we might need into a backpack: water proof jacket, water bottle etc. Then I researched how I could get from Myfanwy's house in Edinburgh to Glencoe. It turned out to be a simple, albeit long, bus trip. The next day I walked down to breakfast dressed for a hike, carrying my pack and Declan's walking stick. Mum froze when she saw them.

"Where are you going with all that stuff," she asked frostily.

"Mum, I've found where Merlin is trapped," I said. "I'm going to Scotland."

"You are not!" Mum said. "It's still two days to the end of term and you have already missed far too much school."

"School won't do me much good if Cadell succeeds in destroying the world," I reasoned. "I've found the resting place of Merlin, the only man who can put a stop to all this. Myfanwy and I have to go and release him. It's the only way."

"You don't have to go," she replied. "You could send those government people or Nain." She paused. "Tom, your father almost died, I won't have you in danger as well. I won't stand for it. I forbid it!"

I shook my head. "Mum, please, this is something I have to do." I took a deep breath. "It's something I am going to do whether you agree or not. I'm eighteen and I can make my own decisions. Please don't make this a fight." She stood ridged for a moment and then let out a sigh and when I looked at her, she wasn't angry or indignant. She was just frightened and sad.

"Be careful," she said softly. "At least promise me you'll be careful." I went over and gave her a hug.

"I will Mum," I said. "I will." I left early enough to meet Myfanwy at the gate as she was going to school. She smiled at me as she came through the gate. I smiled back but I had no time for pleasantries.

"Myf, we have to go," I said. "I've found Merlin." She looked surprised but recovered quickly.

"Where?" she asked. She was already turning around to go back through the gate as I answered.

"Glencoe, Scotland."

Myfanwy took my hand as I came through the gate and we teleported directly to the main entrance hall of Aelred Abbey.

"Wait here, and be quiet, Mum and Gwen are in the kitchen." she said as she raced up the stairs. "I'll be down in a minute." she was back soon after, still wearing her school uniform but with a thick, waterproof jacket and hiking boots.

"Let's go." She said. Just before we left, Gwyneth came out of the kitchen.

"Good luck you two," she said. "Stay away from waterfalls this time." I looked in surprise at Myfanwy, wondering what she had told her, but Myfanwy looked just as surprised as me.

Gwyneth laughed, "Myfwy, do you really think you can keep secrets from me?" she asked. She turned to me. "Keep her safe Tom… no more sleeping bags." I nodded briefly, horrified at how much she knew.

We teleported to the gate and went through to again find ourselves in the dark and musty corridor in the Edinburgh house. We went out to the street and I used my phone to find the way to the bus station. We got there just before the bus left and we didn't have time to buy tickets. Myfanwy just walked onto the bus and waved at the driver.

"You don't need to see our tickets," she said.

The driver smiled back. "No, I don't," he said. "There are seats up the back."

As we sat down I said, "These aren't the droids you're looking for."

She hit my arm. "Be quiet! You'll just make things harder... And yes, I have seen that movie. When I was in year seven I went to Wilson's birthday party. It was a Star Wars marathon."

"Of course it was," I said as I leaned back in my seat. "What else would Wilson's party be?" The bus moved out and soon we were in the Scottish countryside. It was over three hours later that we pulled into the visitors centre car park in Glencoe. We had lunch in the kiosk and then headed out to walk the length of the glen.

It was a wild place. The valley was impressive. The walls were steep and reached up to mountains that looked much higher in the daylight than they did at night. There were still patches of snow around the tops of the mountains and the spring streams were running strongly through the valley. The wind was cold but the sun was shining and it was ideal walking weather. We skirted a lake at the start of the valley and it wasn't long before the shapes of the hills that I had seen when I touched the obelisk became apparent. They were, however, still a long way off and we had a long walk ahead.

It was, however, pleasant walking through the valley. It wasn't just the spectacular scenery. It was that Myfanwy was there and we were good together. Since we were alone together, Myfanwy could relax and be herself. Myfanwy could laugh and Myfanwy could smile. Myfanwy could hold my hand as I helped her over difficult parts of the path. We were also walking towards our best chance to stop Cadell. It was a good walk.

It was about mid afternoon when we reached the obelisk. It was on the floor of the valley near a fast flowing stream. A massive dragon was carved into the rock wall opposite. Both the obelisk and the dragon were hidden by magic and Myfanwy couldn't see them, though to me they were obvious.

"Are we there?" Myfanwy asked when I came to a stop.

"Yes," I said. "The obelisk is in front of us and the dragon is carved into that rock face on the opposite side of the valley." Given what had happened last time, I was reluctant to touch the obelisk but I reached out with my mind, trying to cancel the magic around the standing stone without touching the energy it contained. There was a slight pop in my head.

"Oh, I can see the obelisk now," Myfanwy said then she went silent for a long moment. "Tom, that thing is dangerous," she whispered eventually. "It's a conductor of almost unbelievable energy. We need to destroy it."

"I don't think you would be able to do that," said a voice from the ridge behind us. We turned around to find Cadell seated in a chair-like saddle and, with absurd arrogance, mounted on a polar bear as tall as a large horse. Either side of him were his Neo-Nazi guards dressed in what looked like German SS uniforms and carrying automatic assault rifles.

"Mr. O'Malley and dear Myfanwy, you two really are irritating. You seem to be very hard to kill and you always turn up just where you are not wanted. Not that it matters now. Even if you managed to destroy that standing stone, the process has started and cannot be stopped. Now not even I, the greatest magic user of my time, could bring to rest the forces that have been stirred. Not that I want to. Your world is coming to its much desired end and the time of the rule of the magic users is about to dawn. I will be proud to use my talents to bring order out of the chaos that is about to ensue."

"You've failed whenever you tried to control the world," I pointed out. "Like all the other psychos before you." His face twisted into a creepy smirk.

"Maybe," he said, "But none of the other psychos had this." He held up a plain wooden staff. "I'm sure you know what it is. Did you like playing with your plastic toy?" I looked at the staff he was holding. It was about six feet long, highly polished but unworked: still showing the knots and twists of the natural wood, The most interesting thing, however, was how he was holding it, He had on one of those thick, heat resistant gloves that some foundry workers wear. "Do you seriously think anyone can stand against someone wielding Merlin's staff?"

"I don't know," I said, "but it's not relevant because you can't wield it. In fact, you can only hold it by using an insulating glove and I'll bet that even then it burns," The quick twist of hatred on his face told me I was right.

"Tom," Myfanwy whispered. "I can't do any magic, someone is blocking me, resisting me forcefully."

Cadell answered in a calm but vicious voice. "Allow me to introduce a servant of mine – well, a tool really. Its story is a sad one. Hunted from birth, its own considerable magic talent was concentrated on one thing only: protecting itself from magic." One of the boulders at the base of the ridge started to move. It slowly stood and turned. "I could just get my friends here to shoot you," Cadell continued, "but I have something special planned for you."

The beast from the park stood before us, with its deformed, rock like body. I stepped towards it and for the first time gazed into its eyes. The weathered, olive green eyes gazed back at me with a deep sorrow. Then I knew and it all made sense, in a weird kind of way.

"Ave Michael," I said. "Dominus vobiscum." He didn't give the proper answer but just looked at me with those sad, despairing eyes

"Enough talk," Cadell yelled. "Kill them! Crush them!"

"I know Friar Daffyd misses you," I said quietly. "He looks for you each day at the distribution of the bread." A shudder passed through his body and his eyes seemed to focus on the far distance. A growling noise of some deep but undefinable emotion rumbled from the massive chest.

"Kill them!" Cadell yelled. "What are you waiting for? Kill them now!" Michael turned slowly to face Cadell.

"No," Michael said in his gravelly voice. "I will not kill for you and I will not kill for him." Michael and Cadell faced each other for a long moment.

Then Cadell said, "Fortunately, I don't need you." He turned to his neo-Nazi guards. "Shoot them," he said casually.

"No!" Michael yelled. He stepped in front of us, guarding us from the Nazis. The bullets slammed into his body, shaking him and causing his blood to flow: blood as red as that of any man. The bullets kept hitting him, and he shuddered with each impact, but none could pass through his body. Eventually he stumbled and fell. He struggled to turn and look at me. "Pax vobiscum," he said in a barely audible whisper.

I think it was then that his magic failed because Myfanwy yelled in anger and reached towards the Nazis with her fingers spread wide. They screamed in pain as their guns became red hot and the ammunition exploded within them.

Cadell snarled. "Do you really think you can oppose me Myfanwy? Remember who it was who killed your father and die in despair!" He pointed his finger at Myfanwy. I was filled with fury at what had happened and I reached out to Cadell with an intensity I had never known before: determined that he should not use magic. He was a long way away and thought he was safe, but I somehow 'saw' his magic in my mind and I reached out my hand and took every last bit of it. I left him with nothing.

This not only stopped him from attacking Myfanwy but it also had another consequence; one I didn't intend and didn't foresee. The polar bear was no longer under magical control. It shook off the saddle chair and casually crushed Cadell's skull with a swipe of its paw. It then picked up the body of the greatest magic user of our time in its mouth, shook it like a rag doll and walked off with it. Cadell was gone. The Nazi's took one look at the out of control bear and ran.

I knelt beside Michael. I wanted to help but he had been hit too often and there were too many wounds. There was blood everywhere. He looked at me with pain filled eyes.

"Now I will never be human," he rasped. "He promised to make me human."

"Michael," I said. "He couldn't make you human. You were always human. You are the most deeply human person I know." He looked at me puzzled. "It's not what you look like that makes you human," I explained. "It's how much you love. You have given your life to save ours and I have it on very good authority that there is no greater love than that."

Myfanwy knelt down beside me, her eyes full of tears. "There is something else also," she said. "Not only do you love greatly but you are greatly loved." She leaned forward and kissed his boney, rock-like forehead. Michael looked at her.

"I am loved," he said with a kind of wonder in his voice. Then he closed his eyes and was still. Myfanwy buried her head in my shoulder and I held her tightly, the tears flowing freely down my cheeks.

Chapter 27
Doom of Emrys, Doom Defying.

"So the beast and the homeless guy were the same person?" Myfanwy asked eventually. It was more a statement than a question but I answered anyway.

"Yes, I think they gave him periods looking normal as a kind of bribe to get him to do what they wanted. They used his heart's deepest desire to manipulate him."

"That's awful, but in the end he proved stronger than Cadell," she said.

I nodded. "Br. Theophane once told me that even though the forces against us were great there was a still greater force on our side. I realize now that the greater force was the innate goodness of Michael's heart."

We heard voices and looked up. A group of soldiers was bringing the neo-Nazis, hands on heads, back into the valley. Leading them was Sergeant Fisher of DIAP.I looked at him, amazed.

"How did you get here?" I asked.

"When you didn't show up for school, I checked your GPS trackers and found that you were in Scotland. With the situation around the world so critical, DIAP has decided to take a keen interest in your activities. We worked out that you were going to Glencoe and decided to find out what you were up to. We parachuted into the valley about an hour ago." He was looking curiously at Michael's body. "Things got interesting when we saw these guys running away and a polar bear, a *polar* bear, wandering off into the Scottish hills. What on earth has been happening here?"

"Cadell tried to kill us," I replied. "But our friend Michael here saved us — at the cost of his own life. Cadell then found out that a polar bear doesn't make a very safe pet. He's dead." Sergeant Fisher showed renewed interest.

"He's dead? The rogue magic user is dead?" He let out a long relieved breath. "So it's over."

I shook my head. "No," I said. "Unfortunately Cadell has set in motion events which now have their own momentum. We need to actively calm them down and the only man who can do that is entombed in that mountain." I pointed across the valley to the carving of the dragon. "And that is his staff." I walked over to the ridge and picked up the staff that Cadell had dropped. I could feel a buzzing energy in my hand but I was unharmed. As I picked it up, however, the dragon carving turned and looked at me with brilliant blue eyes. I froze in shock, forgetting that the others still couldn't see the dragon.

"Tom, what's wrong?" Myfanwy asked anxiously. As she was speaking the dragon detached itself from the rock face and leapt into the air, clear for everyone to see, black and terrible. There was a sharp intake of breath from Myfanwy, exclamations and curses from the soldiers and high pitched screams from the neo-Nazi prisoners.

Sergeant Fisher reacted by giving orders. "Take cover! Cotswell, I want the machine gun on the top of that ridge." Two soldiers moved immediately, running from cover to cover towards the ridge top. "Jameison, I need MANPADS now!" Three soldiers crouched behind a boulder and started to unpack some gear. "The rest of you, load armour piercing rounds but only fire on my order." The dragon was circling high above the valley. Myfanwy and I found a boulder and took shelter behind it. The neo-Nazis decided to take advantage of the situation and run. This turned out to be a mistake. Dragons hunt by sight and this one immediately spotted the running figures. It swooped in a low, curving dive and breathed. The Nazis were all lost in dragon fire. They didn't even have time to scream.

"Steady everyone," Sergeant Fisher shouted. "Wait for my order. Jameison, I need Starstreak!" The dragon climbed high and turned on one wing to swoop down on our position.

"Machine gun, short bursts!" Sergeant Fisher yelled. The gun opened up and tracer bullets swung towards the dragon. When they hit, the dragon screamed in pain and turned sharply. It was now flying along the ridge towards the machine gun position. As the dragon breathed, the two soldiers jumped away from the gun. Then the whole ridge exploded in flame.

"Starstreak ready!" called the soldiers setting up the gear. Sergeant Fisher reacted immediately.

"Fire!" he called. A small missile streaked away towards the dragon. The dragon was turning to come around for another run and the missile caught it easily. It exploded just near the base of the dragon's tail. The dragon screamed, a high pitched ear shattering sound, but managed to keep flying. There was black blood streaming from a gaping wound where the missile had struck. It turned, seeking its enemies hiding in the shadow of the river boulders.

This was my cue. I got up and ran towards the stream. The dragon immediately swooped to come after me as I knew it would. Behind me I heard Myfanwy yell "Tom!" and Sergeant Fisher call out "Fire at will." I didn't care. I was running as fast as I could: trying to put as much distance as possible between Myfanwy and the dragon. I reached the stream and jumped without hesitation into the icy water. Above me the world exploded in flame.

I stayed down as long as I could, which wasn't long because the water was really cold. When I surfaced, Myfanwy was running towards me and the dragon was coming in for another attack on my position. I heard an order of "Fire!" come from near the obelisk and another missile streaked out. The dragon saw this one coming and turned sharply but the missile followed it. It dived at high speed into the valley but the missile still caught it easily. It hit the dragon in the chest and the whole creature just exploded in flame and light. There was nothing left.

I hauled myself out of the freezing stream with Myfanwy's help. As soon as I was out she hugged me tight and said, "Be warm and dry," and there I was, warm and dry. There are times when magic girlfriends are really useful.

"Tom, you stupid, stupid boy!" she said furiously, still holding me tight. "You could have been killed." I lifted her face towards mine and kissed her softly on the lips.

"I have to protect you," I said. "It's my job. I'm sure I've mentioned this before."

"What good would that be if you were dead?" she replied. "Who would protect me from your dying?"

Sergeant Fisher came up to us then. "That run was a gutsy move Tom: stupid but gutsy. If you were under my command, we would be having harsh words now. As it is, your run gave us time to ready the second Starstreak. We owe you, big time."

I shrugged casually. "No offense Sergeant," I said, "but it wasn't your men I was thinking of."

He looked at Myfanwy and smiled. "I guess not," he said. "Look, I have two men who need urgent medivac. What are you two planning to do?"

"We need to go into Merlin's tomb and wake him up," I said. "I don't think you can help us with that." He gave a brief nod of his head then shook hands with both Myfanwy and me.

"Good luck," he said. Then he turned and went back to his men. Myfanwy and I went back to the boulders near the obelisk. I gave Declan's walking stick to Myfanwy and picked up Merlin's staff. I looked across the valley and the dragon carving was now gone. At the base of the cliff where it had been, there was now an ornate stone doorway, as big as the doorway of a great cathedral.

"Myfanwy, can you see that grey rock that looks a bit like a chair?" I asked. She nodded. "The door to the tomb is just next to that. Can you teleport us there?" She looked at me as if I were some sort of idiot.

"Of course." She said. She took my free hand and we were next to the rock and at the foot of the massive doorway. Myfanwy, of course, could still only see the rock face.

"Close your eyes,' I said and, still holding her hand, led her through the doorway and into the dark space beyond. I felt a slight 'pop' sensation as I walked through the door, which told me I had passed through a magic barrier. The tunnel had the form of a natural cave with a flat, sandy floor. It wasn't very long. I could already see daylight at the other end. I told Myfanwy to open her eyes. She looked around her but made no comment as we made our way down.

The tunnel was indeed short and we soon found ourselves looking across a vast, nearly spherical, cavern, filled with light. The upper part of the cavern was shrouded in mist, as if it were a cloudy sky, while the lower half formed a forest filled bowl, several kilometers across. The tunnel was exactly half way up the wall, perched between the mist and the forest. At the bottom of the bowl was a lake and in the centre of the lake was a rocky island. It wasn't hard to guess where Merlin would be.

"Myf, I don't suppose you could just teleport us onto that island," I asked. Myfanwy shook her head.

"This is an artificial place, Tom. The position of everything here is really tightly defined. Teleporting isn't possible."

I sighed. "I didn't think it would be that easy. Come on, we need to get going."

The first part of the trip was a near vertical descent, scrambling over rocks. The descent grew easier as we got lower and the tree coverage grew thicker. Eventually we arrived in a deep and tangled oak forest. It was a forest of thick trunks and gnarled branches, tangled roots and thick undergrowth. The light was dim and deep green. It would have been very difficult to make our way through if it were not for a narrow path that twisted its way through the trees.

We followed the path through an unnatural silence; a silence that grew ever more insistent; that pressed louder than any sound. We must have walked for an hour, following the twisting track, trusting, without any real evidence, that it was actually going somewhere. Our world narrowed down, there was the track, the trees and always the silence: persistent and oppressive.

So it came as a shock when we finally heard a sound we hadn't made. There was a brushing sound in the forest: something was moving there. As we moved on we heard it again: something was following us. Then there was a loud crashing as whatever it was raced ahead of us. Whatever it was, it was big and it was fast. Myfanwy almost dropped Declan's walking stick as blue fire raced along it and it turned into a massive pike. This was too heavy for Myfanwy to carry, so I took it and carried it across my right shoulder: Merlin's staff in my left hand.

"I suppose it makes sense that there should be some sort of guard," I said. "But what sort of guard is it that we need a pike like this to defend ourselves?

We came to a bend where the track widened out and the forest was more open. Ahead of us, a black bear, at least as big as the polar bear that Cadell had been riding, reared on its hind legs and roared a challenge. I dropped Merlin's staff and swung the pike around to a guard position. This brought another roar.

"Makes sense," Myfanwy said calmly. "The name Arthur derives from the word for bear. What else would Emrys choose as his guardian?" Myfanwy then stepped forward and started to walk towards the bear.

"Myf! What are you doing?" I yelled. She ignored me and started to recite a long stream of Welsh, most of which seemed to be proper names, in a sing song voice.

"Yr wyf Myfanwy Ferchwyn ap Rhys ap Alwyn ap Cadfael ap Owain ap Cadfan Tŷ'r Pwyll. Emrys yw fy ewythr ac rwyf wedi dod i osod ei rhad ac am ddim. Mae'r rhyfelwr yw Thomas o'r Clan O'Malley. Ef yw fy hyrwyddwr."

I later learned that this was Myfanwy's genealogical introduction of herself; followed by the statement, "Merlin is my uncle and I have come to set him free. This warrior is Thomas of the Clan O'Malley. He is my champion." The bear hesitated for a moment. Then it came down on all fours and moved forward slowly. I gripped the pike tighter, ready to strike, but the bear only nuzzled Myfanwy's hand and turned to lead her further down the path. My pike flashed blue and turned back into a walking stick. I picked up Merlin's staff and followed Myfanwy and the bear.

We soon came to the shore of the lake. We could clearly see the island. It was steep and rocky with only a few stunted pine trees managing to grow. There was a white boat pulled up on the shore and it was beside this that the bear left us. The boat was timber with a high, curving prow and stern. There were no oars or sail. In fact, it had no apparent means of propulsion. Myfanwy got into the boat immediately. I followed, more hesitantly.

As soon as we sat down, the boat started to move silently across the lake. The waters of the lake were black and still. Not even the movement of our boat made a ripple. This, combined with the oppressive weighty silence, gave the experience a surrealistic quality. It was like a strangely coherent dream.

When we got to the island, I jumped ashore quickly; ready to break any magic barriers. There were none, so I just helped Myfanwy from the boat. The same viscous silence coated this island like syrup and made casual conversation unthinkable. We climbed the hill in silence. At the top there was a small building of undressed stone. Its walls were no more than five feet high but it had a high gabled roof of slate. There was only one door and it was low with a heavy stone lintel. We went in. I had to bend almost double to get through the door.

Inside, there were three tall candles each side of a white marble slab and on that slab lay Merlin. He was dressed in a white tunic with a dark blue toga. He could have been a Roman gentleman except that he had wild grey hair and a long beard of pure white. He seemed to be asleep and didn't stir when we entered. Myfanwy went up to him and said, *"Tad, os gwelwch yn dda deffro."* (Father, please wake up.) She reached out her hand but suddenly drew it back.

"Tom, I can't touch him. The thought of it just fills me with hopeless dread." The induced dread was magic and had no effect on me. I walked over a shook him by the shoulder. Merlin still didn't wake up.

"There must be some key to waking him," Myfanwy said. "We just don't know what it is." She looked thoughtfully around the chamber. Apart from the candlesticks it was empty. We had only what we had brought with us. Then she had an idea. "Tom, give him the staff!"

"That won't do any good," I objected. "He can't use it. He's asleep."

She insisted, "Just give it to him. Remember the last line of Friar Daffyd's poem: 'Doom of Emrys, doom defying'. Well, we know it was the power of the staff that caused Emrys to be entombed here, maybe it's also the way to set him free."

I took Merlin's staff and placed it in his hands. Immediately his eyes opened and he turned to look at Myfanwy.

"*Merch ifanc, yr wyf yn falch eich bod wedi dod,*" he said. (Young daughter, I am glad you have come.) I should say here that all of Myfanwy's conversations with Merlin were in Welsh and I only got to hear what was said later. For brevity, from here on I will just give the English translation as Myfanwy gave it to me.

"Uncle," Myfanwy said. "We need you to get up and calm the dragons who threaten to devour the world in their rage." She looked across at me "This is…"

"I know who he is," Merlin cut in. "I've been asleep, not dead. Do you think someone can carry my staff around without me knowing? Do you think anyone can break into my tomb and introduce themselves to my guardian without me knowing all about the encounter? Come! We must get out of here and save this world of yours." He stood up and slammed his staff on the floor. There was a flash of blue and the three of us were standing in Glencoe, at the foot of the rock face. There was no sign that the tomb of Merlin had ever existed.

Merlin and Myfanwy disappeared. Then a moment later, Myfanwy reappeared and took my hand.

"Come on slow coach," she said smiling. Then we were back near the obelisk. Merlin was looking curiously at the body of Michael. When Myfanwy explained who and what he was, Merlin was surprised. Apparently Myfanwy's people hadn't had the same reproductive trouble in his day. She went on to tell him how he had died and he nodded thoughtfully.

"I give him this as a tribute to his courage," he said. He passed his hand over the body and it changed to the body of a thin, young man with dark, lank hair. He was naked and marked with many bullet wounds but this was Michael as I had known him in the park. He had his wish.

Merlin went over to the obelisk and studied it intently.

"Good," he said at last. "This gives me easy access." He then turned to Myfanwy. "Daughter of my house, you need to step away. Do not be too close or this may be too much for you." Myfanwy and I moved over to the top of the ridge, near where the soldiers had set up their machine gun.

Then Merlin raised his arms, holding his staff above his head. He spoke no words, used no incantations, but even I could feel the tingling on my skin as he stretched out his power. Then it started to get cold as he drew on the energy around him. The wind rose and it started to snow. Myfanwy suddenly got very tired as Merlin's demand for energy expanded. I cradled her in my arms and tried to protect her as much as I could. The wind grew stronger still and the air got colder. Soon, Merlin was in the centre of a swirling hurricane and branches of trees and even small rocks were being torn up and thrown about. I bent over Myfanwy, guarding her with my body.

Merlin stood still at the centre of all this, his hair blowing wildly in the wind. He was gathering energy in but you could sense that energy was flowing out of him at an even greater rate. It was as if he was becoming transparent, wasted from the inside. Suddenly, the obelisk exploded and Merlin collapsed on the ground. Immediately, the wind began to die down and the snow started to fall more heavily. I helped Myfanwy over to where Merlin was lying.

"It is done child," he said. "The dragons will sleep for now."

"Are you hurt, my uncle?" Myfanwy asked.

Merlin smiled. "No child, I am not hurt. I am dying." Myfanwy gave a small gasp. "Oh, do not mourn," Merlin continued. "It is a fate long past its time. I am glad to leave this way, with my life force spent in service. I was dying anyway: too old, too tired. I was already dying long ago. Poor Nimwe, if only she had waited a few days…" He started to drift off but then came back with great energy. "When I am gone, take my body to be with my brothers on *Ynys Enlli*. The others who are coming will help you."

"What others?" Myfanwy asked.

Merlin smiled. "My dear child, you can't think that a feat of magic as great as that which I have just accomplished could go unnoticed. They are on their way to discover how this was done." He looked across at me and then turned back to Myfanwy. "Be at peace my child, you have chosen well and you have my blessing." Then he laid his head down and closed his eyes. He gave a long exhaled breath, his hands left their grip on his staff, and he was gone.

I picked up his staff but had no sense of energy. It was just a polished bit of wood.

Chapter 28
Final Farewells

After a while the snow stopped falling and we were left in a quiet world. A short time later the sound of a pony's hooves could be heard on the roadway and a familiar green and red wagon came into view. Almost at the same time, a tall figure in a dark cloak and hood could be seen striding towards us down the walking trail. Nain arrived first but Declan got there close behind her and pulled back his hood while she was still climbing down from her wagon.

"Hello Tom," he called brightly. "There is a release of magic power such as has not been seen since the age of the heroes and you and Myfanwy are at the centre of it. Why am I not surprised?" Nain walked over and gave us a very stern look.

"You two have a talent for finding trouble," she said. "You need to learn the meaning of the word careful." She looked at Merlin's body. "So, you found Myrddin Emrys. Is it over then?"

"Yes," Myfanwy said. "He has put the dragons back to sleep but it took all his life energy to do it. I don't think anyone else would've been able to."

"Nor do I child," Nain said. "Nor do I."

"And who is this?" Declan asked. Looking at Michael's body, half covered in debris and snow.

"That is Michael," I answered. "He is one of Friar Daffyd's ...protégés. He shielded us from Cadell and his cronies. It cost him his life." Declan looked at me with a studied expression.

"There is a story here," he said. "A story worth knowing. What of Cadell?"

"He's dead. He was killed by a polar bear on that ridge over there," I said pointing. Both Nain and Declan looked at me with openly incredulous expressions. "Well, what other mount would be worthy of the greatest magic user of his time?" I asked sarcastically.

Suddenly Declan laughed. "Of all the ways to die!" he said. "The would be ruler of the world, killed by a polar bear in the Scottish Highlands. That will make a good story: a comic story, but a good one."

Myfanwy ignored Declan. "Nain," she said. "Merlin said he wanted to be buried with his brothers at a place called *Ynys Enlli*. Do you know where that is?'

Nain nodded. "Of course," she said. "The island of twenty thousand saints. It's the place now known as Bardsey Island. Yes, it's natural that he would want to be buried there."

"And Michael must be taken to Friar Daffyd's hermitage," I said. "That is where he belongs."

"Right then," Declan said briskly. "Nain, if you could arrange transport to Porth Meudwy, I'll do the rest." Nain looked at him suspiciously but nodded nonetheless. The two bodies were lifted magically and carried as if on invisible briers to Nain's wagon. We placed them in the back of the wagon which was now arranged with two stretcher beds. As soon as the bodies were secure, Declan left saying that he would meet us in Porth Meudwy. Then he was gone.

After Myfanwy and I had climbed up the front with Nain, the wagon set off. The pony kept up a slow, steady trot that, in normal circumstances, would have got us to Wales in about a month, but around Nain all the scenery seemed to go blurry. The pony kept up a steady trot but smeared images of roads and towns, cities and fields, lakes and mountains kept flashing past. It wasn't long before the world became sharp and solid again and we were trotting down a steep road to a small fishing village. Out past the harbour, across a wave tossed stretch of sea, I could make out an island, dark against the red, sunset sky.

The wind was cold, the clouds were dark and low and it was threatening to rain hard. It was no wonder then that the village was deserted. We pulled up at a shingle beach near the town and Declan was there waiting for us.

"What kept you?" he asked.

"The traffic was bad in Glasgow," Nain answered shortly as she climbed down. "What have you arranged?" Declan waved towards the beach and there, resting on the shingle, was Declan's boat. It was a large curragh, made of white cow hide stretched over a frame of dark oak. It was a graceful thing, high at the prow and low at the stern. Nain looked unconvinced.

"You will not be allowed on the island," she said.

"No," Declan agreed. "But Tom and Myfanwy will be and I can at least pull up on the shore. Your wagon would not be allowed at all." Nain reluctantly agreed. "Also, I can take Tom to Annwn under my diplomatic protection to bury his friend." Nain considered this for a while and then nodded.

"Right," she said. "I'll go ahead to Annwn to make arrangements. Also, I need to allay the fears of worried mothers." She pulled a small note pad out of her pocket.

On two pages she wrote 'All well. Tom and Myfanwy safe. Back home later tonight - Nain.' Then she held up both pages and they disappeared into the cold wind. "Now I must arrange to speed up time on Annwn so that you can do what you need to do and still be home at a reasonable time."

The two bodies were levitated amidships the boat and Nain left: her wagon trundling off down the road and through the village. Myfanwy and I sat in the stern while Declan stood in the prow. He raised his hands with his fingers outstretched and the boat moved off across the choppy sea. It moved swiftly and smoothly and soon we were skirting around the island to the small harbour on the far side. Once again, Declan beached his boat on a shingle beach.

"You must take Emrys the rest of the way I'm afraid," Declan said. "I'm not welcome here." I looked quizzically at Myfanwy.

"This is a sacred place and his people once pretended to be pagan gods," she explained. "He will not be allowed here until he is baptised." Fortunately, Myfanwy had recovered enough energy after Merlin's magic that she was able to levitate his body out of the boat and up the road from the beach to the ruin of the old monastery. As we went I became conscious that we were being accompanied by echoes from the past. Thousands of ghostly pilgrims walked either side of us. When we arrived at the monastery it was complete and beautiful. We were met at the door of the chapel by an old man in a celtic tunic and cloak. Myfanwy dropped to her knees, so I did the same.

The man walked up to the body, still floating as Myfanwy had left it, and said, "Welcome home, my brother." He then gestured and six black robbed monks came forward, took the body on their shoulders and carried it into the monastery chapel. The old man looked at us and smiled. He traced a blessing over our heads and he too returned to the monastery chapel. Then the monastery was again a ruin: scattered stones with only part of a tower standing intact. There was no sign of Merlin. We walked back to the boat alone with the last light of the setting sun fading in the west.

"Who was that?" I asked quietly.

"Saint Cadfan," Myfanwy replied. "He founded the monastery about sixteen hundred years ago. It was a place of pilgrimage for over a thousand years." She looked back along the road. "It still is," she whispered.

We made our way back to the boat and as soon as we had climbed on board Declan set sail for Annwn. Declan's boat moved swiftly, even through the rough seas of a coming storm, and it wasn't long before we were turning into the cleft of rock that led to Annwn. There was a sharp contrast as we sailed into the bay at Annwn's entrance. Outside the night was dark and there was a storm coming. The wind was strong and the clouds low in the sky. Here it was still dark but it was calm and the whole of Annwn was flooded in bright moonlight.

Waiting for us on the quay were all of the Council of Nobles, including Nain and Professor Rhys, as well as Friar Daffyd. The spokesperson of the council, the White Lady, stepped forward. She looked more ethereal than ever in the moonlight. It gleamed on her long white hair and dress and reflected brightly off her silver girdle.

"He is banned from Annwn," she said imperiously, pointing at me. Declan answered in a tone so casual that the insult could not be missed.

"He is here on a diplomatic mission," he said. "He is part of my party and under my protection. I will be responsible for him during his stay." He raised his eyebrow as he looked at her. "You are aware that under the terms of our treaty I may choose my own staff?" The White Lady froze in the moonlight, her expression impossible to read.

Then she nodded briefly. "Very well," she said. "But Myfanwy Ferchwyn is to have no contact with the boy Thomas O'Malley."

Professor Rhys coughed. "I don't think my niece has any intention of obeying that decree," he said. Myfanwy climbed out of the boat and levitated Michael's body along the wharf towards Friar Daffyd.

As she passed the White Lady she said, "No, I don't."

As we were also climbing out of the boat, Declan leaned over to me and whispered, "That is important. The House of Pwyll has just declared its defiance of the Council of Nobles. This has been a long time coming. It will be interesting to see how it plays out." We joined Friar Daffyd, who was leaning over Michael's body and weeping.

"My special boy," he said. "My special boy. What have they done to you?" A group of women were gathering back near the cottages.

"They are all mothers of 'mistakes'," Myfanwy said. "I think that maybe word of who Michael is has spread and they are wondering if he is theirs." We went in silent and solemn procession along the river and up the path that led to the Friar's hermitage, our way lit by moonlight and magic. Friar Daffyd led the way with Michael's body floating behind him. Myfanwy and I followed with Declan bringing up the rear. I don't remember much of that walk except its silence, its solemnity and, when we arrived at the hermitage, a great sense of peace.

The hermitage chapel was all prepared with a coffin and six tall, lighted candles. We laid Michael in the coffin and stood while Friar Daffyd recited the Office for the Dead in Latin. When he had finished, I pulled a kneeler over to the foot of the coffin and knelt down. The Friar looked at me questioningly.

"I will be keeping vigil Friar," I said. He nodded and they all left. I was alone; kneeling with Michael's body to pray for his soul. I can't pretend that I prayed all night. I can't even pretend that I was truly awake all night. All I can say is that I was there and that I kept watch.

The funeral was held early in the morning. Friar Daffyd said the requiem mass according to the ancient rites. Myfanwy and I were the only congregation. After the mass the coffin was magically carried out to the rock where the distribution of the bread would take place. The friar gestured and the rock moved to one side. Then a hole appeared and Michael's coffin was placed in it. The friar said the graveside prayers and blessed the grave. I had the feeling that there were eyes watching from the forest. Then the rock slid back into place and Michael was at rest.

"Come children," Friar Daffyd said. "I think I can find some breakfast for you."

After breakfast, Myfanwy and I stayed on at the hermitage. We didn't say much but we kept close to each other and frequently held each other's hand. When the time came for noonday prayer and the distribution of the eulogia, we followed the friar around to the rock. This day, Myfanwy helped with the distribution of the bread and each time she gave bread to one of Friar Daffyd's congregation she would say, "I am sorry, please forgive me."

After the bread had been distributed and Friar Daffyd had given his final blessing, his congregation scuttled and slithered back to the forest. But at the edge of the forest they stopped and turned to face Myfanwy. Then one of them, who looked like a kind of lizard with a grotesquely long neck and a small but human head, opened its mouth to sing the most beautiful sound I have ever heard. It had no tune but was glorious in the purity of its music. Then the whole congregation turned and vanished back into the forest. Myfanwy was weeping so I held her tight for a long time.

We left Annwn that same day in Declan's boat and arrived at a remote beach in Wales. It was night. In fact, it was the same storm threatened night we had left. Nain picked us up and got me home to London about ten o'clock. Mum was waiting for me. She grabbed me in an overly enthusiastic hug as soon as I walked in the door.

"I was so worried," she said. "So very worried."

"It's okay, Mum," I whispered. "It's over. We're safe now." I don't know that she believed me but from then on there were no more stories of earthquakes or volcanic eruptions. The earth was quieter than it had been for a long, long time. The police found Cadell's body about a week later while they were out hunting for a polar bear that had been reported killing stock. A story which no one quite believed until it was actually caught. Cadell's body had been partially devoured and was badly decomposed. No one claimed the body so it was buried without ceremony in an unmarked pauper's grave.

Chapter 29
The words that have power.

That week was Holy Week and all through the Easter ceremonies I kept thinking of Michael and how he had stepped in front of us to save us from the bullets. I remembered the poem by Yeats that had haunted me earlier:

"And what rough beast, its hour come round at last,

Slouches towards Bethlehem to be born?"

Michael's hour had indeed come and his death had, in many ways, seemed more like a birth. I know this wasn't what Yeats had in mind but it was appropriate all the same. I also kept thinking of his declaration.

"I will not kill for you and I will not kill for him."

Who was he? I wondered: this other person who had tried to turn Michael into a killer. For the moment, I left that aside. I had other things, such as going back to school and preparing for exams to worry about. Not that exams were the major topic of discussion when school returned. They had been trumped by another event: the school formal. This was to be held in the second week of term at a reception place on the northern outskirts of London. The talk and planning was incessant. Who was going with whom? Who was going to who's before/after party?

Fortunately, our table was saved from most of that. It turned out that both Wilson and Rachael were planning to go on their own, Phil was taking one of Gabriella's best friends and Gabriella, who was rejoining us for this term (mostly to try and absorb some brilliance from Wilson) was taking the shy little guitarist from the IB stream. He was besotted with her to an embarrassing degree. Gabriella and her friends were going to their own before and after parties. None of the rest of us were going to bother.

Helen and Gwyneth had stayed at Aelred Abbey in order to help Myfanwy prepare for the formal. I think they were more excited than she was. Mum was definitely more excited about it than I was and she insisted on going with me to ensure that I got the right kind of dinner suit.

On the night of the formal, Nain and Gwyneth came to meet us and escort us through the gate. Gwen looked at me critically then she nodded.

"You'll do," she said. She laughed as I looked relived. "Tom you look great," she said. "You and Myfanwy are going to have a great time." We left for Aelred Abbey through the gate. Myfanwy wasn't ready when we arrived so we joined Professor Rhys and Helen in the library while Gwen went upstairs to help her. Eventually Gwen came back.

"She's ready," she announced.

Myfanwy came in. She was dressed in a deep green gown, slightly darker than the green of her eyes, which shimmered as she walked. It was high waisted with a black velvet band. Her hair was arranged high on her head in a complex hair do, held in place by a band of twisted gold wire. She wore a necklace of emeralds and gold. She did look a bit like she had walked out of a Jane Austen novel, which wasn't surprising considering who her mother was, but she was perfect. I had never seen anything more beautiful.

"Breathe boy," Nain said beside me. "Remember to breathe." I realized that I was, in fact, holding my breath. She walked over to me and gave a nervous little half smile.

"Hi," she said. "How do I look?'

"Um..." I stumbled, trying to find the right words. "You look good... um... really good." It was the reply of a tongue tied idiot. I didn't know how she could still do this to me. Fortunately she understood and smiled broadly.

"Have you got my corsage?" she asked.

"Err..." I answered.

"Yes he does," Mum answered and handed me this little arrangement of yellow flowers. I passed it on mutely to Myfanwy who attached it to her dress.

"Thank you, Tom," she answered. I couldn't tell if she was being sarcastic but I think she might've been. We left for the reception place with Professor Rhys driving us in his Rolls Royce. When we arrived there, there were lots of stares and whispers

"Do you suppose they're real..." and so on. It finally dawned on me that if the emeralds in Myfanwy's necklace were real, the thing was worth a fortune. We stood around drinking bad champagne for a while before we got to sit down and eat really bad food. The conversation around our table was a little strained, both because Rachael and Wilson didn't seem keen on talking to anyone and because Gabriella was starring in awe at Myfanwy's necklace.

Finally she said, "That's a really beautiful necklace, Myfanwy."

"Thanks," Myfanwy replied. "It's an old family heirloom."

"Gosh," Phil's partner said. "I wish I came from a family that had heirlooms like that. My family comes from Brixton."

"So, I bet you follow Millwall," Phil said. His partner just looked him blankly. Clearly having no idea what he was talking about. I didn't know anything about Millwall either but I knew Phil well enough to know it was a soccer team.

Myfanwy was away talking when the music started and Rachael grabbed me and virtually dragged me onto the dance floor.

"Come on, dance with me," she said. "I don't have anyone to dance with." The band was a pretty standard rock band playing fairly generic rock music. The music was loud, which made conversation difficult, but Rachael seemed determined to talk.

"So, you and Myfanwy are going to stick together, even after school?" She yelled in my ear. I nodded mutely. "Are you going back to Australia?" Again I nodded. "I know Myfanwy wants to go to university in Wales. How are you going to handle the separation?"

"I don't know," I yelled back. "We'll think of something."

After the first song ended she said, "Thanks Tom but I think I'll sit this one out." I went with her back to the table. Myfanwy was there and as the next song started she raised her eyebrows at me. I took the hint and asked her to dance.

We hadn't been on the dance floor long when she yelled at me, "I don't really like this music." She pointed at the rock band and they started to play a waltz at a much more subdued volume. It sounded a little strange coming from electric guitars and keyboard and the other students looked really confused. "Much better," was Myfanwy's only comment.

I'm no great dancer but it was good to be just holding Myfanwy and trying. However, after a short while, Myfanwy said, "You're the man, you're meant to lead!"

"That's very sexist," I replied. She gave me an exasperated look.

A little while later she said, "You're right. It is sexist. It's also not working. I'll lead." When the song ended the band reverted to its normal genre and Myfanwy and I decided to go and get some fresh air. There was a balcony along one side of the hall which looked out across a garden, towards central London. There were some other couples there but Myfanwy made a small gesture and they all decided to go inside.

"Myf, you look absolutely beautiful tonight," I said. "When I first saw you I couldn't speak properly because you were so beautiful."

She smiled. "Thank you," She said lightly. "And you are by far the most handsome man I have ever met." She was looking out at the view, so I took her by the shoulders, turned her towards me and looked deeply into her forest green eyes. What I had to say was serious.

"Myf, I lo…" She quickly put her finger to my lips. I held her hand and kissed her finger. "Yes, I know.

Words have power. I love you Myfanwy Ferchwyn and I have for a long time now. Words have power and these have all the power my heart can give them." She was silent and still for a while, just looking at my face. Then suddenly she hugged me tightly.

"I love you too, Thomas O'Malley," She said. "I love you. I love you. I love you. You don't know how much I've wanted to say that!" We held each other for a while and then I very gently kissed her.

Then I said, "Myf, I know about your people…I mean, I know about the romantic attachments thing… Does this mean… I mean would you…" I was getting embarrassed and flustered. I didn't know how to ask this or even if this was the right time. Once again Myfanwy put her finger to my lips, bringing me to silence.

"Of course we're going to get married you silly boy, but not yet. You're still too young. First, go and get that marine science degree you've been talking about. Then you can figure out how to propose properly." I could live with that.

I caught a movement out of the corner of my eye and turned just in time to see Rachael go back inside.

Some other couples were coming out onto the balcony so we headed back inside. The band was taking a break and coffee and cheese was being served. The coffee was bitter and awful and the cheese had the consistency of soap but not even that could dampen my spirits. Wilson was sitting alone at the table, finishing a glass of wine. He looked at Myfanwy and me as we sat down. I think that perhaps that wasn't his first glass of wine.

"Tom, how did you do it?" he asked. "How did you win Myfanwy?"

"He didn't win me," Myfanwy objected. "I'm not a prize in a raffle!"

"You know what I mean," he said, waving his hand vaguely in the air. "I'm not very good at that sort of thing. I'm good at equations and things up here.' He tapped the centre of his forehead. "But feelings and stuff like that… I'm not very good."

"Don't think about it. Don't try and analyze it,' I said. "Just be yourself. Just be honest." He looked up and stared at a corner of the hall were Rachael was standing by herself looking out a window.

"You think?" he said. "I'm not sure that worked very well."

"Go and talk to her," Myfanwy said. "Maybe she'll listen." Just then the band came back for their last set. They played a slow ballad in waltz time and Myfanwy and I got up to dance. When next I saw Wilson, he was over talking to Rachael. Actually, he was listening to Rachael complain passionately about something. He did this for the rest of the night.

At the appointed time, we were all herded out of the venue to either go home or go on to other parties. Professor Rhys was waiting for Myfanwy and me and we went back to Aelred Abbey where it had been arranged that Mum and I would stay the night.

When we got back to the abbey, the wind was from the south and the night was warm. As Professor Rhys put the car away, Myfanwy and I decided to go for a walk to the ruins of the old monastery. When we got to the monastery chapel, it seemed to be intact. The door, long vanished, seemed solid. Myfanwy reached out her hand and touched the wood, felt the iron of the handles.

"This isn't possible," she said softly. "Past echoes don't have substance." I opened the door and we walked into the candlelit chapel as it would have been in the 14th or 15th century. We both made a deep reverence to the altar. A black robbed monk was busy tending to the candles. When he saw us he pulled back his hood to reveal the cragged but smiling face of Brother Theophane.

"Sir Thomas! Thou art out late this night. The brothers will soon be arriving for the Vigil Office." He saw Myfanwy then and looked at me questioningly.

"Brother Theophane," I said. "May I present the Lady Myfanwy, Princess of Annwn." The effect of this introduction was remarkable. The old monk struggled to get down on his knees and, I think, would have prostrated himself if Myfanwy had not rushed over and helped him up."

"Reverend Brother, please ease thyself" she said. "My respect for thy age and thy habit will not allow such formality." The old monk got up and sat in one of the front stalls.

"Thank you, my lady. Thou art indeed gracious and most kind." He turned to look at me. "Thomas, perhaps thou hast some prayers thou mayst wish to say whilst I talk to the Lady Myfanwy." I knew when I was being told to go away, so I went and knelt in front of the rood screen. A short time later I saw them both get up, so I went down to meet them.

Brother Theophane looked at me and smiled. "Thy heart hath indeed chosen most wisely, Sir Thomas and I am happy for the both of you. Now, bow your heads that I may give you my blessing." We bowed and he said a Latin prayer of blessing over us. When we raised our head, we were standing in the modern ruin of the chapel with the faint sliver of a new moon rising over the eastern wall.

As we were walking around, back to the front door of the keep, Myfanwy asked me, "How did you know about the princess thing? We never talk about titles." Then it was my turn to give her the exasperated look.

"I'm not stupid," I said. "I've seen your house in Annwn. I've seen the respect given to your family and how the people there treat you. I've also seen how much the three of you worry the Council of Nobles. It wasn't hard to work out."

"Does it bother you?" she asked.

"No," I said. "My girlfriend is a super rich magical princess. I can cope."

When we got into the main hall, we found a reception committee waiting for us, all wanting to know how we went. Over some cups of hot chocolate we explained that we had had a great time. Gwen, of course, had been sent to bed earlier but she turned up anyway.

She took one look at Myfanwy and said, "Well, finally! That took forever." Then she came over and gave me a hug. "Hello brother,' she whispered in my ear. "Welcome to the family."

Once the formal was out of the way, it was back to school and real preparation for the exams. There was no new material, just constant revision, although a lot of the T.S. Eliot stuff was new to me. I particularly liked the ending to his poem 'Little Gidding'. It seemed appropriate somehow.

And all shall be well and

All manner of things shall be well
When the tongues of flame in-folded
Into the crowned knot of fire
And the fire and rose are one.

Epilogue

The exams went well. Both Myfanwy and I got into the University courses we wanted: Myfanwy studying Celtic culture at Aberystwyth University in Wales and me studying Marine Science at Melbourne University in Australia. My departure from London, however, was painful, as was the thought of the long separation ahead. At least it was for me. Myfanwy didn't seem that upset. As I was leaving at the airport, she gave me a gift. It was a copy of 'The Lion, the Witch and the Wardrobe' by C.S. Lewis. I looked at her, puzzled.

"You'll understand," she said. "Don't worry. It's all sorted."

The reference to Lewis' story was further developed by the strange gift from Myfanwy that was waiting for me when I got back to Angle Creek. It was an antique wardrobe. The trouble with the obvious Narnia reference was that this seemed to be a perfectly normal wardrobe. The back was solid and didn't lead anywhere. I know, I tried it often enough.

It was three days later, however, in the early evening, that the door of the wardrobe opened and Myfanwy stepped out. I looked at her with my mouth open in amazement. She gave an ironic smile.

"Well, I'm glad to see you too." she said.

"But how?" I objected. "There's no way you could teleport that distance."

"It's a gate, silly," she answered. "I had Carwyn make it. There's an identical wardrobe in my room at Aberystwyth. The distance between your room and mine is ..." she looked at the thickness of the door, "a little over a centimeter." Just then, my Mum knocked on the door and came in.

"Oh, hello Myfanwy dear. Will you be staying for dinner?"

"Thank you, Mrs. O'Malley. I would love to. I can't stay too long though. I have an early morning lecture." I couldn't stop smiling like an idiot. The surf was running and Myfanwy and I were no longer separated. It had all turned out well indeed and all manner of things had turned out well.

Other Books in the Mfanwy's People Series

MYFANWY
The First Book in the Myfanwy's People Series

Tom is unhappily dragged from his Australian surf to go to school in London. In the middle of an English winter, his unhappiness increases when a mysterious figure magically appears on Westminster Bridge and tries to kill him. Tom soon discovers a whole world of magic, beauty - and danger. In the midst of fighting bullies, being hunted by a psychotic magic user and kidnapped by a secret government agency, he meets Myfanwy, a magic user from a mystical island off the coast of Wales. Their initial distrust soon turns to friendship but this very friendship threatens to upset the delicate power balance in the magic realm.

Tom and Myfanwy must get together to save the world, perhaps even the universe. But how can they, when the whole magic community is trying to keep them apart?

THE THRONE OF ANNWN
The third book of the Myfanwy's People Series

The Council of Nobles is openly trying to kill Tom and civil war is threatened in Annwn if Myfanwy will not agree to marry Alwyn apBryn. Torn between her love of Tom and her love for her people, she accompanies Tom into the high Himalayas, to confront a group of rogue monks who are steering an asteroid towards the Earth.